W9-BZT-670

SALTY SKY

SETH COKER

RIVER GROVE
BOOKS

This book is a work of fiction. Names, characters, businesses, organizations, places, events, and incidents are either a product of the author's imagination or are used fictitiously. Any resemblance to actual persons, living or dead, events, or locales is entirely coincidental.

Published by River Grove Books
Austin, TX
www.rivergrovebooks.com

Copyright ©2016 Seth Coker

All rights reserved.

No part of this book may be reproduced, stored in a retrieval system, or transmitted by any means, electronic, mechanical, photocopying, recording, or otherwise, without written permission from the copyright holder.

Distributed by River Grove Books

Design and composition by Greenleaf Book Group and Kim Lance
Cover design by Greenleaf Book Group and Kim Lance
Cover images: Atosan/Twin propeller airplane landing/Thinkstock; Maciej Bledowski/ Vintage filtered picture of lighthouse/Thinkstock; Ben-Schoenewille/Orange sunset with dune and sea/Thinkstock

Cataloging-in-Publication data is available.

Print ISBN: 978-1-63299-076-1

eBook ISBN: 978-1-63299-075-4

First Edition

This book is dedicated to my family.
With their encouragement, I went from a reluctant writer to
an excited storyteller. With love and thanks to my wife, Melissa;
my daughters, Tyler, Sienna, and Lexi; and my son, Cale.

1993

››› 1

THE THREE MEN exited the side doors before the skids bent the grass. Heads ducked and backpacks jostling, they ran up the hill, ascended the granite steps, and disappeared into the villa.

Alone in the pilot seat, Cale radioed the ship, "This is Flyer. We are on-site. Seeker is on the move. Over."

"This is HQ," the response came. "Roger that. Any surprises? Over."

"This is Flyer. No. Grounds appear empty. Over."

"This is HQ. Roger that. Flyer, power down and keep updates coming. Seeker, do you have radio contact? Over."

"This is Seeker. Roger that. We're inside. No sign of life. Fifteen minutes to objective complete. Over."

"This is HQ. Roger that. We'll stand by for updates. Over."

Cale powered down the bird. He looked west across the Caribbean, toward an unseen Panama. The equatorial sun raced behind the sea. Minutes before, it had been almost directly overhead. Cale took his headgear off and flipped the radio control to the handheld. With the back door open, he listened beyond the tropical soundscape for human sounds while visualizing the start-up procedure and flight path he would use in a few minutes for takeoff.

The radio broke in, "This is Seeker. We'll come out of the west wing on the main level. Five minutes. Over."

Cale checked his watch, then picked up the speaker, "This is Flyer. Roger that. I'll fire up when I see you exit. By the time you cover the 100 yards to me, we'll be ready for liftoff. Over."

The approaching darkness was beaten back as lights flickered on along a low stone wall that stretched out a hundred yards on either side of the helicopter and ran down the driveway. With a jolt of adrenaline, Cale pulled his sidearm. His eyes scanned back and forth. Without looking down, he picked up the handheld. "This is Flyer. Exterior lights have turned on out here. I don't see anyone moving outside. Do you have someone inside? Over."

"This is Seeker. No movement inside. But this is a big place. Over."

"This is HQ. These lights turn on every night—some type of timer or photocell. Over."

Slightly more at ease, Cale set his firearm in the empty copilot seat and resumed rehearsing takeoff, listened for alarming noises, and scanned the area for movement. He checked his watch—two minutes to Seeker's exit. He began to focus on the area of the villa where the men would come out. The glaring lights between him and the doorway blurred his sightline.

The sound of a combustion engine caught Cale's ear. He paused for a second to confirm the sound, then picked the radio back up. "This is Flyer. I hear a car. Over."

"This is Seeker. Roger that. We're done. Heading out now. Over."

"This is Flyer. Roger that. I see moving lights hitting the trees coming up the driveway. Recommend you change exit to lower level. Over."

"This is Seeker. Roger that. We're standing inside the doorway until we identify the bogey. We can see the lights coming into the drive now. Over."

"This is HQ. Roger that. You have permission to go 'weapons live' at your discretion. Over."

"This is Seeker. Roger that. Over."

"This is Flyer. Roger that. Over."

Cale had never heard that particular authorization before, and his fingers trembled slightly as he reset the handheld. He made sure all lights were off in the helicopter. Whoever pulled up might not look toward the field or, at a glance, might not notice the helicopter's dark shape against the darkened field.

A convertible followed by a Range Rover pulled onto the stones in front of the villa's west entrance. Thankfully, the headlights shined at the entrance and neither car cut their lights off. Behind the lights, Cale saw a man in white get out of the driver's seat of the convertible, slide across the hood, and open the passenger door for a woman in a long dress. Four men in black stepped out of the Range Rover. Two of them hurried ahead of the couple, and the other two fell in line behind them.

"This is Seeker. We're going downstairs and will come out below. Over."

"This is Flyer. Roger that. I'll fire up once all six of this party are inside or I see you exit. Over."

Feeling highly visible, Cale watched the party move toward the entrance. The first pair of bodyguards entered the villa and immediately redirected the others back out. They must have either seen Seeker's team or noticed the ordnance wiring. Cale could hear the group's shouts in Spanish as they headed back toward the vehicles. Then one of the guards pointed a hand in his direction. Another one ran to the Range Rover and started it. He drove off the drive and down the stone walkway's entrance through the wall.

No more need for quiet. Cale flipped on the rotors. The blades' *whump-whump-whump* started up. Cale caught a glimpse of Seeker's team coming out of the lower level as the bouncing SUV accelerated and turned onto the grass toward the helicopter.

When it became apparent that the Range Rover was the weapon Cale needed to worry about, he dove out the back of the helicopter and tumbled onto the grass. When the SUV hit it, the helicopter's cockpit crumbled. The spinning rotors tore open the cabin of the SUV and then lodged into its side. The evil sound of metal grinding on metal overwhelmed the night air.

When the noise stopped, Cale reversed course and made his way to what was previously the belly of the helicopter, now on its side. He reached for his sidearm and found an empty holster. He could still hear the radio chatter coming from the cockpit.

"This is Seeker. We've been spotted. Preparing for a firefight. Flyer's chopper is disabled. Not sure of Flyer's status. Over."

"This is HQ. Roger that. We'll have another bird airborne in five minutes, be there in ten. Over."

"This is Seeker. Roger that. If we see signs of life from Flyer we'll engage. If not, we'll stay hidden until you arrive. Over"

Cale heard the car door open. He reasoned that if the door slammed shut again, the driver would come around the wreck from the left; if it stayed open, the driver would circle around the back and come from the right. Cale looked at his watch. Two seconds passed in the Indiglo light, and no door slammed, so Cale crouched low and moved right. He hoped to keep the wreck between him and the driver. He made it around the side of the SUV in time to see a heel pass the far corner of the helicopter.

He looked into the open doors of the SUV. The keys were in the ignition. He briefly thought about driving off, but he couldn't free the SUV from the wrecked helicopter before being shot. He could see the other four men and the woman crouching behind the stone wall, alternating looks between the villa and the wreck. He couldn't circle around the SUV without being seen. He doubted anyone could hit him with a pistol from that distance, but being in the open would further compromise him.

From behind the wall, he saw a flash of light and then heard the long unmistakable *tat-tat-tat-tat-tat-tat-tat* of an Uzi. With an Uzi they could hit him from that distance, and they only needed one out of the sixty shots per second to do the job. The gun, at that moment, was directed toward Seeker's team. He heard but couldn't see the return fire *pop-pop*-break-*pop-pop* of the semiautomatic pistols the team carried. Cale slid feet first under the SUV, uncertain how the driver would respond to the gunfire. Cale looked out from under the open door.

Tentative feet turned the corner, retreated, and then came back into view. They quickly strode to the SUV. Both feet stopped and spread out to shoulder width just in front of Cale. He heard the *thunk* of the driver's gun settling on the car's roof as he prepared for a side shot at Seeker's team.

In one motion, Cale pulled both of the shooter's ankles under his chest as he slid out from under the car. He heard a shot and the immediate ricochet as the bullet bounced off the rotors above them and into the SUV.

The driver let out an "Ugh!" as his back hit the ground, the impact knocking the air from his lungs.

Cale's right fist struck the man's face within a second of his head hitting the ground. He hit him three more times quickly. Cale grabbed the pistol from beside the semiconscious man's hand, put a bullet in the man's forehead, then rolled off him.

Cale edged to the car's tail in a crouch. The sound of the gunfire continued. At least six weapons were being fired, but the dominant sound was the Uzi's *tat-tat-tat-tat-tat-tat-tat*. Cale sprinted away from the gunfight into the shadows, then sprinted to the stone wall and hopped over it, about fifty yards from the enemy. He crept along the curved wall. The man in white held the Uzi. Cale fired on him from behind. Some of the man's hair flew up. Cale thought he'd missed but then saw the gun fall to the ground, followed by the man.

There were more *pop-pops*, and soon, Cale saw Seeker standing in the open, his team lying unnaturally beside him on the ground. Cale stood up. He saw the bodies of the other three men and the woman along the wall. He walked up to the man in the white shirt and flipped him over with his foot.

》》》 2

AS PABLO SET the phone down, a headache began behind Francisco's eyebrows.

Pablo shouted, "*¡Y aún así me siguen probando!*"

The men lounging around the large room grew smaller, stopped moving, and averted their eyes. The young women quietly left the steaming tub; water dripped from their bare, brown-skinned bodies and puddled on the stone floor as they slipped from the room.

Francisco sat stoically as Pablo repeated the refrain—*And yet they still test me!* He knew what Pablo meant. Pablo had killed three presidential candidates, seven supreme court justices, scores of magistrates, hundreds of police offers, and thousands of rivals, and his fate was still continually in the balance. Francisco's face tightened as Pablo's flushed with anger at the audacity that they would believe the results would be different this time. Pablo was the world's seventh-richest man, its most infamous criminal, and his country's most popular citizen. If they wanted to test him, Francisco knew they would learn that Pablo maintained his propensity and capacity for bloodshed.

Pablo's eyes closed as he slipped his head under the tub's bubbling waterline. Black hair clung to the surface amid the white bubbles. He counted up to thirty, then down to zero, and surfaced with instructions to provide his men. Except for the location, the instructions would surprise no one—except, perhaps, the targets—who always seemed surprised when the inevitable happened.

Francisco knew Pablo had little education, and excluding himself, his inner circle had less. Yet, successfully and repeatedly, Pablo employed the same two-part plan. *Plata o plomo*. Silver or lead. Greed or violence. Which did the man on the other side of the table desire? The silver always came first. Since Pablo developed this plan, silver had been abundant.

In this case, the silver had stopped working, so it was time for the lead.

Without haste, Pablo said, "Francisco, General Rodriguez and his staff are dining nearby. Please bring them to me for a discussion."

Francisco was relieved that El Capo's eyes were still closed, because he felt his face betray disagreement with the order. "El Capo, forgive me—did you say bring them here?"

"*Sí, Francisco, aquí*." Pablo's reply smoldered despite no noticeable change in inflection.

Francisco paused before standing. He silently willed his uncle to reconsider. Better to handle the officers in the street or, better still, in their homes, with their families watching. Witnesses to relay the horror to others' ears. Witnesses whose fear would crush their rage and keep them from plotting revenge. Since Francisco's own brother's death and the destruction of one of their family's seaside villas by unknown enemies weeks before, his thoughts had grown colder, while Pablo's seemed to grow more fervent.

If they were alone, he would have argued reason. But not now. Too many people heard the order. Francisco replied, "*Muy bien, Tío*," and motioned two of the lounging men to follow him.

Pablo stood now in the giant tub, visually chafing at the challenge. In earlier years, he would have simply handled the challenge and not felt the chafe. But like all men whose lives tip toward having much to lose and little to gain, Pablo feared someone would take what was his.

Remaining sequestered in La Catedral, his isolation and his sampling of the product magnified his conflicting emotions of vulnerability and invincibility.

In times past, Pablo said to Francisco, "Ambitious men size up their reach. Their power. They want to know whether I'm the Muhammad Ali who fought Foreman or the one who fought Holmes. If these men sat at my knee, I would tell them, 'Gentlemen, do not make this mistake. Do not dance with the *cartel de Cali*. Do not look for soft spots in the provinces. Medellín demands your unconditional love. There will be no successful invasion, and there will be no coup.'"

Francisco knew Pablo was warning him as he prepared him.

The last coup occurred when a twenty-five-year-old Pablo killed his boss, Fabio Restrepo. Restrepo was king of a small but bountiful empire, a growing drug refinement and trafficking business. Pablo yearned to be king and knew there was room for only one, so he took the crown for himself. He repeated the mantra "There is only one king" to all who needed to hear it.

Now Pablo was in his twenty-fourth year on the throne of a greatly expanded empire. He protected the empire's borders but had lost the ambition to expand. This loss of ambition conflicted with Francisco's long-held view of Pablo as a minor god.

Loudly, Pablo shouted encouragement to those around the room, "Remember, all empires are created and maintained from fire and blood." As always when he spoke, heads nodded their assent.

Pablo left the tub and dried off. The prison walls in La Catedral grew too close for his kinetic life—a profitable life rooted in money and violence. He started grave robbing at age ten, taking granite headstones, filing off the inscriptions, and selling the blanks back to the distributors. As a teen, he stole cars. By twenty, he moved through mountain passes, carrying coca paste over the borders of Bolivia and Peru.

This was not Pablo's first arrest, but this was the longest he'd chosen to stay in prison—nearly twelve months. His first arrest happened when he was a young *narco* crossing from Ecuador. When he was released on bail, Pablo first tried to bribe his arresting officer. The noble officer refused the bribe from what he thought was a simple coca paste mule, so Pablo killed him. *Plata o plomo.* The prosecutor accepted the silver and dropped the smuggling case without a trial.

La Catedral was technically a prison and Pablo could not leave, at least not without the risk of not being able to return. However, he could operate his business from within its walls, and his people could come and go. He built this prison wing for himself—more a personal fortress than a prison—as part of his deal with the Colombian government. The deal gave Pablo two victories: First, it helped the Colombian government avoid deporting its most popular citizen; for ten years, even when Pablo served in parliament, the *norteamericanos* called for his extradition. Second, it bought his men time to eliminate the Cali cartel's emboldened assassins.

La Catedral's comforts were similar to those of the four hundred villas Pablo owned around the world. The guards were on his payroll. His multiple phone lines were private. He had twelve thousand square feet of housing, a jetted tub, a waterfall, a full bar, and a soccer field. The warden and government officials asked permission to enter his wing.

Pablo went to his room, dressed, poured a drink, and sat on his bed. One of the young women poked her head in to see whether he wanted her. She had been his favorite this past month. He had taken her from a novice to a skilled lover, and her passion for coupling increased with each lesson. Her new black silk negligee alternately hid and exposed her soft curves. Normally, he would pass his time waiting for the general by enjoying the young skin, but tonight, he silently waved her away with the back of his hand.

Eventually, there was a knock on his door.

"El Capo, Francisco has returned with the soldiers."

Pablo finished his drink. He swirled the ice around the glass twice, set the glass down on the floor beside his bed, stood up, and walked out to the great room.

Francisco seated General Rodriguez and his staff officers in the middle of the room on an oversized leather sectional. As Pablo entered the room, Rodriguez and his men stood. Rodriguez's rise to general correlated strongly with Pablo's patronage. They served each other well. Rodriguez kept the army from focusing its attention on Pablo, and Pablo both eliminated rival officers in the chain of command and kept Rodriguez's accounts stacked with silver.

Pablo wanted to know why Rodriguez now chose to distance himself from the benefits and responsibilities of their relationship.

Rodriguez said, "Representative Escobar, it has been too long. I hope you are finding these accommodations adequate until we can get this silliness with the *norteamericanos* behind us."

It had been eight years since Pablo left office, yet Francisco noted that callers still frequently used the title. He assumed Rodriguez used the honorific because he would want to be called *General* until his dying day.

Before replying, Pablo located Francisco along the wall, and through their eyes passed an understanding. Pablo said, "It is fine here, General. If I stop enjoying my stay, I will leave. Can I get you a drink?"

Francisco had allowed the officers to keep their sidearms. He felt that holding their weapons gave the soldiers a feeling of security, a sense that this was a negotiation. This atmosphere would perhaps help Pablo get more nuanced information than would gunpoint intimidation.

"Coffee, please. The Argentinian Malbec was bountiful at dinner. The Argentines should be proud of their Malbec. Thank you for sending your man to pay for our dinner," Rodriguez said, nodding over his shoulder toward Francisco.

Pablo answered, "Yes, the Malbec and Maradona, no?"

"*Sí*, and when will we see Maradona wearing Medellín's colors?"

Pablo's deepest public disappointment was when Maradona, possibly the greatest football player of all time, refused his entreaties to play in Colombia. Francisco was shocked that Rodriguez was bold enough to broach the subject. Perhaps he had consumed too much of that Malbec.

The small talk between the general and El Capo continued until the coffee arrived. After stirring in his *leche*, Rodriguez asked, "Representative Escobar, may I inquire as to why you requested our presence at La Catedral this evening?"

Whenever this group came together, Francisco was jarred by the differences between Pablo and the general: the general's lack of Indian blood; his proper, well-enunciated Spanish; his formal education and his acute attention to personal appearance. But mostly, he contemplated the differences in each man's sense of pride.

Pablo's pride was in possessing absolute control of his destiny and those within his orbit. If, instead of killing you, he bribed you for cooperation, it wasn't because he didn't think he could kill you. It was because bribing you gave him the result he wanted quicker or easier. He could kill you later if he desired.

The general's pride was that others believed that he was a man who controlled not only his own fate but also the fate of others. The general did not visibly mind lacking the power he projected, and Pablo found this a useful trait. Knowing that the general valued appearance more than silver, Pablo traditionally tolerated this talk as equals in front of crowds.

"Yes, General. I am concerned. You see, I haven't seen much of the world this year. So, I don't understand some of the changes. I hope you can explain them to me."

"Of course. I will do my best, Representative. What may I explain?"

Pablo suddenly sighed, looking tired of the game before it even began. Francisco thought he had spent too many years like a cat flipping mice in the air to enjoy the drama.

Pablo asked, "Why have you not accepted my most recent offering of silver?"

The general stammered, his fear showing. His shaking hand rattled his coffee cup on the saucer. He became aware of the arc of rough men surrounding the door.

Pablo sipped his coffee, awaiting an answer. To Francisco, Pablo seemed to fill more with fatigue than rage.

Once they started, the general's words flowed quickly. Francisco listened to some of what was said but mostly watched the mannerisms of the general's men to see whether there were any worth saving. Certainly, one of these young officers was bright enough to understand the hopelessness of their situation, to step up, be spared, and receive Pablo's patronage to replace General Rodriguez? But Pablo saw nothing of the kind, nothing that would provide any of the men earthly salvation.

Finally, Pablo held up his hand to stop the general. "Thank you, General Rodriguez. I understand now."

The general regained his composure. His shoulders rolled back, and he was the powerful man again, an inch taller and two inches broader. He handed his coffee cup and saucer to one of his men. Although there had been no physical altercation, his thin hair had become disheveled during the explanation. He ran his hand through it to smooth it down.

"It is always a pleasure, Representative Escobar." The general nodded to his men to prepare to leave.

"Likewise, General. Good night."

With that, Pablo raised his eyelids to Francisco. The cannons in his men's hands erupted, and the officers were dead.

When the echoes from the gunfire subsided, Francisco asked, "El Capo, shall I take them to the jungle?"

"No, Francisco, you may leave them here. I will dispose of them."

Francisco questioned El Capo's judgment for the second time this evening. Killing the men here was a poor decision, but making no move to hide the killings was far worse. It would lodge a fiery stick into the government's eye. Francisco considered what this act could do other than force the government into an action neither side wanted.

Unknowingly, Pablo had been right when he spoke to the general: He had not seen much in the past year, and there were changes he did not grasp. He no longer understood the influence of his true opposition—not the Cali or other young bandits, but the powerful *norteamericanos*. The shell government in Bogotá largely conceded its sovereignty to the *norteamericanos*, who sought to eliminate their own country's drug problem by meddling in other countries. It made no difference. The *norteamericanos'* policy ignored the law that supply will always rise to meet demand; a snake can always tunnel a new hole. Francisco understood that it was easier for the *norteamericano* politicians to gain favor by making war in a strange country, rather than among their own citizenry.

The Colombian politicians and generals still accepted the silver or received the lead, as General Rodriguez's prone body attested, but Francisco doubted their ability to stop the foreign army exploring the countryside. Inside these stone walls, Pablo didn't feel this invading army's buildup. He hadn't seen the planes at the airports and the hard-faced men in camouflage driving through the country in armored vehicles.

Francisco approached Pablo to explain these changes, but Pablo waved him off. Pablo picked up the phone and dialed the warden, staring at the men leaking blood and excrement onto his living room floor. Francisco walked away, surprised to realize that Pablo's mistakes would soon make this *his* empire. He found this insight not altogether unpleasant.

2015

»» 3

FOR TWENTY YEARS, he'd flown for Uncle Sam. Now Cale operated a one-man charter business. His twin-engine turbo prop was a workhorse for the East Coast business traveler or hurried vacationer trying to unhurry. Occasionally, there were more interesting folks. At $2,500 an hour of flight time plus expenses, he wasn't cheap, but he wasn't NetJets either.

This was a quick round-trip across the state to pick up friends from his hometown. Cale was hosting a bachelor party at his house northeast of Wilmington, North Carolina, which was a bit of a summer destination. Air traffic control kept the flight at twenty thousand feet, a tailwind pushed the speed over 350 knots, and they enjoyed a high-pressure system, blue skies, and a smooth landing.

The party was for Blake, who—along with Van, Barry, Dan, and Jay—Cale grew up with. Phil was Blake's new friend Cale had just met. The six grew up together the way kids used to grow up together: They'd shared the same neighborhood bike trails, schools, sports teams, and crowd of friends from the ages of five to eighteen. After high school, the guys lost touch with Blake, briefly reconnected for his first bachelor party and wedding twenty years ago, and had seen him fewer than five times since. If Cale were forced to render judgment, he would conclude that in the interim Blake had cultivated his bad habits at the expense of his good ones. But he remained entertaining since a bachelor party was no place to render judgment.

Cale taxied the King Air to the FBO, where his aircraft got fueled, had routine mechanical service performed, and picked up hospitality services. For this flight, rather than order a car service, Cale crammed the guys into his faded light blue Toyota Land Cruiser. He had left the windows open for the three hours he was gone, but the steering wheel was still too hot to grab firmly for most of the short drive to the house.

On the way, Barry asked, "Why'd Toyota stop making vehicles this shade of blue?"

Dan answered, "Because in the second generation of the twenty-first century, there aren't enough people who want to stick out like 1970s pimps to sell a production run."

Cale thought that was delusional, but perhaps he was just being defensive. He figured it was too hard to get the tint right without the lead in the paint.

Cale's house was ideal for both his waterman hobbies and the survivalist instincts he'd honed over the last few decades. The house sat well off a little-used ribbon-paved road, where the entire driveway could be seen from the front windows. Traffic on the road was light enough that Cale recognized by sound any car that did not belong to one of his few neighbors. His lot stretched seven hundred feet from the asphalt to the water and nine hundred feet from side to side. Marsh bordered his property to the north and south, giving a visitor—or intruder—only two means of approach, both of which were long and visible.

And then there was Jimmy, Cale's security team. Jimmy was a 120-pound mixed breed. Smarter and lazier than the average dog, Jimmy held down the fort when Cale was out. Sometimes Cale left Jimmy in the yard, sometimes in the house. There'd never been a problem with the unwelcome sneaking around.

At the water, a long dock extended east across the tidal grass before reaching open water. His twenty-four-foot center-console Boston Whaler with twin 150-horsepower Mercury outboard motors sat on a sling lift. To the southwest, pines shaded the house from late morning on, and a trailer with rotted tires held an eighteen-foot Hobie catamaran.

A bait shop Cale frequented had stocked the Whaler with squid and Budweiser in advance of their arrival. They fished flounder that afternoon in the marshes, with a light breeze and ample applications of DEET. Van saw a sheepshead snacking on barnacles stuck to a pylon. One by one, they tried to hit it with a compound bow that Cale had tied a 10-pound test line to. After a dozen misses, Cale put on a mask, slipped into the water, took a deep breath, and shot it with a spear gun.

Blake passed out on the aft bench of the boat during the afternoon, his face under a towel and his pasty feet soaking in the summer sun. Back in the marsh, Cale found an oyster bed perfectly located just below the waterline at low tide. He'd revisit the oyster bed in winter with a hammer and thick rubber work gloves.

That evening, they pulled Cale's crab pots. They were heavy, filled mostly with blues and a few stone crabs. Cale tossed the female blues out and calmed the jimmies with ice. With each stone crab, he held a claw stationary with channel locks and stuck a screwdriver in the elbow joint. The crab unhinged the endangered claw from its body. Cale then tossed the now one-clawed stones back, wished them well in regenerating their missing arms, and hoped they'd find their way back to his pots.

The main kitchen at Cale's house was outside. He had installed two oversized burner racks twelve inches off the ground, where beer kegs with sawed-off tops served as kettles. The tops were now fastened with wooden cabinet knobs so they could be used as lids. Cale dumped the blue crabs into one while Jay slid the stone crab claws into the other. Barry prepped the fish on a long, blood-stained, plastic countertop and browned the flounder and sheepshead in cast-iron skillets.

Dan helped Cale spread newspapers over the two sun-worn teak picnic tables, and they spent the next few hours cracking shells and shooting the shit, downing beers and tossing the bottles into a plastic trashcan.

When everyone had their fill, they folded the graveyard of crab shells and dead man's fingers, the yellow "mustard," and the orange dusting of Old Bay into the apple cider vinegar-splashed newspaper. They dumped the package into Hefty bags, and Cale put each in a second plastic bag, then placed those inside trash cans and clipped down the lids to frustrate scavenging raccoons, opossums, and black bears.

Cale thought of himself as an environmentalist, but plastic was just so . . . convenient. He wasn't a global warming environmentalist anyway—more a "clean up our waterway day" kind of environmentalist (and, in all honesty, he used plastic bags on those days too).

They left Frogmore stew on the burner to simmer overnight for breakfast and moved to a row of Adirondack chairs facing the waterway for drinks. Van and Barry tossed a set of oversized lawn darts that could impale a skull at improvised targets in the yard. The sun set behind the chairs, but they watched its reflection in the windows on the island across the waterway. In those houses on the other side, there were five CEOs of Fortune 500 companies, three former United States senators, and two hall-of-fame college basketball coaches.

Dan emptied the last bottle of Evan Williams at two in the morning, and they finished the last hand of no-limit Texas Hold'em minutes later, without a clear winner. Then they all fell asleep while Robert Earle Keen played on the iPod to a set of empty chairs.

Friday started early. The men played thirty-six holes of golf, which was thirty-six more than Cale had played in a decade. His clubs' ancient technology did not go unnoticed.

"Hey Cale," Dan said. "I accidentally opened some of your mail. There was a letter from Sam Snead asking for his clubs back."

At the turn, they each buried their first round's sweat-soaked shirts into their bags. The college-age beer cart girls in golf shorts, polos, and soft spikes were seasoned from a summer of flirting golfers. The guys made off-color jokes—more funny than creepy. The girls over-served them, and Barry told Cale as much—Cale objected, but was too drunk to effectively argue the point.

Even sober, he'd never been much for arguments. That's why being a pilot in the DEA fit him so well. He didn't argue about where to go, usually, and nobody ever argued with him about how to get there. Sure, he wasn't a badass who went undercover into the belly of the beast, with a cellphone as his only link to backup stationed half an hour away. Those dudes were nuts. He didn't need to be a rock star. He was content being the horse bringing the cavalry—essential, in the mix, but protected by teammates' overwhelming firepower.

At dinner Friday, the waiter rolled out plastic-wrapped cuts of meat for their inspection, and their picks arrived later, seared to pink perfection and served on white plates. The sommelier earned his pay, bringing them bottle after bottle, and the men's laughter eventually attracted a crowd. Introductions were made. Chairs and wine shared.

After the meal, it was time for the obligatory strip club send-off of the bachelor. The strip club—men at their finest and women on the brink of the world's oldest profession. Cale noticed a lower abdominal scar on "the lovely Roxanne from Calabash." What did her sitter tell the kids? Cale thought about how he'd struggled to break the news to his two daughters about the Easter Bunny.

His daughters weren't debutantes, but they weren't strippers either. At least, not that they ever told him. And they told him everything, right?

Bachelor parties leeched reason out of twenty-year-olds and forty-year-olds alike—even reluctant partygoers nursing a lifelong friendship that hadn't held common ground in twenty-five years. Cale wondered why they were still friends. Emotion? Nostalgia? No reason at all? For some reason, their youthful bond was strong.

Four forty-something women had followed the party from dinner to the club. Van tipped the host and committed to bottle service so they could be seated in an M-shaped combination of sectionals. Time and money disappeared. The women bought each other dances. In his final memory of the evening, Cale found himself in the champagne room being a poor steward of his resources with two of the party ladies and a dancer. One of the ladies poured a shot on the dancer's arched back, and the other drank it off her bottom. Cale took the next shot. It was from a bottle of Patrón but tasted like strawberry lotion.

Cale didn't remember leaving the club but remembered getting cold on the ride home. Too much sun, wind, and alcohol. His dehydrated skin couldn't get warm until he climbed under the covers. He wasn't sure why he awoke on the living room floor, covered by a beach towel and with Jimmy's head creating nerve damage in his calf.

Yes, bachelor parties were no place to make judgments.

»»» **4**

"**NEGOTIATING WITH OUR** enemies is an extremely difficult task. War is easier. War is far more spectacular than peace. I know because I was Colombia's minister of defense; I delivered the most devastating military setbacks to the FARC in their history. Peace, on the other hand, requires patience, discretion, and beating seemingly insurmountable odds. And peace has many enemies. Yet nothing is more urgent than achieving it."

This was the message Juan Manuel Santos, president of Colombia, gave readers of *The Wall Street Journal* as he prepared to sign a treaty with the guerillas, bringing peace to his country after over fifty years of civil war. In this country of fifty million people, over two hundred thousand had been killed. Countless lives had been stunted by the constant shadow of arbitrary violence.

President Santos continued his message, saying, "It is not often that the interests of the United Nations; the European Union; the Organization of American States; and countries like the United States, Cuba, Venezuela, Chile, and Norway, among others, converge for a common purpose."

A strange set of bedfellows created the treaty. Its ink was still wet as Francisco entered Bogotá International Airport. The government won, but so had the rebels. Officials now slept without exploding, and the rebels gained autonomy. Francisco won too, gaining new passports, the ability to move money, and the opportunity to settle his past grievances. All of his rights lost during America's War on Drugs had been restored. Was it a victory for the *recolectores de café*?

Francisco's Tío Pablo once provided the bean pickers with doctors and employment. While to the government, he was El Capo del Mal, to the people, Tío Pablo was simply El Capo. He provided a zoo for entertainment—with statues, popcorn, and carousels to accompany the hippos, elephants, gorillas, and tigers. After El Capo's assassination in 1993, the zoo's equipment was neglected. The ignored animals escaped. Many of the animals, separated from their protectors, were shot or starved. Some went into hiding, living well or barely subsisting in the city or the surrounding mountains.

Francisco found that the zoo animals' fates paralleled those of El Capo's men after his death. A crate of machine guns didn't protect a lone wolf; some flourished, and some perished on their own. Francisco, himself, had been less directly confrontational toward those who could, with a sacrifice, reach him. He had done what was needed for survival—not just for his own but also for that of his family and the hundreds of countrymen whom he supported. He appeared to wear his Tío's mantle effortlessly, but the responsibilities went to bed with him each evening.

Neither the government nor the rebels deserved or would receive the people's loyalty. Speeches of idealism and acts of corruption would be their legacy until the fighting began again. El Capo's discipline and largesse were extreme and rewarded him with bountiful loyalty. Francisco had idolized Pablo since birth, and Pablo, in turn, had taken Francisco into his fold at an early age. Francisco learned how to exploit mankind's wanton core and to nurture its neediest victims.

Pablo desensitized Francisco to the emotional effects of both murder and exacting discipline within the ranks early on. When Francisco was fourteen, Pablo had summoned him to a meeting.

》》》

"**FRANCISCO, HAVE YOU** been at the refinery, learning from Miguel how to turn the paste into powder?"

"*Sí, Tío Pablo*. Miguel has shown me all the steps of the process, from inspecting the paste when it arrives to processing it into powder and packaging it for shipment."

"Do you enjoy your time with Miguel?"

"He is a Panamanian and has so many degrees from the big university. I think that makes him stand a little apart from the rest of us at the refinery, but he has become my great friend. I have learned so much from him, and I am very grateful to him for that." Francisco hurriedly added, "And to you as well, of course, Tío."

Pablo nodded in understanding. "*De nada*. Francisco, I paid Miguel one million dollars in American money last year. Knowing that, do you think Miguel is satisfactorily rewarded for his work?"

"Tío, you are always very generous. Miguel would not make a million dollars in ten years running a Panamanian factory."

"So you agree that I am fair to Miguel?"

Francisco nodded, not knowing where this was leading but feeling a slight unease.

"Tell me, has Miguel taught you how many kilos of powder you can make from a kilo of paste?"

"Each kilo of paste makes a half kilo of powder, because it loses the weight of the water during the refinement."

"Excellent. So when I had one hundred kilos of paste delivered last time, I should have expected fifty kilos of powder in return. Do you agree?"

"*Sí, Tío*."

"But I received only forty kilos. Has there been any unusual waste at the refinery—big spills or batches going bad?"

"No, Tío. Miguel runs a very clean operation. He is always telling people to be careful with your inventory. That is what he calls it, 'El Capo's inventory.'"

"So if there is no waste of my inventory, what am I to conclude?"

"One of the workers is stealing from you? Not Miguel. Miguel is too . . ."

But his voice trailed off. It had to be Miguel. The workers operated naked in the refinery, so they left with nothing. Miguel controlled the keys, the guns, and the guards.

Francisco wondered how he had not seen it. This was his first lesson in how friendship can blind others to your actions and how you can be blinded if you allow yourself to be.

Pablo watched the waves of recognition ripple across Francisco's face and felt a swelling of pride. Pablo handed Francisco a pistol.

"A fish rots from its head. Miguel is the head of the refinery, and if this rot continues, it will eat us alive. Take care of him and whoever you think is helping him. Better to kill too many than too few." Pablo then nodded to a bodyguard, who would drive Francisco back to the refinery.

The ride to the refinery took an hour bouncing across unpaved trails. Francisco thought about his risks in the confrontation. Who was helping Miguel? There was one other Panamanian in the operation, a guard who Francisco had noticed talking animatedly, yet in hushed tones, with Miguel on more than one occasion; he had thought nothing of it at the time. Now, he decided the guard was the accomplice and would have to die with Miguel.

At the refinery, Francisco found the guard on duty. He walked straight up to him and put a bullet in the side of his head before anyone realized he was carrying a pistol. When Miguel ran into the room to investigate the sound, he found Francisco kneeling beside his bleeding confidant. He ran and kneeled beside Francisco.

"Oh no. Francisco, there is so much blood. Do you know what happened?"

Miguel looked frantically into Francisco's eyes and, seeing the determination, backed away. But not fast or far enough. The pistol kicked in Francisco's teenage hands as he unloaded the cartridge into his friend.

››)

IT WAS HARD for Francisco to believe so much time had passed. Pablo had been dead for over twenty years. Francisco's older brother a few months longer. In El Capo's death, a Colombian pulled the trigger, but the *norteamericanos* told him where to stand. The circumstances around his brother's death, long a mystery, were recently illuminated to show that a *norteamericano* actually pulled that trigger.

How to use this new information weighed greatly on Francisco's mind. He, like the leader of the country, had blood on his own hands and had killed many people's brothers and uncles. Blood followed power and wealth. Now, with the treaty's new freedoms, opportunities were opening, there would be new alignments with new partners and, inevitably, new pursuers. A message from a timeless memory of the wrongs they suffered would serve his family well. Exacting revenge against the *norteamericanos* in their homes was no longer a daydream but a bloody message to deliver that would provide protection.

Today, as always, Francisco wore linen pants and a white guayabera and moved briskly and gracefully. By sight, those observing him could intuit half of his life accurately. Strong swimmer. Amateur car racer. Playboy. Although the government officials claimed to never know his location, he was often photographed with young starlets, whose gowns seemed on the verge of dropping to the floor. If those observing him only heard his name, they would know the other half of his life. Most then averted their eyes to not catch his notice. Even the young thrill seekers filled with machismo treaded silently. There was a saying in Cartagena and Bogotá: "*Si los de Medellín aman tanto a los Escobar, el resto del mundo les tiene miedo.*" The fear the Escobars inspired outside Medellín provided a level of safety that Francisco appreciated. His trip to the United States should write the next chapter in his family's mythology.

Francisco's peers were mostly dead, victims of either the war against the state or the *norteamericanos*' war on drugs. Francisco was accompanied by a man near sixty; his young men stayed in the hillsides because their English was inadequate for the trip. They would be joined later in the trip by a young American immigrant from Cuba for whom Francisco had elevated expectations.

"*Alberto, me gustaría un Heineken, por favor.*"

"*Sí, señor Escobar. Un momento,*" replied the older man as he went to order the drink.

Upon his return, Alberto handed Francisco a stemmed pint glass with a handle, a half inch of foam at the top, and a napkin under the base.

Francisco said, "Thank you, Alberto. Let me ask, have you practiced your English lately?"

"Yes, Mr. Escobar. I watched the TV satellite to practice."

"The satellite TV, Alberto. Very good. We all are a little in need of oiling."

Francisco felt progress's buzz ripple through his emotions. He'd begun undoing the damage to his family's operations. Outside South America, his family's role in the trade was severely diminished, displaced by half-breed Mexicans and medieval Afghanis, both lacking in artistry. Their assets were violence, numbers, and a willingness to prey on and then discard the weak. Francisco followed Pablo's blueprint of elevating the weak, giving them strength when they accepted his patronage, and removing them when they did not. Using the new passports, Francisco would expedite the resumption of meaningful trade in Europe and the United States. That, plus exploiting the new legalized marijuana rules sweeping the globe, would provide

Francisco the opportunity to promote his lieutenants into colonels and his colonels into generals. His men were of better stock than their competitors and would rise above them once again. He needed to spend some time assessing his operation's assets and evaluating the risks of running a legal, regulated business.

Looking at his competition, he bemoaned the trade's current lack of romance. How had it fallen so far? Planes no longer dropped bales at designated coordinates that boats with overhauled engines gaffed and raced to shore. No longer did they use submarines to smuggle kilos under the waves. It was now brute force. Coyotes forced fence jumpers to carry backpacks full of product. Now, eighteen-wheelers were half filled with legitimate goods and half filled with cocaine. They pushed so many through the border that they tolerated the loss of a third of their product to confiscation.

The proud *norteamericanos* who murdered and marginalized his family deserved punishment. Perhaps they were already being punished. The arbitrary violence of the new suppliers had ruined their southern playground. A vacation on the cheap in a Mexican paradise just over the border now risked more than bad water.

Nancy Reagan, her "Just Say No" campaign, and her long, skinny finger pointing at Colombia; the first Bush and his *This Is Your Brain on Drugs* ads; the womanizer-in-chief—these worthy targets were too guarded for him to personally eliminate. So Francisco ignored them and sponsored dissent in the Mexican cartels. This could help him gain traction as they accelerated the rate at which their triggers were pulled on each other.

Francisco and his comrades carried no luggage to the airport; all their necessities waited in the States. The security guard gruffly requested Francisco's ticket and passport. Francisco was in a conversation with Alberto and did not respond immediately.

The guard raised his voice. "*Señor, su atención! Necessito un pasaporte aquí. Ándale ya.*"

Francisco's eyebrow arched as he turned to the barking poodle. He handed over his ticket. He reached into his pocket and pulled out his new passport. The guard worked to hold the fold on the stiff passport open; this was the passport's first use, and it did not bend open easily. The guard began the process of matching identification and ticket.

Then the name clicked. His eyes widened. Involuntarily, he looked up at its owner. He quickly looked back at the forms in his hands. With trembling hands, he stamped the paper, his scribble illegible over the official stamp. He handed the documents back. He mumbled, "*Gracias, señor,*" and bowed his head.

Francisco never missed an opportunity to capitalize on fear. This man's revelation of his own fear would save his life after his rudeness. Francisco reached over the guard's stand and grabbed the guard's name tag. He tilted it and studied it for a moment. Without emotion he said, "*Muchas gracias, Rodrigo Villaramos. Buenos días.*"

The airport experience was new. He had never flown commercial. So many lines. So much waiting. His air force, mostly helicopters, was unequipped for traveling the distance to Miami without stopping several times to refuel. The family's Boeing 747 was impounded by the government twenty years prior. He would check into it; the government should give it back. If they didn't, certain officials might start to dream of explosions once again.

In the United States, Francisco and Alberto would find an untraceable car waiting in the parking lot. They'd use it to enjoy Miami before driving to Savannah. There, he would upgrade his air fleet. Three Gulfstream Vs awaited his review. Forty-five million dollars, wired via a Caymans account this morning, sat with the escrow agent. Once he selected the G5, he would board it and seek out what America's War on Terror referred to as *soft targets*.

Revenge. A degree of personal satisfaction. More important, an advance reminder to his soon-to-be business associates of his timeless memory. With his revenge complete, he'd then return to Savannah, drive back to Miami, and fly commercial to Bogotá. The G5 would travel from Savannah to Bogotá directly, with his new crew and any luggage aboard.

Francisco very much looked forward to the week ahead. He could not help but wonder whether a long-ignored arsonist and pilot foolishly did as well.

»» **5**

IT'S A WONDERFUL Life *was wrong. The George Baileys didn't trash their lives when disaster struck the savings and loan. The Potters didn't either. (The Potters chose a different path anyway.) It's those somewhere between Bailey and Potter who fell apart.*

Three good actions: picking up litter, putting the neighbor's dog back in its yard, and listening to a homeless man's story. One bad action: not stopping to help the old woman with the flat tire in the rain. Or one small deception, initiated or accepted.

"I'm sorry I didn't . . ."

For pride. Convenience. Fear. Each of us our own faults. A run on the savings and loan brought the best out of old George. For the rest of us . . . flip a coin.

A profound thought? Maybe, but as Cale switched from dreaming to being semiawake, he lost it. He could still see George holding his little girl. Was that confetti in the air, and if so, where did it come from? A bell rang for Clarence. Was George laughing or crying? The memory wasn't clear. If he'd kept the thought, he was sure it would change things. Silver bullet, that improved it all. Could even get his knees back to where he could dunk a basketball. How proud he was of that at fifteen. How he took it for granted at twenty-five. With fifty in the windshield closer than forty in the mirror, he'd like to do it again.

>>>

CALE FELT THE sunlight through the screens, heard gulls, smelled marsh, and intuitively knew he was at home but not in bed. Each heartbeat resonated in his temples. A cheek stuck to the hardwood floor, the tingle of pins and needles in a leg. He shook the leg. Something was wrong. Adrenaline stoked by the fears of men with long memories from his earlier life woke him.

Oh, right. Jimmy's head was on his calf. He pivoted his leg from the hip. Jimmy stood, circled, and laid his spine against Cale's.

Cale heard *SportsCenter*. *Dun-na-nunt, dun-na-nunt.* His friends laughing on the den furniture behind him were traveling between drunk and hungover. Cale skipped the "between" part and awoke hungover. *SportsCenter* was the white noise behind every morning he'd felt like this. Chris Berman's voice made him shiver.

It had seemed to Cale like a fun idea to fly old friends for a change. Peeling his face from the hardwoods, he reconsidered and found himself wondering whether they would reimburse him for the jet fuel.

The prior night's worship of golden calves and the omnipresent drumline felt like déjà vu. But Cale had married so young and had been so wrapped up in work and family that he couldn't remember from when. And Maggie, bless her heart, had been merciless on him when he indulged.

Once, when his twins were two, he dragged home from a guys' weekend on a red-eye. Maggie met him in the driveway. She was radiant, and his loins stirred despite exhaustion's fog. She was smiling, and he put on his bravest no-way-I'm-hungover-and-tired face and hoped to hide the scratchiness in his voice and the smell of smoke embedded in his clothes.

"How was Las Vegas . . . honey?" she asked.

Wariness should have crept into his mind with the pause before the word *honey*. He grabbed a long hug before replying.

"It was a lot of fun. The undercards on Holyfield's match were better than the main event. The tickets were expensive, but at least I lost all my bets."

The lame joke wasn't acknowledged. "Sweetheart, I'm glad you had fun," she said.

The switch to a different term of endearment was another missed warning. Cale obliviously plowed ahead with a request for quiet time where they could catch up. The request was politely rebuffed, and he was referred to as *sugar*. Maggie steered the conversation to the week's logistics—who needs to be where doing what on which day. Cale felt the sunshine in every dehydrated cell in his body. He daydreamed of getting into his cool, dark house. Finally, he said, "Mags, I'm beat. You mind if I go catch a nap?"

He caught the word *actually*. Something about adults not complaining about hangovers. Then she was gone, and it was a long daddy day for Cale and not the most rewarding one for his girls. Maggie's eyes laughed as the whip tore flesh from his back.

Anyway, tomorrow Cale could return to his pattern of two cold ones a night (preceded by a day or two of detox). Today, he'd take the Whaler to the beach and hope the sand and salt would wear his friends out. Could their livers keep up this pace for a full seventy-two hours?

Going vertical, Cale became slightly dizzy. He procured ibuprofen, antacids, and lemon-lime Gatorade for triage. More *dun-na-nunt, dun-na-nunt* in the background. The lemon-lime tasted like sweat.

Sweat was something Cale knew. Twenty-five years ago, August meant college football preseason. Two-a-days. Eat, heat, stretch, practice, ice, eat, nap, heat, stretch, practice, ice, eat, and sleep. The pizza guy showed up at nine o'clock to give everybody their large pizza for dessert before bedtime. That was two hours after a pasta and hot wings dinner. He didn't remember vegetables, but he did remember lots of bananas at practice.

He missed preseason. But why? Was it the simplicity? The

competition? Camaraderie? Did they still give freshmen swirlies? Could he still play? The height, broad-shoulders, narrow hips, and big hands were all still intact. His feet were as big as ever, which was good for balance. He could take an eighteen-year-old version of himself, but maybe not a twenty-two-year-old version.

No, he'd take the twenty-two-year-old too, just not in a fair fight. Uncle Sam's training took the fair fight out of him. He'd never wanted to fight, but if he needed to, why make it fair? How had he switched from thinking about playing to thinking about fighting?

Time waited for no one, and he now ached when it rained and knew this weekend's hangover would drag until Thursday. Untold hours in the gym and water slowed the atrophy. Twenty straight years selecting hand-to-hand combat training for his continuing education had calibrated his rise, plateau, and slow decline. What a blessing Maggie had gotten pregnant before his junior season—not just because of the twins, but because it forced manhood on him when he wanted more years of boyhood.

His Augusts had gone through several cycles since his playing days. There were the girls' cheerleading camp years. Those were his favorite Augusts for some reason. There was the year of night flights in the mountains. A decade of back-to-school shopping. One August, he crossed a border sixty times in thirty days. The hardest August, was as a new widower with daughters in high school. There was fruit wine miraculously growing in the bushes. White-knuckled trips to the gynecologist. An empty nester at thirty-nine—that was the second-hardest August. He had back-to-back father-of-the-bride Augusts. His next cycle of life was as a grandpa. If his grandkids had kids at twenty, he'd be a great-grandpa before he could collect social security, assuming they were still paying out social security at that point.

Cale grabbed the iPhone to see if his daughters had called. No. This was the part of life's cycle where he loved them more than they loved him.

Maggie, Cale thought, *I could have used you sticking around. I know, I've mentioned this before. I know you've mentioned you wanted to. I did my best as a father. I forced their dates to introduce themselves, even in college. I checked for a smile, a firm shake, a direct look in the eyes. Weather permitting, we'd meet in the backyard, me with my shirt off. I'd show whatever project I was working on. Did my power tools and slobbering dog deter the young men's loins? The girls' social networking left breadcrumb trails. Well, they survived. C'est la vie. They've started families of their own now. Old Gramps can wait for his Christmas cards to arrive and will not complain about it. I know you agree, but sometimes I need reminding.*

>>> **6**

WHAT DID MARK Twain say about life on a boat being like jail with a chance of drowning? How would Twain feel if he paid as much for the privilege as Joe had? Slips, refueling, and provisioning were all expensive. When the captain moved the boat without him and sent him a single bill, it was at least one quick slash of the knife rather than death by a thousand pinpricks.

The boat was really his wife's. She had passed eighteen months ago, six months after the boat was ordered and two months before it was delivered. He had tried to sell it, but he couldn't stomach losing a million dollars on something he'd never used. Now his stomach felt differently. Between the cost of owning and operating *Framed* and entertaining family guests, a million dollars sounded OK.

Maria had said, "Joe Pascarella, this boat will make your sons and grandkids come visit us." But in truth, his sons were busy. They had families and careers. They barely had time for Joe to visit them. He saw his daughters-in-law's hair go gray worrying about their two-year-olds out at sea.

No, he was trying to put himself in a bad mood. He liked the boat, and he could afford it.

Joe's friend Tony Moreno was onboard. As teenagers, they started together as apprentice carpenters. In their twenties, they became foremen together. At forty-two, after twenty-five years, Joe retired from the union to be a developer. Tony's crews worked his local projects. Retired after forty-seven years in the union, Tony was in good financial shape with a nice pension and benefits for life.

On this trip, Joe's nephew and two friends—all three professional fitness trainers—were along as a favor to his sister. He paid to have them flown from Islip to Miami. They were accompanying Tony, the captain, and Joe up the East Coast to Sag Harbor. For the first half of the trip, they hadn't been much help. Then again, the ship hadn't been attacked by pirates, so maybe their waxed chests deterred high crimes at sea.

Joe couldn't get straight what to think of guys whose job was to get stay-at-home moms to do push-ups and sit-ups and who then did the same thing themselves in their free time. Joe had loved baseball as a kid, and his arms showed that he'd swung a hammer for the next twenty-five years. But his gut showed that he didn't buy into the exercise-for-appearances phenomenon.

The trip started with flat seas up to Jacksonville. For dinner Joe, Tony, and the captain went to Hooters and watched the Yankees while they ate. The trainers saw a Jaguars preseason game. The next day, they left early and arrived late in Charleston. They ate Low Country food heavy with butter. The trainers explored town while Tony and Joe retired to the flybridge and pinochle.

>>>

THE THREE GIRLS met two months ago, when they'd moved to Charleston as traveling nurses. They shared an apartment their agency paid for, and they worked the ER, moving between triage stations and assisting general practitioners with minor cut-and-sew operations or setting bones. Occasionally, they took shifts in the surgical center, where surgeons with IQs of 140, coke-bottle glasses, and fish-belly skin dropped f-bombs like drill sergeants. Anesthesiologists, who enjoyed themselves more than other specialties in med school, calmed the patients' nerves as they put them to sleep. The nurses stayed observant, made sure everything went smoothly. They made sure no instruments were left in a belly and no shortage of catgut.

After work, they hit the gym, watched a DVD, and got take-out. On their days off, they lived the traveling part of their titles. In four trips, they'd been to every beach in South Carolina and Georgia they'd heard of. They had closed down The Salty Dog in Hilton Head and stumbled through the pine trees to the Marriott. They had eaten twenty types of seafood at Bernie's in Myrtle Beach. They had drunk Natural Lights with lime at Ocean Annie's, near Kingston's Plantation. They had paddled around alligators at St. Simon. They had been stung by jellyfish at Tybee Beach.

This weekend, they'd planned to drive into North Carolina. The bags were already in the trunk when the big guy had a personal collision with Ashley's car. Now, instead, she awoke to the sound of big diesel boat engines. She felt them more than heard them. The boat left its slip slowly in reverse, then went forward, then reverse again, and finally steadily forward. Without getting out of bed, she pulled back the porthole's curtain and watched the sky behind the sailboat masts that they passed.

"How does the weather look, Ash?" asked one of her roommates.

"Sunny," Ashley said. "Do we have any sunscreen?"

"Sure, here you go."

The cabin was as private as a boat got. It was the only one you didn't go through the main salon to get to. You entered a slow-opening, shock-pressure-assisted door. It opened vertically, and the cabin was down several steep stairs. The only window was an inoperable porthole. The cabin had a small built-in dresser, a really small bathroom, and a queen-size bed. It abutted the engine room—normally crew quarters.

The girls dressed for a day on a boat: bikinis under a layer of light clothing for the morning breeze. Ashley was the first to come out of the hatch.

>>>

LEAVING CHARLESTON, JOE looked back at the city, a special place in the early dawn light. When the first stowaway climbed out of the aft stateroom, Joe spilled Folgers on his Docksiders. She wore a thin hooded sweatshirt and board shorts, and a bikini strap was visible inside her baggy collar.

Seeing Joe, she sang out, "What a beautiful morning. Hi, my name's Ashley Walker. Are you Mr. Pascarella?"

Blonde hair, West Texas smile, Southern California wardrobe. Joe rubbed the pendant on his necklace and smiled.

"Ashley, I never knew how much St. Christopher liked me until this moment." *Where did that come from? It was almost smooth. Well, if she knew St. Christopher was the patron saint of travelers, then it was smooth. Either way, it was flattering.* They locked eyes. Joe noticed that a brightness rose in her cheeks.

Ashley's friends bumped her from behind as they tried to leave the cabin. Joe found a towel to clean up the coffee. Ashley made the introductions, but Joe missed the other girls' names.

After the shock, he learned that Ashley and her friends were traveling nurses. They were stationed in Charleston for the year, working a seven days on, seven days off schedule. They were starting their seven off. He loved the youthful looseness in their plan to get a rental car and drive home from wherever this cruise ended.

A traveling nurse was a new concept to Joe. Apparently, they were well paid and served in the country's most troubled hospitals, like secular missionaries, often in the country's most exciting cities. They worked twelve-month contracts and then picked a new place to go.

The three nurses had been parked in front of Rainbow Row's brightly colored homes. One of the trainers had physically stumbled into Ashley's car, leaving a dangling mirror and oversized knee imprint in the side panel. Of course, the stumbler was Gino, Joe's nephew. The negotiation over the incident ended with the trainers offering the girls a trip up the coast on Gino's uncle's yacht and an agreement that $1,000 would cover the damage. None of the trainers had the money on them. Joe figured, *What's another $1,000, given the upgrade in company now onboard?*

》》》

THE BOAT SPLIT the buoys—red on the left and green on the right. They made it to open water and turned north. The captain promised good traveling conditions this morning. He pushed the throttle down to a cruising speed of twenty-five knots. This was different from a booze cruise.

Joe and Tony's accents were different from the younger guys'. They said their accents were different because there were not as many first-generation Italians and Irishmen in the city or on Long Island now; most of the first generations now were Pakistani or Caribbean. Ashley wasn't sure they believed this was the reason, but she could tell that's what they felt was wrong with their old neighborhood. They didn't use racial slurs or towelhead jokes, but she knew they missed the old neighborhood's communal feel. Maybe it did take a village.

Ashley joined her friends to sunbathe on the deck. They listened to music through their iPhone earbuds. She felt restless and sat on the bowsprit to watch the water below, trying to guess which wave would splash the boat hard enough to spray her. For some reason, that never grew old.

Tony came to ask about lunch. "Girls, what can I make you for lunch?"

"Tony, show us the kitchen, and I'll fix lunch for y'all."

"On a boat it's the *galley*, and youse are our guests. Besides, I can't have you Southern girls frying chicken while we're motoring out here. You'd spill so much grease you'd burn us down. The coast guard couldn't get here quick enough. I will make lunch."

"We're more like stowaways, and I promise not to use the deep fryer. How about you and I fix it together for everybody?"

"Everybody but the Fabios. They have chemicals they eat to get the chemicals out of their bodies. We don't want to get the chemistry wrong and give them pimples; they wouldn't come out of their room for a week."

Tony used plates with a rubbery ring around the bottom to keep them from sliding. He threw potato chips on the six plates, while Ashley ripped apart a rotisserie chicken and mixed the meat with mayonnaise, grapes, and onion to make chicken salad. She scooped it onto the rye bread Tony gave her, peppered it, and sliced the sandwiches diagonally.

The captain skippered the boat from the salon's controls. Joe read a book in the covered lounge outside the main level. The boat had so many spaces that it was hard for Ashley to know what to call each one. She delivered the plates and sat with Joe to eat, while Tony dropped into a chair and picked up the *ESPN* college football preview issue.

"Joe, how do you become a good negotiator?"

She saw that the question caught Joe off guard.

"Why do you think I'm a good negotiator? How could someone who owns this money pit be a good negotiator?"

"Well, you're successful. I don't think you're in the Mafia. So you must have negotiated a lot."

"I guess. Maybe I'm a good business negotiator but a bad personal negotiator. Do you want business or personal negotiating advice?"

"Let's start with business."

"Good, business is easy. The best way to negotiate is to *know* that you don't care if you get what you're negotiating for."

"But aren't there times when I *will* care?"

"Not really. You only *think* you care. Give me any business worry, and I can make you see you don't care."

"Big picture," she said. "I want to start a staffing company that provides nurses. It's what I know, and hospitals always need good suppliers of contract nurses. But I want the nurses to work three ten-hour shifts in a hospital and one ten-hour shift in a shelter for homeless or abused women and children each week. A lot of nurses would love this. Helping people is why they became nurses to begin with, even if, somewhere along the way, they forgot that. But how do I negotiate with the hospitals to get them to pay for the shifts at the shelter? I have ten friends who'd join me tomorrow if we could get a contract!"

"So what do you *think* your concern is?"

"I need the hospitals to pay for the shift at the shelter. I've tried to sell them the idea by saying that they'd be helping the community and that they'd get good press from it. They said they couldn't afford to pay for it. I showed them all the information about how when they see these patients in the ER, they lose more money than if they paid someone to treat them *before* they came to the ER. They still said they couldn't afford it."

"Ashley, I think you got the focus of what you care about scrambled up. I don't think what you care about is getting the hospital to pay for the shift at the shelter. I think what you care about is (a) getting nurses into more rewarding work without giving up money and (b) helping some people in trouble stop their small problems before they become big problems. A stitch in time saves nine. Right?"

"That sounds right, but what's the difference?"

"So now you know you don't care about getting the hospital to pay for the shift. Right?"

"I guess."

"Once you *know* that, instead of 'guess' you do, then you don't have to keep trying to sell them on paying for that shift. You can change your pitch and say the girls—and boys, sorry—will be happier, give better care, stay in their jobs longer, whatever argument you want to use if they get this day at the shelter. You can change it from one day a week to one week a month. Again, whatever argument you can use is great. But now that you know that you don't care if the hospital pays for the shift, what you negotiate changes."

"I don't see it."

"What you care about is the *outcome*, not how it's paid for. Why not ask for 25 percent more per hour and use that to pay for it? Take less profit from running the company. Sell it to doctor offices instead of hospitals. I don't know the answer, but I know if we noodle it around for an hour, day, week, or month, we'd come up with a lot of ways to swing it. It helps in a negotiation not to be pressured to make something happen."

"Maybe."

"There are a thousand ways to skin a cat. You think about it. I'll think about it with my eyes closed for the next half hour." He smiled, got up, and climbed the steps to the flybridge.

Lesson over, Ashley thought. She grabbed the magazine Tony had been reading.

》》》

JOE KNEW THE trainers' plan didn't include the girls staying in their own stateroom. Who could resist the primate grunts that passed for their discourse? He grinned at their disappointment from the first night.

Joe reflected on a good day. During the ride to North Carolina, he spent a lot of time with the nurses, and the trainers kept to themselves. As they headed to port, the sky was sunny, but the waves grew larger. The captain said the first hurricane of the season was six hundred miles to the east. Joe kept wondering what about being around a beautiful woman made the air a little clearer and the sun a little brighter.

>>>

THAT AFTERNOON, WHEN the boat had docked, the girls changed into shorts, sports bras, and running shoes. They found a jogging path around an elementary school on the island near some marshes and did a couple of loops. The path was busy with joggers and dog walkers. A field hosted folks tossing Frisbees. On a concrete basketball court, men played five versus five, with extra players waiting for the next game.

They stopped at a public boat ramp in the shadow of a drawbridge connecting the island to the mainland. It was two hundred yards and several socioeconomic levels from the marina. There were kids crabbing in knee-deep water. Old black men sat on five-gallon buckets, fishing with cut bait. Flat-bottomed metal boats and fiberglass ski boats queued up to get out of the water. Men backed trailers attached to pickup trucks onto the ramp and snapped at their wives as they tried to load the boats onto the trailers. The men from every boat without children dumped empty beer cans into the open-top trash cans in the parking lot.

>>>

IN THE EVENING, Joe and Tony walked across the bridge. They found two stools at a busy oyster bar with seven-foot-high ceilings and ordered two pounds of steamed shrimp, cornbread, and longnecks. The place did good business. After dinner, they bought a pack of Winstons and another round. They tipped out and went to the front porch to watch the busy two-lane street and sidewalk.

The trainers and the nurses were gone when they got home. Joe came across a small urge to track them down and have a couple of nightcaps with Ashley.

>>>

THE TRAINERS WERE in their tight black uniforms, cologne applied and waiting by the time Ashley was ready to go out. The girls hadn't seen much of them that day. Occasionally, Gino tried to awkwardly claim possession of one of Ashley's friends. The intent seemed more a signal to his friends than to hers; her friend was, aside from polite interaction, unresponsive.

Generally, the guys spent the day in their staterooms watching movies, only coming out to sunbathe for a couple of hours. Now they were drinking vodka tonics. The captain poured pinot grigio for the girls, and they had sunset cocktails while he brought out a tray of snacks.

For dinner, they went to a seafood restaurant. A five-piece reggae band played the outside seating area, where there were around thirty people eating dinner and listening to the music. Ashley wondered how much the guys in the band were making for these couple of hours; they were really good. How many times did U2 play for thirty people before they started selling out football stadiums? Maybe that's how her business would have to start.

After the band finished, the girls walked back over the bridge to the island marina. On the way, they passed the trainers, who were following their ears to a dance club across the street. Back on the boat, the girls locked their cabin door and were asleep before midnight.

A secretive knock woke Ashley and her friends. She looked at her phone: three thirty in the morning. The knock became less timid. It grew persistent, even a little angry. The girls, used to sleeping in hospital break rooms, covered their heads and went back to sleep.

>>> **7**

ON SATURDAY MORNING, Barry went for chicken and biscuits and Jay stocked libations while Cale prepped the vessel. He lowered the boat off the lift, topped off the gas tanks from a plastic can, and primed the fuel line. He unlocked the shed, pulled out a funboard, a longboard, and bait from the freezer and loaded them on the Whaler. He added two paddleboards, then fit six surfcasters into the holders welded onto the aluminum rail above the helm.

The veins in his temples pulsed with each step, and the humidity took its toll. His fingers were fatter than Milwaukee's juiciest bratwursts. At one point, Cale found himself holding the day's bait—packs of frozen shrimp and ballyhoo—against the side of his head. He pondered how many times today he'd wonder why he smelled rotten fish. He tossed the bait in the boat's well and sprayed his head with a hose.

The passengers finally loaded at a quarter to noon. Jimmy sat on the end of the dock, his head cocked to the side.

"Sorry, J-man. Hold down the fort."

Hurricane Arlene was hammering Bermuda, but that was good news for the surf report: The sea buoys showed waves four to six feet high, spaced fifteen seconds apart outside Masonboro. That was as close to Waikiki as the East Coast got.

Cale started the Mercuries and slipped into the channel. The first low bridge was a half mile south. A sailboat under motor and a tug pushing a barge of pine mulch both slowed for the noon opening.

Cale wondered how a pine tree could be cut down, mulched, put on a barge, put on a truck, put in a bag, put back in a truck, put in a store, and sold off the shelf for two dollars a bag? What did the guy who sold the tree get? How does three Abraham Lincolns sound? Copper, not paper.

The same thought with bananas. If a bunch three thousand miles away from the trees was bought for two dollars, how much did that guy get paid to shimmy up the trunk and get them down? Cale figured this mental threading was what all pilots did when autopilot had the wheel.

The boom of two Marine Corps Harrier jets grabbed everyone's attention. The jets crossed paths with a floatplane. It would have been a direct hit if they weren't separated by twenty thousand vertical feet.

Jay asked, "Have you flown those?"

His friends always fished to see if he secretly made bombing runs for the military. Knowing Jay meant the Harrier, Cale answered, "Yeah, I've flown floatplanes. Except for the landing, it's about as exciting as driving a pontoon boat."

Watching the floatplane brought back an old memory. While he was flying one in the Keys, he had spotted a cigarette boat in the hook of a small mangrove island. A cigarette boat was de facto suspicious. They were super uncomfortable, expensive to operate, and really, really fast. Their cargo tended to also be expensive and illegal. But hiding one in the mangroves? Come on.

Cale's passenger, Agent Gonzalez, nodded downward and said, "Pilot, buzz the treetops."

They did three loops without finding any sign of life.

Cale picked up the radio and called the patrol boat in the area, "This is Aerial One, looking for Deep Blue. Over."

"This is Deep Blue. Proceed Aerial One. Over."

"This is Aerial One. We have a cigarette boat stashed in the bite on the island just south of Picnic Island. Over."

"This is Deep Blue. Roger that. We are ten minutes out. Over."

Picnic Island had a shallow beach, a few palms for shade, and a forgiving sandbar as its only barrier to approach. It was a popular spot for a family beach day. The mangrove island where the cigarette boat was tethered looked uninhabitable and lacked either a local or formal name.

"This is Deep Blue. Per the charts, we can't access the bite until the tide rises. We should be deep enough in three hours. Over."

Cale was about to acknowledge they'd maintain surveillance until then when Agent Gonzalez picked up the radio. "This is Aerial One. Roger that. Is the . . . lagoon . . . clear for us to land? Over."

Deep Blue said the lagoon was reef free after the channel, so if Cale thought he could land in the lagoon, he should be clear. Cale double-checked his charts. He buzzed the mangroves again and inspected his runway.

As the plane turned around again, Agent Gonzalez asked, "Pilot, any reason not to touch down in the lagoon?"

This was a unique situation. Cale was in charge of the operation of the plane, the safety of his passenger, and the condition of the vessel. But Gonzalez was the operational superior. So if safety in landing wasn't the issue, Cale's thoughts about the safety of investigating the cigarette boat didn't matter.

Cale responded, "Sir, I think the plane can safely land as far as trees, wind, and reefs are concerned."

"Then let's get down there."

"Sir, any reason we can't keep an eye on this site and wait until Deep Blue can check things out with our support?" Cale left unsaid that they would be checking things out with *no* support.

Gonzalez replied, "Pilot, let's get on that pond and unravel this mystery."

A democracy was not an effective organization, but a dictatorship could effectively move you in the wrong direction very quickly—which was where, with his vote torn up—Cale thought they were headed. Gonzalez, he assumed, was rehearsing for his next press conference.

Cale cut down hard over the mangroves and landed with a small splash. The runway he'd chosen led away from the cigarette boat into the middle of the lagoon.

After the plane's momentum dissipated, he turned and brought the plane slowly back toward the mangroves. There was still no movement on the cigarette boat. There was little wind, and Cale cut the engine and coasted toward the trees. Gonzalez got on the loudspeaker.

"This is the United States Drug Enforcement Agency. We have a plane and patrol boat in the area. We need to come aboard your craft. Please come out and identify yourself."

There was no response. Maybe it was abandoned or stashed for later. Or perhaps the four Haitians hiding with their Kalashnikovs' scopes on the plane's cockpit didn't understand English.

Thirty yards from the trees, the plane coasted to a stop. No Haitians yet. Cale unbuckled, pulled on a bulletproof vest, grabbed a collapsible bone fishing pole, and opened the door so he could push the plane the rest of the way. When he stepped onto the pontoon, he knew. The smell of a large decaying mammal was unmistakable. They looked anyway. They both threw up. Cale pushed the plane back and waited for the tide to rise and their friends to tow the vessel out. A great industry, the drug trade. You rarely had to worry about retirement benefits.

Seeing today's floatplane in the sky, the smell came back to him, and bile rose up in his throat. He took his eyes off the sky, cut the Whaler's wake, slipped past the waiting boats, and went under the bridge. The channel broadened, and he pushed the throttle down. The Whaler planed, and he trimmed the Mercs up. The sun, salt spray, and wind cut Cale's hangover.

The channel narrowed. The clearance on the next bridge was nineteen feet, and marinas blanketed both banks. The mate on a forty-two-foot Hatteras sport fisher heading north lowered the boat's antennas to squeeze under the bridge rather than wait for the half-past noon opening. The west bank's bar was slinging beers, tequila shots, steamed shrimp, and fried fish sandwiches. At the east bank's, a guitar man entertained the shrimp-and-grits crowd. The fuel docks had boats rafted up and waiting.

Normally, sport fishers plied the inlet separating Harbor Island from the seven miles of uninhabited sand, saw grass, and turtle nests of Masonboro Island. Today, the high seas advisory kept all but the charter fishers docked. Why did someone who got on a boat every third year think an eight-hour trip to the Gulf Stream in high seas would be fun? The wahoo may bite, and if you weren't chumming the waters, you might reel a few in. You'd get—say—fifteen minutes of excitement over eight hours. Even those lucky few would feel compressed spines the whole drive back to Ohio. Hemingway fished the Caribbean for a reason.

On Masonboro's west coast, the waters were calm. Runabouts tossed cinder block anchors in the shallows, and their passengers waded in the eighty-degree water. The beaches were covered in canned beers, baseball hats, bikinis, menthols, tattoos, and dogs. In the deeper water, a seventy-two-foot Ferretti with Long Island port of call markings sat at anchor, with midsize local cabin cruisers bobbing on either side. Dance music pounded from its decks, and liquor bottles lined its mid-deck bar.

Cale dropped a hook off the bow. Blake and Van wanted to stay with the Whaler to fish. Phil wanted to explore a bit. Dan and Jay took paddleboards to sweat it out. Barry and Cale grabbed surfboards and headed across the island.

At first sight, the ocean confirmed the buoys' report: chest- to head-high swells, nicely spaced. The jetty and its turbid water and bull sharks were a mile north. Cale really didn't like bull sharks—too much testosterone. Every two hundred yards, a surfer pod gathered past the break. Longboarders, far out, caught open swells, while those on short boards chased fully formed curls closer to shore.

Cale took a board of his own, waded through the whitewater, duck dived a breaker, and paddled into the lineup. Breathing hard, his hang-over forgotten, he watched a set form, slipped into position, picked the second wave, waited one-two-three, and paddled. The wave was a left arm break, the board angled down the line, and he rode from the curl onto the face and popped back to the curl. The swell built as the water got shallower, and he got three more turns in before popping over the lip as the break caught him.

The blue sky, consistent waves, no wind, and no chop made ten minutes flow smoothly into an hour, an afternoon. At one point, bob-bing in the waves, Cale noticed three bikinis walking on the beach. The tall blonde in the middle looked like she was here to shoot *Sports Illustrated*'s swimsuit issue. The muscles of her long legs flexed with each step. Thin straps connected the triangles of her black bikini, which covered her most private areas and highlighted her fit, tan, feminine figure. An hour later, Cale noticed the girls again coming back up the beach. He rode a wave all the way into the whitewater to get a better look at the goddess. Except for his realization that she was his daughters' age, the closer look was worth the hard paddle back through the breaking waves.

Barry took his board back to the boat and brought over a surfcaster and a cooler. Pods of surfers left, appeared, and left again. At five, Cale rolled up the leash. His calves were sunburned, his nipples raw, and his elbows aching. His orthopedist had told him he had bursitis in his left elbow. That sounded to him like something you got in middle age. (Kind of like having an orthopedist.) Wincing, Cale pulled off his rash guard, reached past the twenty-five-inch red drum in the cooler, and slipped a can into a koozie.

The low tide had doubled the width of the beach. Three drinks later, the guys headed for the Whaler. A bikinied mom whose kids were with their dad for the weekend floated next to the Whaler in a life jacket, sipping not her first Natural Light of the day. On second glance, Cale recognized Phil floating beside her, hiding underneath a wide-brimmed hat he hadn't possessed earlier.

Barry asked, "Have you seen the rest of our crew?"

The mom pointed, "Two of your friends went to the big cabin cruiser. I haven't seen any others."

Phil climbed aboard the Whaler and grabbed two beers. He asked the mom, "You want a fresh one?"

She climbed aboard for her drink. And sure, she accepted Phil's offer of a ride to the bar. Which bar? Did it matter? Was it appropriate to be there in just a bikini? Why wouldn't it be? The place was on the water, after all.

She hollered to her friends. Her younger dental technician coworker—equally lit, less endowed but with a flatter stomach—joined up. The guys whose beers they had consumed all afternoon gave Phil the evil eye.

Barry pulled the anchor onboard. The Whaler's bow was aground and the passengers moved to the stern to help it release. A wading Phil pushed the bow. Cale trimmed the engines down, reversed the props, and the sand released. Phil wallowed aboard, head and belly first, his legs kicking in the air. He scraped his way across the bow.

Six boats were rafted to the Ferretti. Several liquor bottles now rolled empty on the deck. Bronzed and burned skin was everywhere. Girls in bikinis or Daisy Dukes pulsed to synthesized rhythms. Shirtless dudes grooved off beat. Three massive bodybuilders with deep tans and permafrowns, guffawed like morning DJs and played cards in the shade of the flybridge.

Blake, Barry, and Van were on the flybridge with two Tommy Bahama types and three girls in sundresses. Despite the dress, Cale recognized his goddess from the beach and involuntarily waved. Her head tilted to the side, but she smiled and waved back. Cale found himself involuntarily smiling. He also found himself wondering about this mix of old Italian men sitting with beautiful women above a ladder where three young mastiffs guarded the approach. He tried to remember whether this size Ferretti cost three or four million.

Cale cut the props and knotted onto a Sea Ray's stern cleats. Barry crossed the tie-ups to the Ferretti. Phil, Mom, and Mom's young coworker improvised a dance floor while they waited. Cale, feeling awkward over the wave-and-smile combo, looked for things to fix on the Whaler. Twenty minutes later, Blake and the guys crossed the gunwale with plastic tumblers and the flybridge girls. The goddess smiled at Cale as she boarded. Angst crept over him as he started the engines, cast off, and pointed north.

A DESIRE TO avoid the massive expense of hurricane season insurance on the yacht had pushed Joe to take this trip up the eastern seaboard. Now he was docked in Harbor Island, North Carolina, where hurricane-induced ocean swells were too big for cruising. The stop-and-go of the inland waterway drove him nuts, so their trip would make it no further today. Joe was positive Fort Lauderdale was whitecap free.

As Ashley came out of the aft stateroom just after sunrise, his cynical mood lifted and he grinned.

"Happy Saturday, Joe," she sang out to him.

"To you as well. Did we wake you?"

"No, I had plenty of sleep."

The poor trainers, Joe thought, were apparently so close but still so far. Since Joe didn't want to fight Arlene's waves, he asked the captain to find an anchorage where they could feel the breeze. They cast off, the captain eased from the slip, fast idled less than a mile, and anchored off the north end of a state park. Joe unbuttoned his shirt, knotted the waist tie of his swim trunks, and dove off the bowsprit. He swam the hundred yards to the shallows with his head above water, doing frog strokes. He waded ashore, squishing the clay-like sand between his toes, his seventy-three-year-old lungs only slightly out of breath. The predawn fishermen were returning from the ocean side and loading their boats to head home for breakfast.

Joe walked east, then left the trail and climbed a dune. The ocean advanced in long swells. It looked like a Hawaiian postcard filled with mid-Atlantic green water. He looked west and saw Tony standing on the dive platform, tossing bread to seagulls, and chatting up the nurses. No sign of the trainers. He looked to the south. The island was a long, narrow strip of sand, kind of like Fire Island but without the parking lots and volleyball courts. He looked north past the jetty and saw marinas, condos, and boatyards across the channel. Beyond that, he glimpsed the backs of three-story houses on the beach that were built over carports tall enough to protect them from flooding. The breeze felt great.

Two old-timers sat on coolers. They drank coffee from thermos lids and savored tinfoil-wrapped bacon, egg, and cheese sandwiches. They'd had decent luck, mostly blues. A drum over thirty inches had to be thrown back. A couple of ladyfish. One tarpon that broke the lightweight tackle.

The sand was rougher on the Atlantic side, the tide low but incoming. The big seas washed up new sea wood. Thousands of barnacles clinging to a former pylon gasped for water. Joe picked up a few shells that caught his eye and tossed them into the water.

He walked north, toward the jetty, and watched a fisherman drag a three-foot shark out of the water. Surfers bobbed in the waves a hundred yards out. A pelican dive-bombed a bait ball in between the surfers and the fisherman. For not the first time, he wondered why people surfed jetties. Were the waves that different? A pair of paddle-boarders stroked into the swells as they came out the inlet. Everyone and everything was crowding the jetty.

It was midmorning when Joe started for the boat. He passed the nurses cutting through the island, wet from their swim. Ashley gave him a hug and a lingering squeeze on his upper arm. He could feel the wetness on his chest where her bikini fabric had pushed against him. They said the boat was quiet; the trainers weren't up yet when they left.

Reaching the muddy sand, Joe aimed his swim for the anchor line. The tide was stronger than he'd expected. He barely grabbed the dive platform. Standing on the platform, the breeze and sun took the water off him and his skin tingled with the slight itch of drying saltwater.

Tony and the captain were playing Scrabble, and Joe joined them for a second cup of coffee. For someone with a ninth-grade education, Tony was excellent at Scrabble.

Tony said, "Did you see my girls in their bikinis?"

"Yeah. It was about enough for me to fake a heart attack to get some reviving."

"You think they brought any little blue pills with them?"

Joe laughed, "I thought you'd graduated to a pump," as he went below. He changed into Bermuda shorts, fastened his floral shirt with the wooden buttons, and slipped on his Docksiders. The trainers assembled egg white omelets and protein smoothies in the galley. When he was their age, he and the other foremen would knock back two shots, two beers, and a roast beef hoagie during lunch and then go work another five hours. These princesses had three gin and tonics over an afternoon and started slurring. Maybe they needed the yolks.

On the boat's leeward side, the captain used a remote control to lower the dinghy via a motorized pulley. The dinghy hit the water, and Tony grabbed the cable and walked it to the dive platform. He released the carabiner attaching the dinghy to the pulley and secured the bowline to a cleat.

Nodding at the dinghy Tony said, "Hey, Joe, let's check out the neighborhood."

A couple of minutes later, Tony and Joe boarded, lowered the propeller, key-cranked the engine, released the bowline, shoved off, and pushed down the throttle.

The permanent inflatable had a hard bottom and a thirty-five-horsepower outboard. The US Navy and Coast Guard used larger versions for fast access into shallow water. Tony sat in the skipper seat, and Joe sat to port.

Tony was a natural-born icebreaker; he didn't even know there *was* ice. Old, young, male, female, pretty, ugly, rich, poor, busy, bored, alone, in a group, drunk, sober—it didn't matter. As a result, they met the couple on the Waverunner up from Murrells Inlet for the day and the guys in the leaking johnboat with the forty-year-old, 15-horsepower Evinrude. Tony chatted at the sandbar with picnicking families, their anchors stretched out along the beach beside their umbrellas, folding chairs, coolers, and unleashed dogs. Tony and Joe drank canned beer with some fellow carpenters. These Southern carpenters—with their sun-bleached hair, sunburns, and blurred tattoos—were not union men.

At two o'clock, Joe phoned the captain to prepare sandwiches. Travelling back to *Framed* but still half a mile away, Joe heard his nephew's music. Smaller boats were rafted alongside the big Ferretti. A small party seemed to have started while they were out.

"Tony, was it the music blasting that got the first boat to raft up? And the second one rafted because a first was rafted?"

"I'm betting Twitter. Gino probably tweeted to the local weight-lifting community that he was having a party today with all you can drink protein shakes. We should have told the captain not to give him the proper location."

"I think we're stuck with the *boom-ta-boom-ta-boom-boom-boom* the rest of the day."

After a brief pause to survey the Ferretti's decks, Tony added, "Of course, there is a bright side to having young visitors too."

Tony brought the dinghy to the dive platform, and Joe secured it with the raft's bowline. They would wench it up after the rafters left. Twenty people were spread out across the yacht's main deck, and a makeshift bar was set up in the lower console. Joe shook a few hands, watched some interesting dance moves, and climbed to the flybridge.

Eating his roast beef sandwich, he flipped off the flybridge's speakers. He watched the nurses come across the dunes, enjoying the view enough he almost didn't hear the music below. He finished his Budweiser and twisted the cap off another. He stretched out and opened his book. The fiberglass canopy shaded most of him. The heat, shade, breeze, and Budweiser overpowered the *boom-ta-boom* and hysterical shrieks of laughter from below, and Joe fell asleep.

At five thirty, he awoke to Tony sitting across from him, showered and shaved and with a highball in each hand. Joe blinked out the sleep, sat up, and took the drink that was offered. He looked to either side of the boat and saw more boats tied on. He took a sip and gurgled the booze around to take the taste of sleep out of his mouth.

"Nothing attracts a crowd like a crowd," he said. "You sleep?"

"No. Too many interesting people onboard. The things you can pierce. It's a brave new world."

"Is that why you're so scrubbed? Getting something off or trying to get something on?"

"Old dogs still hunt," Tony laughed. "Good for you to remember."

"Yeah, but what if you catch it?"

"Hang on as long as you can."

Thumping up the ladder, a big, good-looking full head of gelled hair peered into the flybridge, followed by a pair of massive tanned shoulders. There was not much kindness around the eyes and probably not much intelligence. The confidence was a consolation prize for a mediocre soul. Seeing his nephew made Joe tired.

"Hey, Gino, how's the party?"

"It's great, Uncle Joe. Can I tell the captain to run the little boat into the village and buy some vodka? I think we're on the last bottle. Also, could he pick up some lean steaks and whey protein mix?"

"Gino, if he wasn't here, who would know what button gets the anchor up or how to start the boat?"

"Hey, Gino," said Tony, "who told you girls want tall, dark, and needy? With your shiny hair, milkshake muscles, and cabin on this boat, you start with first and goal and don't even score a field goal. It was like the Giants before the Tuna."

"I got something for you, Tony. Fifty bucks says I could have any girl on this boat today. You want some of that action?"

"If you had a fifty, I'd considerate it, but I don't need fifty more of your uncle's money. We played pinochle yesterday."

"Use gin, Gino. Those girls aren't going to know the difference."

"Uncle Joe, we could really use some vodka. It's got fewer calories than gin."

"Mary and Joseph, help me. You're worried about your own lady-like figure, not your company's. Gino, I haven't heard you say 'thank you' for the vodka you already spilled. Go enjoy your friends with some gin."

"Whatever. Yeah. Thanks."

"Eh, big guy, before you go—is Ashley back?"

"How should I know?"

"Well, if you see her, let her know she is welcome to join the men up top for a cocktail."

"Why aren't I invited if she is? I thought you said it was for old men only."

Tony looked at Joe and laughed. "You can figure that one out, Gino."

The chiseled face disappeared down the ladder.

Tony cocked an eye at Joe. "Maybe you do think an old dog can still hunt?"

Joe grinned. "How long would that square neck have lasted as an apprentice?"

"Sweet Mary, mother of Jesus, he wouldn't have made it a day, much less a three-year apprenticeship. A boy that strong and proud would have broken his thumb with a hammer by 10:00 a.m. If he made it through the morning, can you imagine him going to lunch at the Rolling Pin with the crew? Trying to show he was a bigger man than everybody else and then heading up the scaffolding in the afternoon? He would be dead before the afternoon smoke break."

"Pattie might have been able to make a decent guy out of him, though. I'll never forget my first day with Pattie. His hard hat's brim an inch from my mouth. Telling me I had no pride because of the way I stacked the two-by-fours off the delivery truck."

"I had no pride because my shirt was untucked. 'You want to be a union man or a day laborer?' My chin was soaked with his spit. He might have used a few racial epithets to describe me that aren't so kosher anymore."

Joe and Tony knew the stories; they'd been there together. Memories of good times. Pattie was a stand-up guy, had his nail pouch on by seven thirty. The smoke break was at ten, lunch at a quarter to twelve. Back from lunch at twelve thirty, smoke break at three. The nail pouch was off at four thirty. Nobody started late, took different breaks, or left early. Drink at lunch if you want—Pattie did—but you had four hours of sawing and hammering after lunch at the same pace.

"Pattie was right," Tony said. "I had no pride. I wasn't worried about ruining that lumber. Stacking it sloppy on uneven ground. Letting it bow or rot in a puddle. He taught us what pride looked like, huh? No wasted material. Clean cuts. Straight nails. Use a four-inch nail when you need a four-inch nail and a three-inch nail when you need a three-inch nail. You need a galvanized nail, use a galvanized nail. Always sweep jobsite at day's end."

"I've never been so proud as when my apprenticeship ended. At the banquet, I wore a tie my mother bought me for the occasion. That was one of the only times I've worn a tie since Vatican II. At the bar afterward, when Pattie told half the Chapter I could run a crew on his job anytime but that 'some of you sorry excuses for foremen need me,' I didn't know if I should laugh or cry."

"Old Pattie was a good egg. Never seen more men laughing at a wake or crying at a funeral. Not many like Pattie."

The conversation lulled into a comfortable silence. Joe wondered whether the sea would lay down tonight. If not, no rush. He'd fly the trainers home if the trip dragged. He finished his highball and swirled the ice counterclockwise. Tony set up the backgammon table. The captain delivered a tray of snacks: pickles, deviled eggs, sardines, and crackers.

The captain asked, "Joe, would you like to anchor out for the evening, or do you want to head back to the marina? I checked and a slip is available."

"Tony, what do you think? Fresh air or fried oysters and the Yanks on the tube at a bar?"

"I'll lose more on backgammon than we'll spend at the bar. Let's get the oysters. Besides, maybe the bicepsketeers will go out, and we can put some real music on when we come back."

"Captain," Joe said, "we'll watch the sunset over the marsh from here, then head to the marina."

The captain kept up a brief conversation with his employer, then went about rechecking the boat's equipment. Tony refreshed the highballs while Joe prepared the board. He looked at the sunspots on the back of his big hands above his scarred knuckles. He thought of his wife. He forced himself to think of her as she lived. Wrestling with the kids. Her calves in front of the range, getting breakfast ready. Soaked and panting after a tumble. In an evening gown from a fundraiser two years ago, her cleavage nestling a crucifix. Was it only two years?

He remembered a conversation about dying she'd had with the boys when they were young. Their eldest asked, "Mommy, if you die, what do you think will happen?"

She answered, "After I die—and we all die—I am going to watch you and your brothers. Each morning just before you wake up, I'm going to kiss you so you will be forced to smile first thing every morning." Her voice rose to make sure she had his attention. "This is important stuff. Remember, when I'm gone, you don't have a choice but to smile first thing every morning when you wake up, because who couldn't smile when they know they've just been kissed by an angel!"

She went so quickly from striking beauty to bedridden ghost. He dreaded the tubes and beeping machines. Tough decisions—awful decisions. "No, son, we won't fight it. She won't fight it. Let's celebrate the time we have left." Then she's at peace. There was more crying. The wake and the family, hugs and laughter. The service, the eulogy. The family's stay through the weekend. Then the empty house.

He visited the kids, even though they had just left. He took the grandkids to Disney World, on Disney Cruises, to Disney on Ice. He went to the office more, then spun off the business. He sold off his properties at the right time. That was luck. He set up new wills and trusts and living wills and revocable trusts and got the executors set. The financial planners ran with the cash and made more of it. The tax accountants made plans; he made gifts. In fourteen months, it was done. Then he could feel pain.

He turned his right hand over and looked at the calluses. The heel of his hand was tanned where the hammer's rod shifted back and forth. Carpentry was a different business now. Engineers drew plans showing exact details of wall cavities, materials, and placement. Mexican crews framed ten thousand square feet a day. Air guns hissed and popped. Stairs were assembled in factories and dropped on the job site. How many guys today could cut a stringer in the field? Trusses were made in factories too. Nothing required the same skill, so the price carpenters charge went down. The price of building went down. More buildings were built and built quicker. Was this a good thing? In the end, he used factories to make his stairs and trusses. He used crews with foremen with half the skill he had at nineteen. It seemed like a bad thing, but the buildings weren't falling down.

He looked at the sunspots on the back of his left hand and the calluses on the palm of his right hand together. These were gifts from a life lived in the sun with a hammer—weakness on the back and toughness on the front.

"Well, luck be a lady tonight," Tony laughed.

Joe picked his head up as the nurses climbed the ladder.

"Tony, why don't we see sundresses like that in Brooklyn?"

"Because they wear little black dresses in Brooklyn?"

"Not when the sun's out. How do you climb a ladder in those shoes?"

"Joe, let the ladies keep their secrets. I just hope Gino isn't catching a peek while they climb the stairs. A weak-minded man could be tempted."

"Girls, welcome to the flybridge. This is a men's-only establishment as it relates to males, so you won't see any boys with waxed armpits or pedicures. But as the eminences-in-residence, we do maintain carte blanche to invite ladies to join us."

"Joe, youse weren't going to ask the ladies about their waxings, were you?"

"Forgive Tony, he rarely talks to women he doesn't have to tip."

Ashley and her friends carried drinks mixed with various tonics, sodas, and lemonades. Joe wasn't sure whether they were poured with vodka or gin. Ashley's hair was wet. When she moved, Joe could see the dampness on her shoulder straps. She crossed her legs above the knee and leaned back into her seat. She settled on the bench underneath Joe's outstretched arm. Her French-manicured toes held her shoe up by the toe strap, the shoe's heel dangled in the air.

The talk was light but good. The girls had seen sea turtle tracks on the beach. They watched dolphins playing in the waves and saw an unidentified sport fish jumping offshore. They'd watched seagulls harassing beached crabs as surfers bobbed in the swells. The owners of small, old boats seemed to have unending ingenuity in what they used for anchors: a dumbbell, window weights, tent stakes. The current's strength was surprising, and they watched the beach grow and shrink with the tide. How great the day was. Joe learned he was the only one who took a nap, but he was first on the beach too, so he didn't feel so old about it.

Tony excused himself and climbed down the ladder. The girls talked about how sweet Tony was, even if he had a touch of ladies' man in him. Joe admitted Tony had been quite the hound; it had taken more than one wife to settle him down. That was an easy problem to have when happy hour happened at twelve and again at five.

Lunchtime happy hours were a myth to the girls. They had heard jokes about two-martini lunches, but they were just jokes. Joe knew this was an age difference. They were born after Nancy Reagan had embedded "Just Say No" into society. MADD and SADD were fixtures in their middle schools. As adults, they didn't even smoke in bars. When "Free Bird" was played, ten thousand smartphones were the lights.

The girls didn't understand why five o'clock happy hours ended so punctually in big cities. But they were Southern girls; a train schedule never dictated their day.

Joe enjoyed the smell of Ashley's shampoo. Was it vanilla, coconut, or something totally different? Didn't matter, he liked it. It relaxed him. He zoned out of the conversation, then answered some questions about the boat, about growing up in Brooklyn, normal get-to-know-you stuff. They asked about the changes to New York City—from good to bad and back to good—or if not good, at least safe but still with some character.

One of the girls had worked in a Brooklyn hospital. She jogged the Brooklyn Bridge to Manhattan before work, stretched in Battery Park, and jogged back. She went with friends to Peter Luger Steak House once. They didn't know you had to pay cash, which had made the end of the night a little tense. She went to a seafood bar under the bridge, where beer was sold in thirty-six-ounce Styrofoam cups and the walls were lined with cut ties.

Ashley laughed, "Y'all think those ties belonged to Wall Street interns? They didn't notice their coworkers stuffing ties in their pockets as they walked in."

Joe laughed back, "The pups probably couldn't decide if they were more afraid of Mom asking where their Brooks Brothers Christmas present was or of returning to the office improperly attired."

The nurse who had worked in Brooklyn added, "I think the ties got cut off at guys' retirement parties."

The conversation drifted along. Joe showed pictures of his kids and grandkids on his phone. He realized the girls must have known about his wife, because that topic was never raised. He answered questions about business. Joe moved his hands so much when he talked that someone suggested they play charades. They went in a circle and tried to act out movie titles.

Joe started with *Taxi Driver*, which took the girls a while to get because they'd never heard of it. One of the girls did *Avatar*. Another did *Harry Potter*. Ashley went with *Titanic*. They did books next. The first girl spanked her bottom and then humped the coffee table. The other girls shouted out *Fifty Shades of Grey*. Joe had to have the book explained to him. He let the explaining, which was a group charade in itself, go on longer than needed.

Tony returned with two young guys—well, fortyish guys, distinctly younger than Joe or Tony and distinctly older than the trainers. They were flushed with sun and beer. They struck Joe as stand-up guys. They must have struck Tony that way too, and Tony usually called it right.

The not-so-young guys were on a bachelor party trip. The one with the sunburned feet was the betrothed—Blake. Not to his first bride. They took seats, and the captain mixed their drinks. Their manners were good, and they waited for the others to refill their glasses before they drank. Their accents were Southern but not country. Outside of a few *y'alls* and one *dadgummit*, Joe figured they'd have carried a barroom conversation in the city with no problem.

Sweat from his glass beaded and dripped over Joe's fingers when he picked up his drink. With Tony back and the new guys needing seats, Ashley scooted herself farther under Joe's arm. The bachelor was in the cups and locked into a conversation with one of the other girls. The nonbachelor, Van, showed a quick wit and good cadence on his delivery. He and Tony bantered back and forth.

"So why does someone from New York or New Jersey—or do they just call it Jersey now—have to choose either Nets-Jets-Mets-Islanders or Knicks-Giants-Yankees-Rangers? What type of self-hating person would choose the Nets-Jets-Mets-Islanders? None of those teams win, and half those teams don't even play in New York. It's like someone from North Carolina rooting for the Bullets—I mean Wizards—Panthers-Braves-Hurricanes."

"Yeah, I've been hearing for years there are some nice cities here in North Carolina. So I visited Charlotte and Raleigh, and the people are all real nice. But where is the city?"

Lunge. Parry.

Another tanned fortyish guy with a round face and glasses peeked his head up the ladder.

"Joe, Tony, girls. Meet our compatriot, Barry."

"Barry, you look an honorable sort. What are you doing consorting with these two? Look at this lush you're traveling with. He's rubbing thighs with a maiden who I'm pretty sure is not his bride-to-be. And don't get me started on this other piece of work."

"Is he sharing a few opinions?"

"Does the pope wear a funny hat? Have a drink. Maybe you can improve the conversation."

Everyone shifted around to make room. Ashley's full body now pressed against Joe's side. His arm had fallen asleep. It wasn't enough to make him move. His bladder was full. That wasn't enough to get him to move either.

Barry pointed out the runabout that brought him onboard, Van, and Blake waved to their friends aboard it, who weren't looking up. One guy and two girls were dancing on the runabout. A second guy—tall and muscled, with his shirt off and floral board shorts—was fiddling with the engine. Joe watched him hop into the water and clear finishing line from his prop.

After one drink, the tanned, round-faced man (Barry, was it?) motivated the bachelor and the nonbachelor to get moving. The nurses were ready to get into town and left with them. The runabout looked overloaded casting off. Joe took the opportunity to descend the ladder and use the head.

He chatted with the trainers, but didn't find any common interest other than the logistics of when they were going to shore and where they were docking. Joe watched the trainers play hearts for a couple of minutes. After seeing the queen of spades mishandled two hands in a row, he moved on.

Why did they want the party if they were going to play cards? It struck Joe that these guys, behind their big talk, were more comfortable looking aloof than engaging with the world around them. They were cool in appearance but terrified the world would see through them if they risked reaching out. That nugget of insight put their behavior in a different light. He figured after a few more drinks, they would break character and give themselves the excuse of "being hammered," as they called it, if they failed.

Joe scanned the main deck. Tony was chatting up a woman with a minimal outfit and a sly smile. Joe thought that if she'd had pale winter skin, a sweatshirt, and dungarees, Tony wouldn't have noticed her. That wasn't right; he reconsidered. Tony noticed everyone. He was a true gentleman—in the important ways, at least. But the tone of his conversation would have been a lot different without glimpses of bronzed nipple in the strappy bikini.

Turning the other way, Joe began to search out the owners of the boats rafted alongside them. He introduced himself, met some good people and some who took advantage of good people. He let everyone know he was pulling anchor pretty soon and that he hoped to see them at the bar tonight. With notice given, he retired to the flybridge and prepared a cocktail for the sunset.

When Joe was midway through his drink, Tony came up the ladder. No words spoken, he made his own drink and sat next to Joe, watching the orange light sink into the tree line behind the marsh. Below, the last of the rafters tossed off their lines and headed somewhere else. Sitting, watching night take over, and with Ashley's scent embedded in his memory, Joe felt like he was beginning a journey.

»»» **9**

ASHLEY GOT UP early on Saturday, hoping to get a jog in before the day's travel. Joe, Tony, and the captain were already up and about when she came out of the cabin. They were preparing to cast off. The Atlantic was too stirred up for travel. Instead, they doubled back south on the Intracoastal a short ways and anchored offshore an uninhabited island of small sand dunes.

She watched Joe swan dive off the front of the boat into the water and swim toward the sand dunes. Something pleasant brought a smile to her face: The dive and his strokes looked like the old black-and-white Tarzan movies or TV shows, or whatever they had been. She'd always seen them on TV on Saturday mornings. Saturday mornings in her house, before everyone woke up and whatever trouble the day would bring started, was her favorite time at home—probably the only time she actually liked being at home.

Following that mental thread took her too far down the memory trail. The memories that came next took the light out of her and made it hard for her to breathe.

Why had her mother stayed with her father? Because she was a drunk? Her mother knew what he was. Was it because she didn't want to leave the double-wide trailer parked at the front of the mobile home park where her husband worked? Because she didn't want to burn that last bridge she hadn't burned? Was it just because he needed her so badly in his chest-pounding, bullying way?

Why did her father need her mother so much? When the booze faded her looks, did he still feel like more of a man for having her with him? When he sat on the porch in his white plastic chair and shot bottles pinned to the clothesline, did he need her to see how good a shot he was? During his evening rounds in the mobile home park, collecting rent door to door with a pistol in the small of his back, another strapped on his ankle, and a blackjack on his side, did he want her to see how tough he was? Was that why he had her inch their red Ford Ranger along behind him while he made his rounds?

Ashley sat in the front seat for many of these trips. She had watched her father collect money from their neighbors. Or intimidate them if things weren't as they should be.

Kids yelled out, "Momma, rent man here," when they saw him coming. Nobody had a checking account. Some paid with money orders. Most used cash. Her father stuffed the money orders and cash in a fanny pack strapped across his stomach.

Sometimes, folks disappeared on him in the middle of the night, leaving a balance and a trashed trailer. Her father fixed, cleaned, and rented the trailers. Some folks didn't pay and wouldn't leave until her father marched them out. More than once, he needed the pistol to get them to leave. Waiting for an indifferent court system wasn't his style. Despite his obvious weapons and ability to use them, a full fanny pack of cash was a strong motivator for the hungry to take risks. More than once, she had heard the commotion of would-be robbers paying for their efforts.

He was good at his job. He could sell. He could fix things. He could collect. She knew his problem wasn't his skills. It wasn't good tenants, bad tenants, or muggers. His problems were, in the language of the preacher at the Primitive Baptist Church they went to on the first Sunday of each month, the demons inside him. He fed his demons, and they grew strong. Greed made him skim cash from the owner, and pride made it so he couldn't stand to even hide what he was doing. She'd hear him say to her mother, "Weren't for me, he wouldn't get nuthin' out of this place. I'd say he owes me this little extra and then some."

When Ashley was thirteen, he'd had the job for seven years. By then, his records showed each week that he collected more than he turned over. He wanted the owner to know he wasn't stealing from the tenants; he was stealing from *him*—the owner, his boss. For a while, he kept an extra hundred dollars a week. That grew to an extra five hundred dollars.

Finally, in front of the house, the owner showed up with two deputies. Ashley was getting off the school bus. She saw her father cuffed and marched to the cruiser. She saw her mother come around the side of the house. From a hundred yards off, she recognized her glazed eyes. Her mother half concealed a pistol at her side. Ashley froze. Her mother raised the pistol. Ashley didn't know whether she was going to shoot the sheriff's men, the owner, her father, or herself. She hoped she wouldn't fire at anybody.

Her mother fired at the owner. She missed. A deputy tackled her. The pistol slid through the dust under the lattice that edged the bottom of their mobile home.

As her parents were put in the back of the car, Ashley walked past her double-wide, eyes straight ahead. She followed the figure-eight loop around the park. The other kids ran to tell what had happened. She heard a door open and someone yell, "Rent man's wife shot the lawman! There's blood everywhere!" The story grew. Folks came out of their trailers for a looksee.

When she felt too many eyeballs, she climbed a post and jumped the barbed wire fence separating the park from the ranchland next door. She stayed out of sight on the ranch until dark, and then headed for the road so she wouldn't have to walk past all the trailers. Along the road, she walked in the dry drainage ditch. She lay flat when she saw headlights.

She returned to the trailer park. Her home was unlocked, so she sat in the dark in her mother's cloth recliner and crushed a pack of Newports. It felt peaceful in the empty house. She kept the lights out. She pulled on a bathrobe that was on the floor beside her, reclined back, and slept.

She didn't go to school the next day, and nobody came to check on her. She grabbed a newspaper from a neighbor's patio to see whether her parents were in it. They weren't.

That night, she searched her parents' bedroom. It didn't take long. It was only eight feet wide, ten feet long, and seven feet high. There was a dresser, a bed, a lamp. She found her father's mason jar of cash above a ceiling tile. It wasn't hard to spot. The ceiling tile was stained from where his fingers pushed it up and set it back in place every day. She found two pistols and the blackjack and the phone number for her grandfather. She recognized the name, but she had never met him, and she didn't know where he lived. Her mother barely knew him. She said he went to sea when she was a baby, and her mother left with another man before the aircraft carrier returned.

She called the number, and a man answered. She hung up. Her hands shook. She grabbed a phone book and looked up the location of the area code. San Diego.

She packed the money, guns, blackjack, and two changes of clothes in her backpack and set the alarm clock in her room. She slept under the bathrobe on the recliner again. Her alarm went off before sunrise. She brushed her teeth, grabbed a pair of Mello Yellos out of the refrigerator, and added her toiletries to her backpack. She put on her mother's cowboy boots. The boots took her to five foot eleven. She put on an Exxon trucker hat and slipped her blonde ponytail through the back. She locked the trailer, walked to the Ranger, and started driving west.

The Ranger traveled the state road for two hours before she

stopped for gas. At the first gas station, she didn't pull in close enough to the pump to fill up the gas tank. She backed up and bumped a trash can. She panicked and pulled back onto the road. Thirty miles later, at the second gas station, she parked and fueled without incident. She bought an atlas of the western United States, a two-liter Mello Yello, and a package of pork rinds.

That night, she slept in a Walmart parking lot. The Ranger's seat didn't recline, so she leaned against the driver's side window. She used the bathrobe as both blanket and pillow. The second night, she slept in the parking lot of a casino. By noon on the third day, she was parked off Cabrillo Freeway, near downtown San Diego, staring at a pay phone and hyperventilating.

She dialed. He answered. She hung up. She dialed. He answered. She got out "Grandpa" and then sobbed. Her first tears. He listened. She added three quarters before she was calm enough to be understood.

He came to get her. He brought a neighbor to drive the Ranger. They went back the way she had just come, to his house on the east side of San Diego.

She settled down, and he checked on her parents. They didn't make bail. He got her mother to appoint him guardian, and she enrolled in school. She called him "Chief," like his friends did, after his final rank in the navy. He died shortly after she graduated from college. She missed him.

Turning back to the east, Joe was now walking out of the water and into the dunes. She went to her cabin. She imitated the knocking pattern from last night. Her friends made seductive calls back to her knocks. They were tying on bikinis and laughing when she entered. She took her suit off the hook and put it on. They went to the galley, sliced cantaloupe and watermelon, filled a platter. A box of Cheerios, a strainer full of blueberries, and stacked bowls were on the table. There were carafes of milk and orange juice in a bucket of ice. This she could get used to.

Tony sipped coffee and worked a crossword puzzle on the couch in the salon. He winked at the girls. Ashley noticed there was a bottle opener built into the bottom of his flip-flops. She was pretty sure he didn't know it was there.

The captain cleaned salt off the windows and portholes using a squeegee attached to an extension pole. He dunked the squeegee in a bucket and leaned slightly forward so he could see his work. He made several slow back-and-forth motions with the sponge, then spun the pole in his hand and made long, clean, upward pulls with the rubber blade. Not for the first time, Ashley wondered whether this type of work was something he loved more than something that needed to be done.

After breakfast, they swam to the island. Joe came through the dunes from the ocean side, discretely pulling in his gut when he noticed them. This made her feel good, and she gave him an extra squeeze with his hug. She found herself wondering how old he was. How many years would he still be active? And if she wasn't trying to deny the truth, attractive. Ten? Twenty? She guessed he was near sixty.

On the ocean side, it was breezier. They walked south four miles, talked a lot about not much. It was pleasant. Birds ran away, and ghost crabs scuttled into holes. Ashley found a sand dollar still whole, brown, and slightly fuzzy. A broken piling lay in the sand. It was covered in barnacles that were alive. Their shells opened, gasping for water. The mass dying made Ashley queasy. Pretty funny for an emergency room nurse, she thought. Queasy over barnacles.

They didn't talk much as they headed north into the breeze. She watched a surfer in floral shorts ride a wave nearly two hundred yards before hopping off his board in ankle-deep water less than twenty-five yards from them. She had watched his fluid physique and movements on the long ride and was surprised that up close his face, unlike his physique, indicated he was middle-aged.

The girls couldn't figure out which path to take across the dunes, and it didn't really matter. They were just going to end up too far north or south. When they got to the mainland side, they saw the boat and reoriented themselves. There were plenty of sunbathers on the waterway side of the island. The girls waded in the warm water. The bottom was between sandy and muddy.

When they were parallel to the boat, they started to swim out. Halfway across, they were twenty-five yards behind the boat, so they swam back to shore and got a lift. A party was in progress when they arrived, the music pounding. Ashley shut the door to the main salon as she went in, dulling the noise from outside. She fixed a late lunch. She stood in the galley, eating and flipping through an entertainment magazine—oh, the struggles of the rich and beautiful once they became famous. Taking in the yacht's salon, she wondered whether for her, getting the rich part would be worth the cost.

When she finished eating, she went outside and danced with her friends. She twirled away from a couple of guys who wanted to dance with their manhood pushed a little aggressively against her backside. She talked with Tony for a bit while her friends were getting cleaned up. She was the last to go into her cabin to shower.

She put on a spaghetti strap dress and high-heeled sandals and joined her friends on the deck. Gino told her they were invited to the flybridge, so she climbed up and scooted in next to Joe. She smelled the day's salt, sweat, and suntan lotion on him. The smell fit a leader at ease. She again tried to pinpoint his age. Tony entertained the girls, then left and came back with two guys she hadn't met. One guy's feet were so pink that a whole tube of aloe wouldn't have helped. He sat next to one of her friends. She couldn't hear their conversation, but her friend was all smiles and sparkly eyes.

At Ashley's friends' request, they left the Ferretti with Pink Feet and his friends. They hopped into a small boat whose owner, she realized, was the guy she'd watched surfing. Ashley sat in the bow and looked back, hoping to catch his eye, but he was focused on his work.

10

IN THE AIRSPACE over the Caribbean, the drawing took shape on the notepad. At the top of the page were Francisco's initials in blue ink. From there, three branches connected down to other men's initials. These limbs forked to more initials, and the limbs below those were no longer identified by individual initials but were labeled by a combination of roles and locations such as *Peru, paste transport.* Subsequent levels continued the naming convention of location and role.

The page was a rainbow of highlights. Green highlighted occupied positions, yellow showed positions of concern, red indicated positions where changes were needed, and blue marked unfilled positions. The blue fields were largely tied to the long-neglected markets in Europe and the United States, although a few referenced China's edges in Macau and Hong Kong.

With a black pen, Francisco put asterisks beside his priorities. A mental aside grabbed his attention. He picked the blue pen back up and circled the family members on the tree to see whether any branch was either neglected or overloaded. Too many brothers running one branch of an operation was an invitation to insurrection that Francisco might be slow to see if he was focused on growth. As the information began to visually pop from the page, Francisco scratched over and moved initials to get the skills and loyalty balance he wanted.

With family accounted for, he then looked at the green highlighted limbs without family member initials to see whether those running successful operations could move to a red or blue role. Did they have the skills to start a new operation or only those for maintaining an existing process? Did they develop talent in their organization to be able to replace themselves, or would their group fail without them?

Francisco asked, "Alberto, tell me, what do you know of the Uruguayan, Alfonso?"

"He is very . . . ," Alberto paused. He struggled to find the exact English words. He looked in Francisco's eyes for permission to switch to Spanish and saw it was denied. Unable to find the precise wording, he resorted to a longer description, "He is very good at his men getting to the right spots. He employs good men."

"Does he have a man trained who could do this in his absence?"

"Yes, his brother Jaime is very good."

"Excellent, does he have a wife and children?"

"Yes."

With that, Francisco wrote Alfonso's name over a blue highlight on a limb far removed from the one his brother Jamie would now operate. He added a note to move Alfonso's family to one of his villas in Colombia.

Throughout the long flight, he continued the process of reconfiguring the map of his soon-to-again-be-global operation. He promoted greens, filled in blues, and addressed reds with his long continuation of Pablo's policy of *plata o plomo* by drawing either a dollar sign or bullet over the initials.

Francisco needed this exercise to order his world. He was a good leader but a reluctant manager. He bonded well with his people and got more from them than they would have provided another boss. Although he did not admit it to others, he felt he had surpassed even El Capo in this manner. He had his people's hearts. Machiavelli would have approved of his mastery of being both loved and feared. But he needed to force himself to deal with the tedium of daily operations. This tactical exercise of evaluating where to focus his improvements was enjoyable. But experience had taught him that the daily process of holding his people accountable was one that needed to be delegated to his inner circle.

The return of growth would be good for his family but it needed to be thought through. If he stopped the business today, money would not be an issue for ten generations and a thousand relatives. But ambition, ambition was an eternal issue. His cousins and nephews needed to find new markets and add to the family's grandeur rather than squabbling over its vast remains.

He recollected a long-ago conversation with a retired Royal Air Force pilot Pablo had employed to fly the family's Boeing 747.

"Francisco, why do you think people everywhere speak English? It is not an easy language to learn nor a particularly beautiful language to the ear. It does not smell of sex like French or convey excitement like Italian. There are not many native English speakers compared with Mandarin, Hindi, or Spanish. So why?"

"That is an easy question to answer. Because the *norteamericanos* speak English. Because to do business with them, you have to speak English."

"That's an inadequate answer for a lad with your noggin. The world didn't start with business being done in English or with the bloody Yanks. Have you ever heard the saying, 'the sun never sets on the British empire?'"

"Of course."

"Tell me why a small island in the north Atlantic should have had such an empire."

Quickly tired by the pilot's Socratic style, Francisco said, "No, stop this. You tell me why you think this small country of people with bad teeth and fragile skin had an empire across the world."

The pilot promptly replied, "The law of primogeniture." He looked at Francisco and saw the small roll of his eyes. "Ah, you don't believe me, young master. You thought I was going to say because of the queen's dominant navy. Or perhaps you thought I was an ethnocentrist and believed it was our naturally superior intelligence and appearance. But no, that would be rubbish. It was the rule of law—and particularly this law—that gave England the world's greatest empire."

Despite his desire to stop the old pilot's show of superiority, Francisco was curious to hear the reasoning. "OK. Tell me what this law is and why it made everyone speak English."

The old man explained. The law of primogeniture gave the family's full inheritance to the eldest son once the father passed away. In the rest of Europe, when the father died, the inheritance was split among the sons. Therefore, many Englishmen who were raised in wealth grew up under the specter of needing to make something of themselves to avoid being impoverished once the eldest brother received his due.

With England being a small country with modest physical resources, these men were forced to take their education and breeding into the world, colonizing it for mercantilism. In addition, the eldest son, who had full control of an undiluted inheritance, could invest the money in large projects in trade or manufacturing. By contrast, the six sons of an Italian count were each given a sixth of the count's lands. Then, their six sons were each given a sixth of their father's lands—enough to live without the motivation to avoid hunger but not enough to make investments to change the world.

Francisco never researched the story's historical accuracy, but even if it was only a fable, it held wisdom. He needed new markets to send his ever-expanding list of working-age nephews and cousins into. Let them take the lessons he had taught them, as Pablo had taught him, to new markets. Let them stand on his shoulders and help him conquer the world, or let them be gobbled up by others trying. If they stayed within the current operations, they would eat each other up with petty grievances, and eventually, there would be internal warfare.

He had watched with interest as other families had turned their guns inward. He would not let this happen to his empire.

Yes, Francisco needed to capitalize on this growth opportunity. And of course, he did not divide up his inherited or accumulated wealth, so he was willing and able to make world-changing investments. He well knew some investments were repaid in currency, while others were repaid in blood.

The long highway drive to Savannah had alternately run through overcrowded urban areas and long stretches of barely populated farmland. As Francisco now rocketed southwest in his new G5, he wondered why more *norteamericanos* didn't fly private. The minimal effort and maximum comfort on his first flight in his new jet reinvigorated him for the tasks he faced. He chose this Gulfstream because the seating arrangement allowed a cabin with a door to be built around the back couch if he desired.

Sitting in his plush leather seat, he reflected on his brief stay in Miami. The city was so changed from before. He wondered where the Jews and blonde-haired *norteamericanos* had gone. Rich Hispanics and Russian service workers were all he met in his explorations. He had spent the prior evening—morning, technically—behind a velvet rope at a nightclub with a grass-sod dance floor in the company of a certain type of Russian service worker. A new grass floor each night! Who thought of these things? He liked this new Miami. It cost more, but more was for sale.

The copilot came over the intercom. "Excuse me, gentlemen. We touch down in Sanford in thirty minutes. A white Porsche Cayenne with the starter fob under the driver seat is parked at the FBO for your use this afternoon. Unless directed otherwise, I will refuel and wait for your return. With your permission, Estella will begin preparing the cabin for landing."

This was the type of service you should expect at $14,000 an hour. Two pilots and a stewardess manned the G5. Francisco instructed the bilingual crew to speak English in the United States. The crew, hired before the G5 was purchased, had met the men in Savannah. The pilots, career commercial carrier veterans, collected pensions from bankrupt companies. The stewardess was in her early thirties, a modern Colombian beauty with dyed blonde hair and extremely enhanced silicone breasts, extended eyelashes, and long curved fingernails. She wore a V-neck blouse, a short skirt, and stilettos. He was confident she would pay him, as the owner, special attention when he required it.

This morning's stop would be brief. "Alberto, where are we meeting Mr. Radcliffe?"

"In her wife's office."

"You say, '*his* wife,' Alberto. Where will the wife be?"

"We have made a date for her with a new client in Orlando. The client will not show for their lunch meeting."

"What does Mr. Radcliffe believe is our visit's purpose?"

"To lease the vacant storefront below his wife's office. She owns it, but he leases it."

"And where are our supplies?"

"They were delivered to the vacant storefront already inside of five-gallon paint drums. The Cuban arranged it."

Francisco knew all of this. And he knew Mr. Radcliffe would die by fire as he lived by fire.

A family lawyer found Mr. Radcliffe's identity with a few lucky keystrokes and his location with a few more intentional ones.

Wikipedia provided a summary report of the twenty-year-old raid on Francisco's family's beach villa. It was under a section of thousands of pages, titled "DEA War on Drugs: Colombia 1985–1998." Francisco was in the process of having these documents read to learn more. There were more names to learn—*norteamericanos* and Colombians. *Exploding dreams yet, my friends.* Francisco knew his family's memory and reach must be known to be long. It was part of the mystique. It was part of the fear that protected them.

At the time, the capital had taken credit for the raid. The government announced it had "enforced the laws of the people" and destroyed the structures. Francisco remembered an above-the-fold newspaper headline: "*El gobierno destruye la villa de playa de Escobar.*" It was all propaganda. The cartel's black market income was greater than the country's GDP. No system that taxed honest citizens could sustain a military and legal system that could destroy the cartel. The capital would need not only support from the *norteamericanos* but also propaganda that convinced the populace that their victories were their own and not those of the *norteamericanos*, who would abandon them once their own needs were met.

In the raid report, the names of the leaders were blacked out. The names of the helicopter pilot and the explosives agents who carried out the mission were not.

The report detailed how Mr. Radcliffe and two associates put the explosives in place. Before the charges were set, Francisco's older brother arrived at the residence with a female companion and four bodyguards.

A firefight ensued. Two DEA agents were fatally shot. All five Escobar men and the woman were terminated; Mr. Radcliffe and Mr. Coleman, the surviving DEA agents, carried the Colombians' bodies into the villa. The fallen DEA agents were loaded into a new helicopter that arrived quickly, and explosives were set on the disabled helicopter. The new helicopter took off with its passengers. The charges were detonated, and the villa and disabled chopper were leveled and then engulfed in flames.

Francisco had never known what happened to his brother yet instinctively knew his disappearance was tied to the villa and that he was dead. When the Escobars learned nothing from selectively bribing and torturing government officials, they knew it was the *norteamericanos*, who obviously had kept the secret from their Colombian counterparts.

The secret was out now, and the score would be settled.

11

ON THE WEST bank, Cale saw his paddleboards lashed together. He eased across the channel, parallel docked, cut the engines, and tied the spring and bowlines to the dock cleats.

On the elevated deck, Dan sat, his shirt unbuttoned, in a plastic chair at a plastic table under a Sunbrella awning. Two buckets of empty longnecks were being carried off as a new bucket replaced them. The captain and mate for a fishing charter shared the table. Their tanned faces, sun-bleached hair, and white visors were their profession's uniform.

Longeck in hand, Jay was a table over, talking with a couple. The man, whose back was to Cale, wore seersucker pants, Ferragamo loafers, a white polo, and wire-framed Ray Bans. His wife's sundress was low cut and accessorized with tall heels, a straw hat, and oversized sunglasses. The couple drank juleps in highball glasses.

Cale's passengers departed. He managed another smile at the goddess whom he was very disappointed in; he assumed now that she was a call girl, escorting a couple of uberwealthy old guys and their bodyguards on a pleasure cruise. He stowed the paddleboards onboard and used the dock hose to wash sand out of the Whaler. A stevedore's work was never done.

He called Maggie. In his mind, of course; he was still sane, just a little sad below the surface. No real news. In these talks, the girls were still sixteen and tired from practice. They exchanged *I-love-you*s. The family would go to church in the morning and over to her parents' for lunch and a low-key day on the lake. The Ski Nautique was out of the water, but the Jet Skis could pull the girls if they wanted. No worry, he'd behave so he could safely fly the group home tomorrow. Another *I love you* and *I'll see you tomorrow*.

Fans cooled the dock's open-air bar. Cale's passengers mingled with marines from the big base thirty miles up the road. He grabbed a bottle from Dan's bucket and sat with Jay and the couple drinking juleps. They exchanged names, but over the background noise, he didn't catch theirs. He did catch that this was his third marriage, her first. Plaintiff litigator, former pharmaceutical sales rep. They had his kids from wife number one every other weekend but not this weekend. The breeze, shade, Jay being Jay, Cale's own fatigue, and Mrs. Julep's on-display assets made the afternoon pleasantly glide into evening.

The fishing charter crew sitting with Dan took off to prepare for tomorrow's charter. There was a lot to do with a fat buzz in the dark: set the rigging, cut the bait, fill the ice chests, fuel the boat, clean the head, and so on. Dan flipped his chair around and split the Juleps, his chair between theirs. The Mrs.'s arm and leg now brushed Cale's. He scooted over slightly, and she followed.

Dan, who never knew a silence he couldn't fill, said, "Cale, these good folks were telling us earlier that they are going to visit Colombia in January. Didn't you work in Colombia for a few years with the DEA?"

"Yeah. I spent time there off and on, but I was never stationed there. All the pilots were stationed domestically."

Mr. Julep said, "The place seems to have settled down. They just signed a treaty formalizing the peace between the government and the rebels. It seems that areas of the country that Westerners haven't seen in decades are now open for business. One of my clients is inviting us on a couples' trip."

Cale supposed "Northerners" was more accurate than "Western-ers," but he got the point.

"From what I remember, it's beautiful country," he replied. "Mountains. Lots of forest—sort of a jungle-like forest. Mild temperatures. Maybe it's the latitude, but I remember it seemed to be night twelve hours a day even in the summer."

Mr. Julep seemed intent on staying in Bogotá. "Did you know that within a week of the peace treaty happening, the US signed a free-trade agreement with Colombia too? A lot of good things are happening down there. Probably real opportunities to make money for someone familiar with the terrain."

Macroeconomics in a barroom? Cale didn't engage, since no proof or specificity was required other than the strength of the speakers' convictions—or the loudness of their voices. Also, like all DEA agents with classified records from Bogotá, he never discussed Colombia, because those they battled had long memories and ample resources. He made a mental note to call Sheila at the agency and check the scuttlebutt on both the treaty and the free-trade agreement.

Cale changed the conversation's direction. "I really wasn't there long. I spent most of my career harassing hippies out of pot fields."

This piqued the Mrs.'s interest. She grabbed the top of Cale's wrist with her hand and asked, "And how did you harass hippies out of fields? Did you sneak into the fields at night wearing camouflage and face paint with machine guns drawn and floodlights lighting up the night sky?"

Cale sensed how she pictured this breathless adventure and was tempted to draw it but refrained. To him, it was more about fire ants, wet shoes, and general discomfort. Was there anything worse than wet socks? He smiled, hoping to convey the message that he couldn't live up to those expectations.

"Nothing so exciting for me. If I flew you over Northern California across the Sierra Mountain range, you'd see one-acre pot plots everywhere. Some of the pot plots are on private land, where the owner has no idea he is in the agricultural business, but most are in the federal forests.

"In a normal field day, we'd take the helicopter out, set down in the middle of the field, take a couple of sling blades, and whack the plants down. We'd spray commercial-grade Roundup everywhere, hop back on the bird, and find the next unnaturally cultivated pot plot."

"Did you ever surprise people? Did they ever put up a fight?"

"Sometimes. But there were usually a lot of us carrying a lot of guns, and they just wanted to disappear into the woods before they got arrested. Also, because I was the pilot, I was the last out of the bird, and any action was over before I'd unhitched my seat belt."

Seizing on the comment about Roundup as an opener, Dan launched into a story about Roundup, gasoline, yellow jackets, and yelling "fire in the hole." Mrs. Julep's hand grasped Cale's knee as she tried to gain control of her laughter. Cale briefly wondered whether Mr. Julep was drawn to her by her good sense of humor or the warm firm grip of her long fingers, but mainly, he relived a mission her questions had inadvertently brought to mind.

》》》

THE DOORS WERE open and the engine off. Sweat soaked Cale's cotton clothing. He retraced his preflight and mission checklists. The mental distraction lessened his urge to unlace his right boot and dig fingernails into the itchy skin he couldn't reach with his pencil's eraser. Afternoon boredom had obliterated the morning's adrenaline.

Radio reports from other teams informed the agents that four suspects stood beside four white pickups at the intersection of two county roads. A few miles from the road, through woods at the lake's edge, additional suspects awaited a delivery. One sat on a three-wheel ATV with an empty large rear basket. The other rested on a Jet Ski in the shallow water. No change had been reported in over two hours.

Cale visualized the six men: denim overalls despite the heat, sleeve-less Rusty Wallace T-shirts, a few impressive mullets. He figured even odds the guy on the Jet Ski was wearing cut-off jean shorts.

A sharp voice came over the air, "This is Alpha team. We have visual on a small plane flying low coming out of the south. Over."

"This is HQ. Roger that. We see it. Hold your positions. Over."

Nothing to report from Bravo team. Bravo sat in a small, circular clearing in the woods. Around the circle's perimeter, undergrowth had taken advantage of the sunlight and had grown thick and tangled. Beyond the perimeter, the forest was hardwoods, with a few old pines that had not yet been crowded out. The radio report jolted everyone to attention.

"This is HQ. Looks like the plane will be on the water in two minutes. The men at the trucks have seen the plane. One is now on his CB. Over."

"This is Alpha. Roger that. Visual on suspect on the three-wheeler. He has picked up his CB. Over."

Unconsciously, the teammates leaned forward to absorb the infor-mation. They shifted the placement of their hands on their firearms into ready position.

"This is HQ. Roger that. The plane is below our line of site. Alpha, do you have a visual? Over."

"This is Alpha. Roger that. The plane has touched down on the water. The Jet Ski is approaching. Looks like they have more to unload than can happen in one run. Over."

"This is HQ. Roger that. Alpha, report when the plane is unloaded or the three-wheeler starts to move. Whichever is first. Over."

"This is Alpha. Roger that. Jet Ski is taking two duffel bags to shore. The pilot set two more duffels on the pontoon. Pilot is in the cockpit looking anxious to leave. I think this will be the last trip. Over."

The pseudomilitary radio chatter's rhythmic, repeated refrains always reminded Cale of biblical poetry, if you substituted "Roger that" for "and it was good."

"This is HQ. Roger that. With four duffels and four trucks, we need to modify plans. These could be three decoys and one real McCoy. We are unprepared to track in four directions."

"Bravo team, proceed to the crossroads. Lock down the pickups before the three-wheeler arrives to offload. Alpha team, walk from the lake up the trail toward the pickups behind the three-wheeler. Your goal is to keep the three-wheeler from backtracking into the woods. We have alerted the FAA to track the plane. We'll have somebody in the air out of Charlotte in five minutes. At a minimum, we'll photograph the plane and get its call sign. For the perp on the water, if his friends don't turn him in, it's his lucky day. Copy. Over."

"This is Alpha. Roger that. Leaving position to backfill trail. Over."

Although he was not the head of Bravo team, he was the pilot, and, in this case, that trumped seniority. Cale clicked in. "This is Bravo. Roger that. Starting engines. Proceeding to crossroads. Over."

The bird fired up. A rush of hot air blew from the air conditioning vents and pushed the sweat off Cale's nose and into his eyes. The big props circulation elevated the team gently. The takeoff lacked the muscular effort that jumbo jet passengers feel as their plane's engines dig for the required speed on a runway of limited length. Cale slipped on sunglasses as they rose above tree-dappled light into full sun. He flew less than five hundred feet off the ground—low enough to be difficult to spot but high enough to adapt to the topographic changes.

The stealth advantage desired from the low altitude flight required line-of-sight steering. The horizon provided a series of landmarks that directed the flight path. Cale progressed through them until he locked in on the two roads that stretched away from the forest. A visual on the intersection of the roads was hidden by the tree canopy. He felt confident that he could guesstimate the intersection's location within a hundred yards or so. The mission's rehearsals never included this scenario. Cale tried to picture where to set the bird down and what obstacles he'd find beyond a bunch of startled guys with guns.

The road grew larger behind the tree canopy, and he began

shedding altitude. As the bird crested the forest's edge, the trucks were suddenly directly below. Cale skillfully swiveled the bird in a tight circle and descended. On landing, the blades' spun within ten feet of the two trucks.

The three passengers jumped out as the skids settled on the ground. Quickly, the Bravo team forced two suspects to the ground. The other two suspects backed to the wood's edge, then took off running, roughly north, along the side of the road, presumably looking for a place to cut into the woods. Two agents took off after the fleeing men. The Bravo team lead knelt into the back of each prone man and cuffed their wrists. Given the mayhem, Cale shut down the chopper and stepped out to help. Another improvisation.

When the chopper's noise and wind diminished, Cale heard the whine of the ATV moving through the woods. He glanced at the running agents. They were over a hundred yards away and still going. He was surprised; four grown men went straight into a dead sprint, and nobody pulled a hamstring. The Bravo team lead had rolled one of the handcuffed men onto his back, putting his right leg adjacent to the other suspect's right leg. With one suspect's right knee facing up and one suspect's right knee facing down, the agent zip-tied the pair's legs tightly together. This awkward position made it almost impossible for them to travel any distance if they had to be left unguarded. The Bravo team leader now also heard the ATV and locked eyes with Cale, who was waiting to assist.

"Coleman, get onto the trail and force the ATV to stop or turn back toward Alpha team."

Cale was ready to help but wondered why he was going after the ATV with just a sidearm while the man with the intimidating long-stock semiautomatic guarded two tied-up guys. As Cale entered the woods, he took off his sunglasses and clumsily stuffed them into his pants pocket.

The combustion engine's noise increased as the distance between

Cale and the ATV decreased. He ran at three quarters speed into the woods. Thirty seconds into the woods, he saw a confluence farther down the trail where three trails joined to form the one he was on. Which trail was the ATV on? Did it matter?

It didn't. What mattered was getting to that trident's confluence. If he stopped him here, the suspect would U-turn out a different trail, negating Alpha team. Without the chopper airborne, it would also be impossible to track him in the maze of hills and trees. Cale sprinted toward the confluence, but as he approached, he realized the fallacy of his logic. This was probably not the only intersection, just the last intersection. He needed to prevent the ATV driver from making the U-turn.

Cale backed up to the trident's handle and found a white oak that split into two large trunks on the trail's edge. He searched the nearby underbrush and found a decent-size limb with small branches and dead leaves still attached. He dragged the limb onto the trail just after the white oak. He didn't use a log, because the suspect likely went down this path in the morning, and the sight of a new log would be suspicious enough to trip the driver's dormant survival alarms. A new branch was just a nuisance.

Playing hide and seek, Cale braced himself four feet off the ground between the trunks in the white oak. His right foot settled in the bottom of the V. He checked to make sure it wouldn't stick when it was time to move. He put his left foot partway up a trunk, bending his hip and knee to fit it in place. He deemed himself sufficiently invisible from the trails. The sound of the motor grew. His breath slowed like it used to before the snap of a ball.

The engine's sound changed as the driver laid off the accelerator. Would he stop and move the sticks or slow down and ride over them? The engine revved slightly; he was still feeding it gas. Looked like only a slowdown.

Finally, the front wheel was in view. Cale dove. The ATV was moving faster than he had anticipated. He extended himself as if the landing would be on water. His right hand caught the back of the driver's hair—one more reason to appreciate the timeless mullet. The suspect was pulled backward off the three-wheeler. Cale turned his own body enough in the air to land on his shoulder instead of on his belly. The driver landed on his back and rolled into a crouch. Both men gasped for oxygen after the hard landing.

The driver took off into the woods in a crouched stagger. Cale popped onto his feet and tried not to wobble as he started his pursuit. Five steps in, he stopped. He had the goods and the driver's partners—surely, they would roll over and identify him. Cale doubted the ATV driver was the evil mastermind behind the operation. Did it matter if he somehow eluded capture?

So he let him go, walked back, and climbed onto the three-wheeler, which had decelerated unharmed in the middle of the trail. Sitting astride the machine, he put his hand on the throttle and, for the first time, noticed the fistful of long blonde hair clinched in his palm.

》》》

IN THE PARKING lot, the marines and passengers from the Whaler played cornhole while the night crowd arrived beach style: the men in golf shirts, khakis, deck shoes, and even a few clean shaves. The women wore sundresses and makeup and carried clutches. The day crowd holdovers stood out with their T-shirts, shorts, cover-ups, flip-flops, red faces, loud voices, and glassy eyes. The Natural Light Mom and her coworker that Cale had brought over from Masonboro were still in bikinis and enjoying a considerable amount of attention. Cale caught the waitress's attention and bought them bar-branded T-shirts in case they got cold or were overcome by a sudden desire for modesty.

The big Ferretti that was anchored off Masonboro lit up the channel, heading north, hugging the starboard side, and running faster than Cale felt it should. Its wake pounded the boat slips as it passed. Cale growled, waiting for the waves to roll into the Whaler. The boat's bass overpowered the bar's music a hundred yards off. The big boat cut speed and turned to port. As it approached the dock, it pointed back to the north. The captain let the helm go and stepped to the side rail. He used a joystick to control the bow thrusters and rear props. As the captain kept the stern a foot off the dock, the two Tommy Bahamas and three bodybuilders in black T-shirts hopped onto the dock.

The Bahamas and Jerseyites grabbed drinks at the bar. Van caught a Bahama's eyes, and they exchanged waves and smiles. The bar's TV was changed to the Yankees game. The Bahamas leaned against the bar and looked at menus. The mastiffs hovered behind them, then walked toward the cornhole game. Blake and a flybridge girl sat canoodling on a masonry wall. When one of the Jerseyites noticed the pair, his posture changed; f-bombs and Italian f-bombs exploded.

The girl looked puzzled at the verbal attack. The f-bomber grabbed her arm and pulled her up. Blake stood and then one meaty hand pushed him backward over the wall.

The Whaler passengers and the marines started to react, and the exchange grew noisy. Cale excused himself and scurried toward the confusion. He knifed through the crowd and inserted himself between the big man and the girl's body. The big man squeezed her arm tighter. Cale shook his head slowly side to side as he looked into the eyes of the enormous younger man.

Being in the open would be better. Being this close to the beast made Cale uncomfortable. There was less chance for bad luck in an open space. Fortunately, the big man was proving a typical bully, incapable of envisioning a scenario where he'd find a worthy adversary. The bar crowd quieted. Metallica now played clearly in the background. Cale wondered when Metallica changed from fringe metal into acceptable background music.

The men's eyeballs stayed a foot apart. Cale was curious. When would the big man release the girl's arm? Was he smart enough to put the girl between them before he did?

One of the Bahamas, whom Cale had tracked in his peripheral

vision, stepped between the two men and peeled the Jerseyite's hand from the girl's arm by turning his thumb outward.

The Bahama finished leashing the black T-shirt with one hand and thumbed out $1,000 from a large cash clip pulled from his shirt pocket with the other. The Bahama handed the cash to the flybridge goddess, who had squeezed in beside him, whispered something to her, and returned to the bar with one hand dragging the black T-shirt with him.

Maybe he was the Don. Don Bahama was a silly name, though. Cale guessed the flybridge girls now wouldn't finish their cruise. He definitely heard the words *hotel* and *fly* in the whisper. What a tragedy for someone with that appearance and smile to live the kind of life she had settled for. The Bahamas and the bodybuilders headed to the far side of the bar's deck.

The forty-five seconds of conflict sucked the life out of the cornhole game. Blake and Van decided to take the girls—with whom Cale still hadn't exchanged names—clubbing. The goddess the Bahama handed the money to was so stunning that Cale wasn't sure he could get his name out if she asked. Of course, as Sherpa, stevedore, and bodyguard, he was just here to work, so no worries. He stepped into a new role as tour guide and walked the group to the turnout, where a taxi waited. Van keyed Cale's address into his phone's map function before hopping into the backseat.

Now that he was walking alone, the heat and lack of breeze on the road made Cale head back to the waterfront, and a small marina's sailboats drew him down the gangway. He loved sailing. Well, loved the idea of sailing. Flapping sails, swinging booms, and rope burns killed the actual love of sailing. He did like being at anchor, though. Or even tied up to the dock. Maybe he liked camping.

The gangway had knee-high louvered lights. They did a great job illuminating everything below ankle height. Each boat slip had hose water, drinking water, and shore power. All of the boats appeared to be less than fifty feet. Most were docked stern-to. It was a mid- but rising tide, and the lines were slack. A forty-eight-foot trimaran occupied the end slip. The boat's technology was mind-blowing, unrecognizable to a sailor of fifty years ago. Automatic reefing systems for mainsail and genny. Pointing and spinning antennas for the GPS. Other electronic systems that he couldn't identify also covered the masthead. A sailor could empirically know the weather, depth, tides, wind speed, and fish location. Yep. Probably a real-time Bloomberg console too.

The trimaran's red and green running lights were off. It was named *Tri Again*. Home port: Hamilton, Bermuda. Big taxes registering a boat in Bermuda. Canvas and steering were controlled from the center cockpit. Currently, it was snapped tight. Soloing the Atlantic on *Tri Again* seemed reasonable. The journey might not be fun, but Cale knew he'd enjoy the anchorage in Spain.

He wasn't sure whether he felt or heard the footsteps on the gangway, but something made him turn in time to see the Jerseyite who'd grabbed the flybridge girl. He was peeling off his shirt and setting it on a white fiberglass dock locker thirty yards away. He emptied his beer's contents on the dock. Shame on him, Cale thought, wasting beer that way.

They locked eyes. The Jerseyite growled, "I don't want your redneck blood on my shirt or any beer splashed on me."

You see, those invariably unintimidating and unwitty comments were why Cale didn't speak before an altercation. The scariest pre-altercation stance he'd seen was a silent twenty-one-year-old Mike Tyson staring down his woofing opponent while getting the referee's instructions. No referee tonight, but Cale doubted this would last the ninety seconds it took a young Iron Mike to dispatch his opponents.

"You want to swim? Might cut youse-self on the barnacles. Youse might find them real sharp when you're scrambling around. Might be your best option. Of course, I'll greet youse when you come to shore, so you might have barnacle cuts and still need a new face. Without fifteen friends and a hundred witnesses around, youse look like you want to mind your own business. Why so quiet? Too scared to cry uncle?"

He spit the word *uncle* like it was distasteful.

Quite the monologue. Cale was tempted to deliver an equally long response. Maybe the Gettysburg Address? *Four score and seven years ago, our fathers . . .* Or perhaps Mark Antony's speech at Caesar's funeral. *Friends, Romans, countrymen, lend me your ears, for we come to bury Caesar, not to praise him.* But he figured the humor would be lost on his audience. Probably the historic and literary references as well.

The big man rolled his neck side to side. He circled his shoulders. He shook out his arms. Maybe he was here to do calisthenics.

Cale watched the empty beer bottle in the Jerseyite's right hand. He cupped the bottle's neck in the webbing between his index finger and thumb. Cale knew the big man would be better off throwing a straight punch than swinging a roundhouse with the bottle at the side of his head. The bottle would hurt a lot less than knuckles to the chin and provided more time for Cale to move or block. He chose not to share the advice.

The approaching footsteps' cadence embedded in Cale's brain. His breath slowed. He slid his right heel twelve inches behind his left, his left toes pointed at the big man, his right toes pointed sixty degrees right, knees bent, and his weight balanced. His left hand rested on his thigh, his right arm slightly bent and his thumb on his board shorts' waistband. A six-foot-three, 210-pound rattlesnake waiting for the lumbering six-foot, 250-pound bull.

A rattlesnake could always strike a bull. But was there enough venom to bring it down? What's with the mental commentary? Nobody was placing bets. Stay focused. Cale tried to remember he'd lost a couple of these before. (Yeah, but that was when he fought fair.) Big man, be smart, still time for you to turn around. Cale pondered making a small offering to the big man's pride to try and stop the altercation. Even saying something innocuous like, "Hey buddy, I got no truck with you" might divert the energy flowing to this intersection, but Cale couldn't bring himself to do it.

The big man now rocked his torso as he continued forward. He lifted his fists. Right hand slightly out wide ready to swing the upturned bottle. He closed in. Cale took two quick steps, split the upraised hands, and unloaded on the sternum. *Boom!* He grabbed the big man's hair with his left hand. He pulled the head downward and brought his right elbow up, crunching the eye socket. *Boom!* Cale kept his left hand on the back of the meaty head. Grabbed, straightened, twisted, locked the right arm at the wrist, dragged him past and toward the ground. Cale gambled and dropped onto the locked arm. *Crack!* He rolled onto the enormous back and slammed an elbow into the right ear. *Boom!* The broken left eye socket bounced off the deck boards. *Thump!* The big man was out cold.

Bounding up, Cale scanned for danger. A nonpartisan witness, he hoped. The other two big men, he hoped not. The pounding heart told him to leave the destroyed big man. Adrenaline in overdrive. Body twitching. Slowly, he left the old fight-or-flight reptilian brain. He embraced the cognitive mammalian brain's return. He reminded himself to breath in through the nose and out through the mouth. His lungs filled with the smell of salty sky, and he relaxed.

There were questions to be answered before he'd know exactly how to proceed. Who were these guys? Bad drunks mooching a trip from a fading playboy? Were they the Bahama's bodyguards? Thugs wreaking havoc up and down the Atlantic seaboard? Good guys with wives and kids gone overboard on a guys' trip? That could describe a few of Cale's friends this weekend. Did the other meatheads and Bahamas know where this dude was? Nobody expected Cale here. The big man must have tracked him from a distance without being noticed. The thought that he had grown so obtuse as to not notice a two hundred fifty-pounder hiding behind lampposts made Cale feel soft around the middle and jowly around the neck.

The big man was breathing, but needed a hospital. Cale took the big man's cell from his shorts pocket, dialed 911, and held his nose talking to the dispatcher. "I need an ambulance on the docks at Lumina Marina." The dispatcher asked for clarification. He repeated the need and location then tossed the phone into the channel.

Doubling back to the bar, Cale grabbed a Bud and sat. He noticed Mr. Julep in the parking lot smoking a cigarette. No smoking in bars in North Carolina—how'd that happen? Philosophically, it was a horrible law. Practically, it was very nice. The Mrs. returned from the lavatory even more talkative with her husband away. Reseated, her leg once again pressed against Cale's, despite the extra space at the table.

She put her hand on his arm and asked him, "Our hero has returned. Weren't you scared?" He wondered how she knew, and he tensed up. She continued, squeezing his forearm, "Over there, when the big guy was yelling at the girl and you ran in to break it up."

He relaxed, now knowing what she meant. Cale answered, "Maybe. I really didn't think about it."

Mrs. Julep added, "Don't you think that whole group—the old guys in particular—look like guys in the mob?"

Cale didn't acknowledge that he had the same thought. He heard the ambulance whine increase and then cease. He used the beer bottle as an ice pack on his knuckles. The ambulance lights weren't visible. The street and parking lots to the north were on the west side of the buildings, and the patio was on the east, overlooking the waterway. Cale scanned the crowd for the Bahamas and the other big guys. They stood at the bar, getting animated in their review of the baseball game. The old guys seemed to have made friends with their neighbors. Nobody seemed anxious for the missing bodybuilder.

Fifteen minutes later, the ambulance siren hadn't restarted. A good sign the damage wasn't too bad. Although that arm had to be broken.

Of course, if the ambulance didn't leave with the big man, he would return to the bar, and then it would be best to be gone. Cale paid the waitress for the table, which included the Juleps' bill. Of course, you're welcome, ma'am. No, no thanks necessary. Ah, sure, here is my card. Dan rounded up the bachelor party members, less Blake and Van, and the men cast off. It was ten thirty. They would be home in twenty minutes—probably too early to get a bachelor party to call it a night, but worth a try.

12

WHEN THE SUN ducked fully behind the horizon, the captain hoisted the dinghy back on deck with the crane. Joe clicked on the overhead lights and started reading while Tony rummaged around for his glasses, which he belatedly realized were pushed up on his head.

After a few minutes Tony said, "Hey, Joe, is it me, or is it quiet downstairs?"

"Must be time for the big boys to get their evening attire ready. I think they're in their cabin doing *oms* to make sure they'll make the right clothing choice."

"Hmm. Black jeans and a black crewneck T-shirt or black jeans and a V-neck T-shirt? You think to get in those sausage-skin jeans they wear they help each other pull up their zippers with pliers?"

"As much as they talk about getting action, would they need to call one of their buddies to help them get out if something did happen for them?"

"Nah, they would go Incredible Hulk-style and flex their quadriceps until . . . pop . . . nothing but ripped clothes."

After a few more laughs, the conversation lapsed, and the captain could be heard finishing the departure preparations. Joe enjoyed the relative solitude and felt a little sentimental gratitude toward Tony for coming on the trip. He could shed a tear if he kept the thought in his mind too long. He laughed softly to himself and went back to his book.

Once it was started, the trip into the marina was quick. The captain drove the boat at about half its cruising speed yet still kicked up a big wake. The captain believed the inland waterway was a highway. If you wanted a dock on the side of a highway, that was your problem. Joe didn't know enough to agree or disagree but noted the angry dock owners they left in their wake. Even if it made no sense to put a dock on the side of a highway, it wasn't the dock owners' fault. They'd just bought the most convenient spots they could afford. The blame should go to the local politicians who approved the construction. But they were just responding to their constituents' desires and increasing the ad valorem tax base at the same time so they could fund the schools and the sheriffs' offices. So it wasn't really their fault either, but the fault of developers like Joe, who made money on the deals. But was it really the developers' fault? Weren't they just responding to what the market wanted and the laws allowed?

Joe found this a pretty good example of the tragedy of the commons. Wouldn't it be wonderful if we could go back and turn the Intracoastal Waterway's banks into national parks? Vladimir Putin could make it happen today and not even worry about compensating the current dock owners. Joe worried slightly that America's government was showing Putin-like tendencies, drifting toward fascism under a socialist banner. Federal and local governments seemed to show systemically less respect for the Fourth Amendment in the name of security and used eminent domain for reasons as thin as increasing the ad valorem tax base.

The captain was talking with Tony and almost overshot the bar they wanted. Once the boat was appropriately situated, Joe and Tony hopped off, followed by the trainers. Joe figured the trainers would stick close through dinner to save money. He thought it might be worth it to give them money to go eat elsewhere but didn't want to set a precedent. He brought a stack of cash to close out after each drink so they wouldn't run up a tab. He didn't put it past them to buy champagne or expensive liquor on his tab for some girl they were afraid to talk to but wanted to impress.

〉〉〉

ASHLEY'S GROUP GOT drinks and played cornhole. A few enlisted guys happy to be both out of the desert and off the base joined them. Ashley bought the marines a round in appreciation of their service. She paired with Van, and they won their first two cornhole games before losing and having to sit out.

She noticed the parking lot was filled up and the dock thinned out as the nighttime crowd drove over and the daytime crowd took off after a long day of sun and drinks. She watched Joe's big boat plow up the channel before quickly shedding speed. The captain steered the boat into a hover beside the main walkway to let everybody off. He then took the boat down to the slip. She walked a few yards away from the group to watch him work the boat into the slip. He used the remote control as he walked around the deck, using different engines to keep the boat between the pylons and the walkway. Finally, he tossed lines to a deckhand, who helped him secure the boat.

〉〉〉

JOE HEADED TO the bar and ordered a bucket of PBR. If there were too many calories in the Pabst, then the trainers could buy their own beers. They got the bartender to find the Yankees game. The Yankees were up in the third. There was a good chance they'd make the series this year. It was still strange to see someone other than Jeter wearing the captain's band.

Shouting caught Joe's attention. He turned to see his nephew holding one of the nurse's arms, spittle coming out of his barking mouth. Joe said, "What the—" and stopped, letting his head droop.

"*Paesano*, that boy pisses in his own cornflakes," Tony said, shaking his head side to side.

"Hey, Tony, you think it's too late to sign him up for military school?"

"Military schools are too close to home. Let's check on the Merchant Marine."

〉〉〉

ASHLEY SAW GINO pull her friend off a wall and onto her feet by her arm. He then pushed the guy with the sunburned feet over the wall into the plantings. That brought heat to her ears that she was sure flushed her face red. She wanted to slap Gino harder than she knew how. If it cost her getting reimbursed for her mirror, so be it. If the trip ended tonight, she was OK with that too.

In that moment, she wasn't seeing Gino pulling her friend off a wall, but her dad pulling her mom out of the recliner that defined their double-wide's living room. Growing up, Ashley spent as little time at home as possible. She tried to come home as close to dinnertime as she could. Sometimes she'd find Mom sprawled in the recliner, deep in an alcohol-induced slumber, her body at angles that would normally keep a human from falling asleep. The platinum-dyed top layer of hair, which usually magnified her sexuality, appeared grotesquely artificial against her brown roots in that unnatural position. When her mom was day drunk, her responsibilities were always half done. Maybe the clothes brought back from the community laundry facility, wet and ready to hang, were piled on the floor at her feet. Her tight and short polyester dress was wet where the clothes sat before they slipped down to the dirt-tracked floor and her chipped toenails. Or maybe there was a half-finished dinner—peas, carrots, and corn, partially boiled, peeled, and shucked, a store-bought lasagna starting to smoke in the twenty-four-inch-wide range.

If she found the bottle, empty or not, Ashley tossed it. Then it was the sprint to get Mom up before Dad came home.

"Mom! Wake up. Mom, you need to get up!"

A mumbled reply, "Go back to bed, Ashley . . . just a bad dream."

She would pull on her mom's eyelids with her fingers, slip a finger into her throat, pinch her cheeks—anything to induce a reaction. "Mom, you have to get up."

Another mumble. "Ash, you're home from . . . early . . . school."

Then she'd stand in front of her mom and try to pull her up, hoping when her body became vertical that she'd remember to engage her own muscles before gravity took them both down.

Sometimes it worked, and her mom got coherent while Ashley completed the unfinished chores—hung the clothes, removed the layer of burnt cheese, opened the windows to get the smoke out. Sometimes Ashley got home too late to get things fixed. At the time, she felt it was her fault for not wanting to be at home. Now, she knew it wasn't her fault, but emotionally, she still felt it. If her mom could have just let her know when she would be a mess, Ashley would have come back early or not left at all. But would it be twice this month or four times this week? There wasn't a pattern Ashley could pick up on, and she blamed herself.

If Ashley got there too late, her dad would be home before her mom was up. He'd see Ashley pulling on his wife. He'd see Ashley frantically doing his wife's chores, hoping she'd have better success waking her mom later but still before he arrived.

He was quiet in these moments. If Ashley wouldn't leave her mom's side, he might backhand her. Not in anger. Short slaps to keep household order. Certainly nothing like the belt-buckle-inflicted scars he collected on his back and legs growing up.

When he got Ashley out of the way, he would take his wife by an arm and drag her out of the chair. He'd let her fall as her body wanted. If her head did or didn't hit the floor, it didn't seem to matter to him. If her dress caught an edge and ripped, he just kept pulling. He'd pull her down the short hallway, past the trailer's bathroom, and past Ashley's closet-size room to the master.

He'd shut the door to their room. She could hear her mom being dragged onto her bed by that arm. Then she'd hear the shuffling as her clothes were pulled up or off and he did the same with his own. And then she'd hear her dad start in on her. In such a small home, devoid of sound insulation, there are no secrets in good times or in bad, and in this home, the bad had far outnumbered the good. Her mom always woke up before her dad finished. There would be a change in the sounds—some brief struggling, then acceptance, and occasionally excitement. It wasn't exactly rape, at least her mom never thought of it that way. But it identified more closely with punishment than pleasure for all in the household.

So now, seeing Gino pull her friend up made Ashley too angry to see straight. A crowd had formed between her and her friend. She saw the guy with the floral shorts fly in from a different angle to stand nose to nose with Gino. She fought to get through the crowd, ready to unload on Gino wherever she could hit him.

》》》

JOE SIGHED, THEN hustled toward Gino. He slipped the fray, grabbed Gino's thumb, and got him to release the girl's arm. Without releasing Gino, Joe turned to Ashley, who appeared behind him, and handed her money from his shirt pocket.

He whispered in her ear, "I'll fly these goombahs home tomorrow. Why don't you and your friends get a hotel tonight? Try to be back to the boat by noon tomorrow. Captain says we have a five-hour ride to our next stop."

Her eyes went from angry to vulnerable as he spoke. He saw her hands were in fists that slowly relaxed. She nodded, understanding.

Walking to the bar, Joe belatedly turned back to apologize to the nurse for Gino's behavior, but she wasn't looking his way. He noticed the bachelor being helped out of the bushes and onto his feet. He didn't seem any worse for wear. His pride wasn't even dented; he was cracking jokes before he had even gotten the planter's dirt brushed off. He'd gone from romance to conflict to the bushes and then to joking and ready for romance again.

>>>

ASHLEY LOOKED AT her friend's arm and saw the red finger impressions that would be bruises by morning. What did Joe call Gino? *Goombah*? That was a new one for her. She thought Joe was wonderful but had panicked over how he was going to react when she saw him get to Gino before she did. Would he support his nephew just because he was his nephew? She was unconsciously putting TV-land, father-figure expectations on Joe, thinking he must support right over blood instinctually with a level of ethics she never experienced from her father. This expectation of someone to behave as a father figure was a new one for her. She had never let herself put these expectations even on Chief.

There was no fun for her friend left at this bar with Gino still present. The group prepared to leave, and Ashley tried to catch Joe's attention. He and Tony were laughing, pointing, and facing the TV.

>>>

WITH THE DECISION made to send the trainers home, Joe's spirits were up, and his energy returned. He would leave it to his nephew to explain to his sister why he was home so soon. He pulled the captain aside and asked him to book the trainers' flights.

Joe could feel Gino steaming. One of the trainers tried to redirect the energy and asked Joe a question. "Hey, Joe, how'd you come up with a gangsta name like *Framed* for your yacht anyway? Youse not some kind of Mafia guy like the old men we see playing chess on the street, are you?"

Tony answered, "So you know what Joe and I did for a living, right?"

"Yeah, youse was carpenters."

"And you know what carpenters do?"

"Yeah, they nail wood together. So what?"

"Part of what carpenters do is build the building's envelope, its walls and floors and roof, right?" Head nodding. "Well, that is called framing. Joe is retired, and the past tense of framing is . . ."

The trainer had stopped listening to the lecture. The food arrived, and the conversation continued only between Joe and Tony, who ate facing the bar. The oyster po'boy was delicious, and the Pabst cold. Tony and Joe watched until the Yanks won without having to bat in the ninth. Like many days, it was a good day, despite the extended family mayhem. As the saying goes, you can't pick your relatives. But for better or worse, blood is thicker than water. Right or wrong, Joe had grown up knowing to look after his own.

The sun and booze caught up with Joe. The trainers were somewhere behind him. He only noticed them the last hour when one reached into the beer bucket.

As they left the bar, Joe and Tony said good-night to two of the trainers. Gino was absent. Joe told them he was flying them out in the morning and for them to tell his nephew when he showed up.

Onboard *Framed*, Joe ate four Chips Ahoy! cookies, downed a glass of milk, and called it a day. He looked forward to his kiss just before he awoke.

13

THE GUYS RELOADED beers and sat in the Adirondacks. Widespread Panic played on the Jawbone. A burner heated leftover stew. Cale unloaded the Whaler while Jimmy slept on the dock, his head resting on his front paws.

When he'd finished unloading, Cale iced his right hand in a cooler and drank a Gatorade with his left. The dock was mostly dark. He hoped the others wouldn't notice the improvised physical therapy. He wasn't sure why, but he hadn't mentioned the fisticuffs. He hoped the incident was simply in the past, although he knew hope wasn't a good strategy.

These things had a way of not staying in the past. Wasn't he a bit long in the tooth for such behavior? Would his personal umbrella insurance cover a lawsuit? He imagined his daughters' mothering eyes if they heard old Gramps had gotten into a fistfight (again). The mental image of their expressions surprised him and brought out a laugh, which he figured was better than crying.

For some reason, an old fight flashed through his brain. It was in New Orleans during a bowl game. They'd won. Maybe next season a national title. He played well. Felt good. The coaches turned a blind eye to the hotel exodus, and he made plans to catch the guys on Bourbon Street, but first he had a date with Maggie at Pat O'Brien's.

As they entered the crowded courtyard, two alumni gave up their wrought-iron two-top to him and Maggie in exchange for handshakes and a photo op. When he was handed a Hurricane, Cale copped James Bond's line, "The best drink of the day is just before the first." (At the time, that sounded cool, but now he appreciated the insight.) He clinked his oversized glass against Maggie's water goblet.

The tropical vegetation was vividly green for January. Maggie wore jeans, a tank top, and a white cardigan. He wore the team's travel outfit: khakis, a golf shirt, and a sweater with the university's mascot stitched onto the breast. Fans in gold, blue, and green took more pictures with him as they left. In a moment of peace, she told him she was ten weeks pregnant.

Surprising himself, he was stoked. The preamble was over; life started now. That national championship run was forgotten, getting a degree was forgotten. Her smile at his reaction lit the table.

She unleashed daydreams. Where they'd live. How they'd pay for things. What the baby boy would look like. She was sure it was a boy until the ultrasound fifteen weeks later. (Stress *a* and *boy*—wrong and wrong.) Cale took the straw from his hurricane and bit it in half, slipped it into itself to form a circle. He grabbed Maggie's hand. "I'm sorry I haven't asked your parents' permission, and I'm not sure what I'll tell Father Malloy, but Maggie, will you marry me?" There were few times when he'd gotten life exactly right. That was one.

"Yes." Kiss.

He didn't notice the place filling with orange-and-blue fans. Didn't remember even to order a new drink. Eventually, he did use the restroom. As he returned, he saw two guys in orange standing beside Maggie. A third sat in his seat. Maggie's glow was undimmed and there was a little mischief in her eyes.

"Excuse me, mind if I grab my seat back?"

"No, this seat works for me. Go back to the grain fields. We'll take good care of this little lady. She looks pricey, but I'm sure we can afford her." The talker was out of college but not by much—maybe a law student or a bank analyst. A little kindle caught fire in Maggie's eyes.

Cale responded, "Fellas, we appreciate you visiting, but it's time y'all left our table."

"Oh, we're good, Hoss. I'll even buy your drink. Just mosey on now. I'm sure your coach is worried about you."

"Cale, honey, let's just go. It's late anyway. I'm sure your coach *is* worried. With these three strapping young adversaries, I'm worried about you too." Fake drawl, grin, needle in his adversary's pride. Troublesome vixen, she was trying to get them out of trouble but not willing to walk away in full defeat.

"Well, no, Maggie. Coach thinks I'm asleep, and I like our table. Guys, seriously, this has been great fun, but time to move on."

"Or what? You hit me, you'll have to hit these guys too. Then some of the other guys from inside. Then, whether you're standing or not, the cops will arrest you, and your football career is done. Coleman, we all saw *SportsCenter* reports of when you were arrested last year for fighting. This one gets you packed off that lily-white campus. No football. No scholarship. No degree, if you were actually planning on getting one. So, Hoss, we're not that worried. So go on out, and we'll entertain your friend. Maggie, right?" The soliloquy and spotty reasoning made Cale conclude they were law students.

All three orange guys stood. Maggie got up and backed away. She must have known that if she'd gotten bounced around in the altercation, Cale's rage wouldn't stop even when their heads hit the brick patio pavers. The guy talking had his head tilted so much his ear almost touched his shoulder. Was that supposed to be intimidating? A show of intellect? What was he trying to convey? His neon orange rugby shirt was stained from a long tailgate. The other two smirked, confident in themselves, their friends, or how much Cale was worried about playing football.

Bad calculus. Fist to the nose of guy on left. *Crack*, blood, down.

Elbow to the talker in the middle. Down. Guy on the right cracked Cale's right temple. That was a surprise. He recovered and unloaded a right into the man's left shoulder. The blow knocked the man off balance. Cale reloaded and dropped another right to the left side of his jaw.

When the fight was over, he was arrested. There were journalists and photographers. His hands were cuffed behind his back, and he sat on the curb while drunk orange-and-blue fans taunted him.

But Maggie kissed him. "That was a good one to go out on, big papa. Now no more from here on."

Oh, if that had only been true. Cale thought, *I've tried, Maggie. You know I have tried.*

Man, in the memory, she looked too happy. "The arresting officer says you're heading to central lockup. They'll set bail in the morning. I'll let your coaches know before the media finds out and meet you there in a few hours to bail you out. I love you."

Central lockup was cold, foul smelling. There was a little throw-up, a little urine, a lot of body odor. The first cell held over a hundred people. There was a line to use the pay phone. Were there still pay phones in jail, or could you use your cell? The prisoners were ninety percent black, ninety-five percent drunk. He was shuffled from cell to cell, with no obvious reason for the location changes. They served grits and hard boiled eggs for breakfast. He never got the orange jumpsuit.

Memory over, no smiling Maggie to tease him this time. Back in the moment, stars were everywhere. The wind picking up. There were no mosquitoes, but a few no-see-ums.

His phone vibrated—a text from Maggie: "Stop lap dance—put down beer—check weather." All right, it wasn't really a text from Maggie but a warning text from a weather service he'd registered with. Arlene had hooked left. Category 2. Projected downgrade to tropical storm when hitting land. Expected landfall, North Carolina coast. Rain to start by dawn. Winds arriving by noon.

Cale texted back, "Thx. Beer down, will prepare house when

lap dance over! Send guys in car Mon, see you Tues—if all OK. Love you. Tell girls sorry I'll be late." The no-reply texting service bounced back a minute later. He wasn't sure why he did that. Maggie died before texting took over the world.

He started the storm prep process, grabbing extra lines to secure the boat. Arlene showed prescient timing: The King Air was on the tarmac, its normal hangar closed for the week for floor resealing. He left a voice mail at the FBO to see whether they could move it to a different hangar. He was sure it was too late unless other owners had flown inland.

There was much work to be done to put the house in the best position to weather the storm. He needed to close the storm shutters, secure the kitchen, and lash down the outdoor furniture. The house would survive; it always did. It was high enough to avoid flooding. The hip roof deflected the wind. A barrier island and the marsh protected it. Maybe there would be some missing shingles or a pine tree would fall inconsiderately, but there'd be nothing too severe. He wasn't sure about the plane or the boat and tried to be philosophical, thinking his insurance company couldn't make money on him every year.

He moved the potted plants from the front porch. He and Jimmy bumped into each other repeatedly. The moving from place to place was messing up Jimmy's sleeping patterns. A minivan taxi pulled into the driveway, and Blake stepped out. That was an inaccurate description. Blake fell out into a stagger with his arm around the girl from the cabin cruiser. Van folded a seat forward and, with another girl, got out of the rear row. The mind-numbing hot blonde from earlier sat in the front seat and paid. She was joking with the driver. The driver laughed and thanked her for the tip. The driver seemed more than a bit smitten.

Hmm. These working girls lost their ride and were crashing at his house? If the blonde could carry a conversation, she could marry more money than she'd know what to do with. Odd touch of class for a working girl, paying and tipping the driver like that. Cale would have thought she'd only open her wallet to put money in. What a waste.

"Big maaaan! I didn't know one song at the club, but my dance moves were still golden. You like this one?" Blake demonstrated. "It never goes out of style. This one is timeless too. Check it out. Look at you, midnight gardener carrying your flowerpots around. That would be a boring movie. Taxi almost hit a deer back there. You say taxi and deer in the same sentence after the word movie, and you can't help but think De Niro, right? I'm a raging bull! Road is craaaaazy dark. You remember everyone? Good, good."

Cale started to respond, but Blake's mouth started first.

"Been bragging you have the coldest beer in the state. Only way I could get everyone back here. They said they've had extremely cold beer in South Carolina before, but I say South Carolina beer can never be cold enough to taste as good as my man Cale's beer. Check out those palmetto bugs running on your porch. My ears are ringing, and my mouth is singing. No Louis Armstrong songs; this night is just starting. Whew." The door smacked closed as they disappeared into the house.

The girls in the driveway were comparing something on their phones as Van walked over.

"Lord, he is rolling," Van said. "What a clown. That jackleg will get you into trouble in a second. You saved him once tonight. I pulled him out of trouble who knows how many times at the club. Hard to keep up with him."

"No girls, no energy. But if he gets a whiff of it, you can't stop him."

Van's face was incredulous and almost weary at the thought of the shared cross they'd shouldered for the weekend. "He has been like white on rice with that one. If he wasn't marrying somebody else in two weeks, I'd think she was Mrs. Right."

"She might not be Mrs. Right, but she is probably Mrs. Right Now. She doesn't seem too upset about losing her client," Cale offered.

Van double blinked. He looked like he'd been punched. He bent forward, laughing, and tried to gain control. He put his left hand on Cale's shoulder. His head hung down, facing the crushed gravel. Water dripped from his eyes. Cale couldn't help but start laughing without knowing the punch line.

The girls looked at the laughers and started walking over, suspicious they were the brunt of the joke. Van pulled it together and whispered, "Big man, what kind of circles do you run in that those are your thoughts? These girls are working girls, and they do work together, but they aren't *that* kind of working girls doing *that* kind of work together."

The shorter girl waved and went inside with Van, who hooked his elbow to hers. Cale watched them go inside and heard them go out on the back porch and yell down to the others. He turned to the blonde and felt a little intimidated. Neither her smile nor her sundress, which stopped mid-thigh, was untying his tongue. But he was a diligent host, so, finally, he said, "So you'll find this so funny. I was just telling Van I thought you were a prostitute. You know, a lady of the evening. And your clients were the old Mafia-type guys from the boat and bar. But he says you don't even have to pay to have sex with you. Isn't that the funniest thing ever?"

Actually, he didn't say that. But that thought ran through his mind, and Cale capably returned her smile. She finally started the conversation.

》》》

"SORRY WE DIDN'T get introduced before. I'm Ashley Walker. Thank you for what you did with Gino. You know—the big guy in the T-shirt. That was a brave thing to do. He is . . . " she started and then shook the thought out of her head.

She studied Cale. His hair was thinning. There were deep sun lines around his eyes, and his skin was a golden tan like hers, not dark olive like Joe's. His face looked friendly, reminiscent of a successful municipal politician. Confident. At this point in his life, he had probably earned that face. The honesty and the laugh lines—he had a nice smile.

She noticed his proportion hid his size well. His arms were roped with muscles. He held the cement pots without effort. His T-shirt fit a V-shaped body. She thought maybe he wasn't being brave with Gino. He might not have had reason to be scared.

She surprised herself. "I saw you surfing." Now, embarrassed, she kept talking. "You look busy. Can I help you with something?" Suddenly, she was rambling. "I don't want another drink, but I know it will be a while before they are ready to go, so I might as well be productive."

Ashley paused for half a second, thinking over her use of the word *productive*. Who said *productive* on Saturday at midnight? She got her mouth going again. "I got the driver's cell number, so I can call him directly when we're ready to leave. He said to give him a half hour heads-up. I gave him a pretty big tip, so I think I can count on him to want another."

>>>

HER NERVOUSNESS RELAXED Cale. He wondered how in the world she could be nervous unless it was from constantly being pursued. He wondered if he hadn't spent most of his adulthood following drug dealers whether he would have assumed she was a call girl. He told her about the hurricane.

Ashley asked, "Do you think I need to call Joe and let him know about the storm? Or will the captain know?"

"That is a heck of an expensive boat. His captain ought to know."

"I don't even want to know how much that boat cost. It would make me even more convinced Joe was in the Mafia, and I don't want to think that." She wanted to change the conversation from Joe and said, "Well, at least it's good that it's going to just be a tropical storm."

"The wind is less intense, but sometimes the rain is worse because the storm doesn't move on as fast. I think that was the problem with Katrina. Once it got onto land, it stopped moving but kept raining until the flooding got out of control."

"Could something like that happen here?"

"I don't think so. The land isn't as low. No levees that I know of, not as many people. Sometimes the hog farms have their waste lagoons blown out, and that gets into the rivers, and all that bacteria gets built up and comes down and ruins our oysters. There was a real bad storm like that in the mid-nineties."

Hmm. Cale wished he hadn't said "mid-nineties." She was probably thinking, *Oh, I remember reading about that when I was in preschool.*

"Is a waste lagoon what I think it is?"

"Only for a couple of hundred thousand pigs. You should see the lagoons from the air. Drive to or from the coast on I-40, and there is about a fifteen-mile stretch of road where you catch the scent."

"I think I'd rather see it from an airplane than smell it on the ground."

She helped Cale wedge twenty-four potted plants against a section of shadowbox fence away from the house. They took the front porch furniture into the house. He showed her how to unhinge, shut, and lock down the storm shutters, turning the house into a fortress. They took care of the outdoor items except the Adirondacks and part of the kitchen, which were in use. None of their friends paid any attention to the preparations. He learned about her job and how the trip evolved. The process took an hour.

Ashley needed to use the restroom. They stepped inside. Cale took the opportunity to straighten things up. Seven guys in a small space put a lot of things out of place. When she got out of the restroom, he noticed her studying his picture wall.

"Is this your wife and daughters?" she asked, looking at a picture taken on a ski slope ten years prior. This was the first time the subject had arisen.

He answered yes, and preempted the follow-up. "Maggie, my wife, died not too long after this picture was taken."

She glanced at his hand then responded, "I'm sorry." She caught Cale noticing that she was looking at his hand. Her next statement came out awkwardly. "I guess . . . I guess . . . I just assumed you were . . . still married."

He spun the silver ring on his left with this right hand. He did this often. Caught in the unexpectedly awkward moment, he said, "When I'm not paying attention, I still think of myself that way." Hoping to stay at the surface, he changed topics and pointed to another picture. Three men stood in flight suits, arms outstretched like crosses, their fingertips touching. In the background stood a sequoia with a trunk whose girth exceeded their outstretched arms. As the tallest, Cale was, for symmetry, set in the middle. "Have you ever been to Northern California?"

"Just once. Chief and I—that is, my grandfather and I—drove to Yosemite. The trees and rocks are from another world. Did you work there?"

"A good bit while in the DEA. My favorite assignment. Even the bad guys were good guys."

They took the conversation outside and joined those who were still awake. Blake's date sat on an arm of his chair, her legs across his lap, ankles resting on the far arm of the chair. Her side leaned into the chair's back, and her arm ran across the back of the chair behind his head. They looked quite familiar with each other. He was still on fire.

"Big man! So what were you going to do at the bar if that frog decided to jump? I was just getting into ninja kung fu mode when you jumped in. Man, I'd have torn that big gorilla apart. Done it silently too. You might have forgotten: I took several karate classes at the Y in the mid-eighties."

Mid-eighties. At least Cale said mid-nineties. If his girl did the math, she would realize she was at least minus five at the time.

"And don't forget," Blake continued. "I had the famous Bruce

Lee–Chuck Norris fight in the warehouse on tape growing up, so I know some moves. Speaking of Chuck Norris, do you know why Chuck Norris kills two white guys each week? To prove he's not a racist. Author. Movie star. TV star. Republican pitchman. I bet he would win *Dancing with the Stars.*"

He was funny. Really funny if you were cross-eyed but not so cross-eyed that you couldn't keep up with his stream of consciousness. Cale sipped some water and tuned out. It had been a long weekend that he was ready to see wind down.

Ashley placed a hand on his thigh. Oh yes, he quickly tuned back in. They started a side conversation, a discrete tête-à-tête. What island was in front of them? Where were they now versus earlier today? She got that the coastline basically ran north and south but with a lot of jut-outs and jut-ins going east and west. That sped things along. Somewhere, they left geography and weather. He found himself talking about Maggie and the girls. They didn't come any smoother than a guy who thinks you're a hooker and then tells you all about his dead wife. Maybe he should mention how great it was to be called Grampa. He noticed her hand left his board shorts.

›››

ASHLEY WONDERED WHETHER that was what rejection felt like. When she had flirtatiously touched Cale, he changed the subject to talk about his grandkids. *Was that the message he wanted her to hear?* At the same time, listening to Cale, Ashley, for the millionth time, imagined growing up like other kids. What would life have been like having loving parents, siblings, this year's styles, and normal teenage worries? *Does he like me? Does she like me? Will I make the team? Does this outfit look good? Am I cool? Hot? Smart?* Not *Is Mom about to shoot the sheriff?* Not *Excited my parents are in jail and social services forgot me.* Now, despite the perspective that hard knocks were supposed to provide, she had the normal worries of a person in her mid-twenties. *Am I a good person? Why don't I have a boyfriend? Do I want to have kids? Do I drink too much? Do I like work? Where am I going with this life?*

>>>

IF SHE WAS flawed, it was deeply hidden. Perfection. Physically, for sure. Cale, due to some unresolved adolescent self-consciousness, refused to mention that he noticed her on the beach. He still couldn't show his underbelly. Surfing today, when he saw her walking, he let a good set go past so she could get a little closer to watch him.

She was funny, quick, self-deprecating, and seemed tough, too. Not calloused-hands tough, more rode-through-the-badlands-and-came-out-the-other-side tough.

He checked himself, because his judgment was probably not operating at optimal levels. The fight, the three-day bender, and the hurricane heading to town might have made him focus on the positives. So his house, recreation, and livelihood were at risk with a big storm heading his way? Was there any reason he should be off center?

Cale maintained a running mental commentary beyond the conversation. Of course she had Maggie's good characteristics and none of the bad. Now she was a goddess down to the flower picked and tucked behind her ear. Two hours ago, she was a lady of the evening. Things changed fast. Good to remember that.

She did have the flaw of not being his girls' mom. But it'd been a long time and wasn't his first rodeo since Maggie passed. He wasn't sure this was even his outcome to choose, although there was certainly a connection between them. At least, he was connected now that he didn't think she was a westernized geisha. He knew he didn't own the outcome, but he owned the intent.

The drunks sitting uneasily on the wagon understood. You rechoose everyday. Most days, you lined up to stay out of harm's way. *Lord, do not lead me into temptation . . .* but life wasn't lived in a bubble. There were old friends, enabling families—crabs in the bucket pulling you back in when you had one claw over the edge. The drunks still took business trips. They still had fancy meals with clients, pressure for sales. Would the clients buy more if you loosened up like you used to?

You didn't simply choose life once and press autopilot. The PTA, a comfortable house, a college savings plan, Wednesday date night, pickups from practice, a shoulder to lean on, your own shoulder leaned on, volunteer boards. You earned and unearned your life. Generally, life just happened whether you deserved the outcome or not.

Cale noticed he was talking about his kids and grandkids again. Doing a good job presenting himself as a father figure. Not Lothario or Fabio or Brad Pitt. Actually, Brad Pitt had a bunch of kids, so maybe the message was blurring. Was forty really the new thirty? Maybe for people with two-year-olds at forty, not nineteen-year-olds at forty. (Forty? Who was he kidding? What was a twenty-year age difference between friends? He hoped she was older than his daughters.)

A series of *woo-hoo*s turned their heads. Clothes had been kicked off in the yard. Running buttocks were more noticeable at night than you'd think. Bare feet thumped across the dock. What were the odds of someone snagging a splinter on the dock? Would they know now or wonder where it came from in daylight? Someone doing a splay-legged head-over-heels flip was first in the water. The landing was loud and the splash high. Good height on takeoff, but Cale guessed it was an over-rotation. Next, a two-footed jump off the dock. Legs straight, toes pointed down, hands covering breasts. Then a dive. The show ended with a pair of synchronized cannonballs.

>>>

ASHLEY HOPED CALE would and wouldn't join in—cross impulses. It would be nice to see spontaneity behind the wall of duty. Outside the surfing, all she had seen him do was work. In the water, she could create a situation without making a decision, some incidental contact underwater perhaps. Something easier than two sober people consciously crossing the Rubicon.

But she wasn't even looking across the Rubicon yet. If he shed his shorts and took off for the water, she'd have to corral various emotions to reach her decision to join in or not. If he went, she would have to choose between rejecting him now or rejecting him later.

》》》

CALE TOOK THE road less traveled. His knees weren't up for the dash. He hadn't ingested as much joint lubricant as the others. He stood and pulled Ashley up. He gave her a small grin and a wink. They walked to the dock. He reached under the handrail, opened a small plastic box, and flipped on the under-the-dock floodlights that pointed at the skinny dippers.

Blake's manhood telegraphed his thoughts. He embraced the literal and figurative spotlight and went into a dead man's float. "Eh, check it out. The Washington Monument. Tallest building around."

Van added, "Shave 'em on back, Blake. It'll add a half inch to the presentation."

"Man, chicks dig this seventies motif. You boys worry about your shrinkage and your landscaping issues. Ladies like an all-natural man."

One of the girls asked, "Is it always that skinny?"

"What? Sweetheart, you are mistaken. The tremendous length has your perspective out of focus. Come a little closer. You'll see. Use your hands as a measuring device. It's like a redwood. The height makes you not appreciate the girth until you're right up on it."

Laughing, Cale cut the spotlights, and flipped on an LED rope light that wound up the ladder from the water to the dock. He opened a pressurized storage locker and pulled out five towels and set them on the dock for the skinny-dippers. Pilots should never forget they were in the service industry. The laundress in Cale rationalized *what's one more load?*

Walking back toward the house, Ashley asked, "Should we put the outdoor kitchen stuff away?"

"Good idea."

They finished the cleanup by the time the others were out of the water. Being sober, Cale felt the late hour more than the others. Or maybe—being middle-aged, or as they called it for the last twenty centuries, *old*, he felt the late hour more than Ashley, who also seemed clearheaded. Ashley headed into a powwow with her friends. Cale whistled Jimmy over and snuck off to his bedroom. He paused, then locked the door and put in his earplugs. A clean conscience was a beautiful thing.

>>> **14**

RADCLIFFE'S ARMS AND legs were duct-taped to a chair. He searched the room for a means of exit or defense. He spotted paint roller extender sticks and sheetrock putty knives. Mediocre weapons in a hand-to-hand fight if he was free, but nothing to help in this situation. He looked at the alarm panel. If he made it there, could he hit an emergency button? Maybe, but he realized, with no tenant, he didn't pay to have this space monitored.

He followed his training and used the downtime to think through his options. If his arms or legs had been duct-taped together, he could have flexed and retracted and rubbed to loosen them, weakening the material's tensile strength. But this was not how he found himself. Each arm was taped individually from bicep to wrist to the chair's back spines. Each leg was taped individually from knee to ankle to a chair leg. Very effective. He leaned forward and looked at his hands turning purple. He felt the swelling of his feet against his shoes. If he was cut free, it would take minutes before either his hands or his feet would work.

There were three men in the room now, speaking casually off to the side. He could hear their conversation but tried to block it out. Reconnaissance wasn't needed. Survival was.

The men represented three generations. The middle-aged man was in charge. No introduction with the middle-aged man was necessary despite this being their first meeting. Radcliffe hadn't seen a photo of the man in twenty years, but his name often crossed his mind. Being in the situation he was, he definitely knew who he faced.

Radcliffe's mind sifted through the cleaning and paint schedules for the office. He thought about his wife's plans for the day. Was there a chance someone would discover the situation? He wasn't really sure how much time had passed. He prayed no one came along. No more victims. Nothing short of a SWAT team would save him anyway. Was he the first, or was his old pilot already dead?

When he had come to show the space, it was to just the one younger, darker man. He'd noted the man was Hispanic before unlocking the door, but this was Florida, and he couldn't be wary of all Hispanics he didn't know. Radcliffe and the young man's conversation alternated between English and Spanish. The young man said he was Cuban, and the accent agreed. He certainly did not use the elegant Colombian Spanish that would have concerned Radcliffe, so he let himself relax.

They had made it through the entry lobby and a tour of the first two office spaces. The Cuban had asked good questions that made him think he was a serious prospect. Radcliffe hadn't seen the short hose until it was swinging toward the side of his head. He was semiconscious through the taping. Now the combination of time, pain, and adrenaline had him fully alert. Radcliffe watched Francisco nod to the older man, who ripped off the tape covering his own face. Radcliffe yelped and noted half his mustache stuck to the back of the tape.

Francisco asked, "Mr. Radcliffe, are you ready to tell me about the villa?"

Radcliffe rubbed his face into his shoulder. Red trickled from the missing mustache. A bloody smear soaked into his shirt's shoulder. Radcliffe numbly answered, "I am sorry; I don't know what you're talking about. I was in the DEA, but I worked a desk and now I collect a pension."

Left unsaid was that Radcliffe always felt this was how his life would end. He needed this torture to end before somebody stumbled upon them. If, by chance, Escobar didn't know the whole story, Radcliffe needed the trail to go cold with his death.

The old man approached again. He took off Radcliffe's shoes and stuffed paint-thinner-soaked rag strips between his toes. Radcliffe felt the wetness, smelled the odor, and heard a lighter flicker on and off behind him.

Radcliffe watched the look pass between Francisco and the man standing behind him. The younger man moved in front of Radcliffe and bent down with the lighter. Before the Cuban could ignite the rags, Radcliffe's head sagged dramatically. With feigned meekness he said, "OK. OK. What do you want to know?" This was his chance to sell Escobar the lie.

>>>

THE CUBAN RELEASED the lighter's trigger and stood up. Francisco asked several questions about the event. All of the answers agreed with the report he had read, but his face showed Radcliffe only skepticism and disdain. Finally, he said, "How many terrorists did it take to kill my brother?"

Radcliffe paused, "There were three of us. Two of my men died. I was the only survivor. When I shot your brother, everyone else was dead. I radioed for a backup helicopter."

The Cuban did not need to be told. He knew Francisco did not like this answer. He bent down and lit the rags on both feet. Radcliffe screamed. He bounced his metal chair. Twenty seconds. Forty seconds. A minute. The rags began to burn out. Radcliffe's screams turned into whimpers.

Francisco said, "Mr. Radcliffe, if there is nobody else to see, I have nowhere to go. This can take a very long time. Should we see if your wife would like to join us?"

There was no reply besides the whimpering. Francisco poked at the charred feet with his shoe and the intensity of the whimper changed. He nodded to Alberto, paint thinner glugged out of the bottle's wide mouth onto Radcliffe's thighs and lap.

"Mr. Radcliffe, I am going to ask you again. Who else killed my brother?"

Radcliffe met the inquiry with silence. He seemed no longer able to meet Francisco's gaze. Francisco concluded Radcliffe knew his eyes would betray his desire for mercy.

"You still do not want to answer? Then let me tell you a bit about what I will do with the extra time I have now that I won't need to find your accomplice."

Francisco waved toward the tools he would use. At first, Radcliffe stared only at the floor, but then Alberto pulled his head up by his hair to show him his future.

There were water buckets that would put out the fire on Radcliffe's lap before the next one started on his shirt. Sandpaper to remove the burned skin down to the muscle. Finally, the relief, the razor knife Francisco flicked open that would end the misery once he'd heard the truth.

As the Cuban bent to light the pants, Radcliffe, with a genuinely meek voice, confirmed Mr. Coleman's involvement, and as the flame lifted to his crotch, he frantically—and somewhat pathetically, it seemed to Francisco—volunteered that Coleman killed his brother and explained exactly how. He seemed to have no other helpful information.

At this point, Francisco ended Mr. Radcliffe's life with a slice across the throat. Reaching through the wound, he pulled the tongue through the hole. Alberto took a picture of the corpse with its signature necktie lolling on Radcliffe's chest. The body would be burned too badly for the necktie to be seen by the authorities. But later, when Francisco was in Colombia, they would make the pictures public while denying any complicity. Part of this killing's purpose, after all, was for the image to make its way into the public's consciousness.

The confirmation Mr. Radcliffe provided of both his own and Mr. Coleman's participation was appreciated. If the report had been incorrect, Francisco didn't mind killing an innocent *norteamericano*, but he did mind the thought of the guilty living on. Twenty years were enough. Mr. Coleman's end would not be as painless as Mr. Radcliffe's.

As they returned to the G5, Francisco said to Alberto, "You did well. You have not lost your touch."

"Thank you, Mr. Escobar. We still have good men in Florida who provided the information and supplies. They are the ones who first introduced us to the Cuban last year. I feel he does very well for one so young."

"Yes, he again did very well. Very clean." Francisco paused, thinking of a role on his notepad the Cuban might play. He then added, "Please reward these good men generously. We will be spending more time in Florida and need good men." Francisco looked in the rearview mirror and saw the Cuban following. "Do you think the Cuban would be helpful for the rest of our trip?"

Alberto agreed and pulled out his phone to make the arrangements.

>>>

FOCUSED ON THE growth of the business, Francisco walked away from Alberto and the Cuban, who sat in the front row of the Gulfstream. Francisco sat on the couch at the back of the cabin and picked up his notepad. He felt good that the pad's red was now overlaid with new initials, but there was still too much blue. He wrote the Cuban's initials and a question mark beside one critical spot of red.

Unfortunately, he saw no choice but to form an alliance, even if the Cuban succeeded. A smaller Mexican cartel seemed obvious. These were the relationships he was developing. The men from the

Yucatan were more similar to the former *recolectores de café* that his family employed in his established territories than were the Aztec, Apache, and Pueblo descendants in northern Mexico.

Francisco looked forward to filling his men's passports with stamps. They had the financial resources for the growth. They had the skill set. They had the product, and there was demand for that product. They had firepower. But they lacked manpower. His men were largely old or unproven. There was too much death in the middle. Could the Cuban be trained to not only perform but also to lead?

He ruminated on the old RAF pilot's comment about the rule of law allowing England to rule the world. There seemed validity in this idea. In the failed states of South America, it was true: There was no rule of law. Even in Mexico, law only took hold within pockets of the citizenry. Certainly, there were laws, but the justice and value of these laws were not embedded in the culture. The creation of value that came from honoring deals or respecting property rights was little understood. There was no understanding of the fact that if there were no dishonor in stealing, then everyone's property would soon be stolen, except the smallest amount they could physically protect.

Better to partner directly with the Americans and Europeans rather than the Mexicans or Moroccans. The westernized criminals with whom he would deal were culturally bound to honor deals. Their deceptions would only occur when it was in their best interest. A calculated gamble. These partners would realize they made a choice to steal and would understand the ramifications. The men who grew up without the rule of law stole because they could at that moment; they didn't consider the consequences.

The Americans and Europeans were also sheltered. Even their poorest grew up with doctors to treat the sick. They rarely saw youthful deaths from poor health or violence. The untimely passing of a single friend traumatized them; a mass grave was a fairy tale. The idea that law enforcement officials could be left hanging from street lights was unfathomable.

Using the Western men would save lives. The reminders of his violent capabilities would be needed less frequently. Another benefit of dealing with the Westerners was their fifty years of equal rights movements. He could align with women as well as men. Certainly, his socially repressed competitors under their turbans or machismo wouldn't. The old RAF pilot would probably say that the Western world ruled today, because it allowed women to contribute. Francisco could hear his cockney accent, "Lad, how do you not use half your population and move forward? Do you think if I cut the engines off on the left side of the plane we'll get there as fast as if they were all trailing blue flames?"

>>>

ESTELLA INTERRUPTED HIS thoughts. "Mr. Escobar, would you like a drink?"

He looked up and replied, "Please. A Heineken."

He had missed the pleasure of watching her approach. He did not repeat the mistake as she walked away, taking the time to absorb her fluid motion. As she walked, she traversed a tight rope, each foot landing almost exactly in front of the other. Her shanks cocked up and down with each stride. The tucked-in shirt highlighted her narrow waist and straight back. The slit in the skirt's back stopped just below his imagination. She bent at the waist and opened the undercounter refrigerator in the middle of the cabin. This was for his benefit; it would have been more comfortable for her to bend at the knees. He started to relax. It had been a good day. As she returned, he watched a drop of water from the cold bottle land in the open fold of her button-down shirt and slide first sideways and then accelerate vertically down between her breasts.

Handing the bottle over, she asked, "Is there anything else I can get for you, Mr. Escobar?"

He motioned for her to sit. Estella drew the curtain separating the plane's lounge from its passenger rows before sitting. Silently, he enjoyed her fragrance. He felt the skin above her knee as it turned to soft inner thigh. He turned toward her, and their eyes met and held. A knowing look of pleasures to come passed between them. Francisco felt it was a shame he had not already upgraded the back of the cabin with a wall and door.

Francisco did not find the limited privacy inhibiting. Estella soon wore only her heels. Two of Francisco's buttons were lost on the floor. From the sounds Francisco heard and the quivers he felt, the missing wall did not detract from Estella's experience either.

"HE SPEAK TO the cops?" Joe asked the two nervous trainers who'd awoken him with the story of the attack on Gino.

"Yeah, he was telling them the story when we were at the hospital. Oh, and the docs won't release him before eight."

"OK. Thanks. I'll get him in the morning." Dark thoughts of retribution seeped into Joe's brain. A moment of silence passed as they stood on either side of Joe's cabin doorway.

One of the trainers finally said, "Mr. Pascarella, one more thing."

Where did all this "Mr. Pascarella" come from? Joe nodded for him to proceed.

"Do you mind calling Gino's mom? He asked us to, but, you know, you're her brother or whatever, and maybe she would take it better from you."

When they waxed their pubic hair, it must have pulled their balls off too.

"Yeah, I can do that. Oh, I was going to tell you in the morning, but since we're all here: The captain got you a Hertz car to drive to Raleigh and fly home tomorrow. Assuming Gino's OK to fly, he has a seat on the plane with you."

There was no reaction from the two man-boys. Joe remembered he'd told them earlier in the night. He turned and shut his door. He cut his light and fell onto his bed. He heard the trainers leave. He lay on top of his sheets until he heard the rain start. Somehow, he fell back to sleep.

》》》

TONY HAD COFFEE ready when he got up. The conversation between the trainers and Joe woke Tony last night, so he was up to speed. Fortunately, the captain had already picked up the rental car the trainers were to take to the airport. He and Tony could use it to check on Gino. Leaving *Framed*, Joe put on a yellow raincoat, flipped the hood up, and filled a to-go cup. They hurried through gusts of rain to the small rental SUV. None of the console buttons were where Joe thought they should be.

"Anthony, you think Gino was attacked?"

"Hard to imagine somebody looking at him from the front and then choosing to beat him up. Hard to imagine him admitting it if they did."

Clear as mud. Joe hated to see his family get hurt. Hated that he thought such uncharitable thoughts about Gino every time he saw him.

Forty years ago, Joe had hammered scabs taking jobs from his guys. Those guys' mistake was wanting to feed their families. He didn't feel so good about that now. He and Tony never relived those memories. Some of those guys were just back from Vietnam, too, already emotionally torn up and maybe trying to kick some bad habits. And when they tried to make a living . . . Joe didn't want to follow that thought.

He just wasn't sure about Gino. He'd talk to Gino and see whether he could figure it out. He wouldn't rush to bust open a scab today, but if somebody cowardly attacked someone under his care . . . Really, if somebody cowardly attacked anybody and Joe could do something about it, he would. Processing the situation, he felt a spark catch in his gut.

Ignoring the technology in both the dashboard LCD and their phones, they wrote the directions on a sheet of notepaper.

The hospital parking lot was under construction with a new oncology wing coming soon. Hospitals always grow. Demographics pushed the hospitals' expansion destiny, which was to grow or die. Funny thought for a business dealing with death. There were good margins in hospital jobs, lots of change orders, and late-stage customization. You could turn five percent profit into fifteen percent quickly.

Gino was having breakfast—what else—a smoothie. His right arm had a hard cast bent eighty degrees from straight. Not plaster, but hard. It was wrapped in fiberglass mesh tape like sheetrockers use. How much would a plaster cast around Gino's ham hock arm weigh?

Gino's face was a mess. It was hard to tell with the swelling and discoloration, but Joe thought he looked depressed. A good butt whipping could do that to you. Although Joe noticed that somehow, he'd ripped the neck of his blue paper gown enough to show his hairless chest.

"Eh, Gino, how you feeling? I hope better than you look."

He mumbled, "Uncle Joe, cut me some slack. I can't believe it. Doctor says I'll need this cast for four weeks. Then a smaller one another four weeks. Then they'll look at it again to see how much longer. I probably won't work out for three or four months by the time it's healed. I'll lose a lot of mass in four months."

Diminished appearances. The source of depression was identified. Joe thought to mention that, as appearances go, he, not Gino, was the "after" picture.

No reason to pile it on. Gino spent his life creating those muscles. He didn't need them in a conventional sense. He didn't pull a plow, hammer railroad ties, grapple giant crab pots onto boats in freezing waves. He needed them to substitute for a personality—personality from physical presentation. Saved effort on thoughts, words, or actions. Joe felt a little bad for him.

"So, Gino, what happened?"

"Uncle Joe, I went to look at the boats. I stopped to take a whiz off the dock. I had my johnson in my hand when that sucker with those flowery shorts cracked a tire iron across my arm, popped me in the head a couple times when I was bent over, and left me. He stole my phone and the cash out of my wallet, too."

"What did the police say?"

"They asked if I knew his name or any way to find him. I didn't. Here's the police report."

Joe could track him down. The nurses knew his name or his friends' names well enough. He could almost remember the names of the guys on the boat. He figured the captain would remember the name of the boat itself. Gino could have figured this out. Joe didn't think he'd mention it.

He wasn't sure about Gino's story. Joe read the report. Why was his shirt off to whiz? Christ Almighty, what was he thinking? Gino would take his shirt off anytime he got the chance.

The doctor made her rounds. The CAT scan and MRI were clear. She scribbled on the chart at the foot of the bed. Gino could fly home. She prescribed pain pills, advised an orthopedist, and moved down the hall. Two minutes tops. Gino said he'd never seen her before.

Tony and Joe helped Gino into his pants. Neither one's knees felt good bending down, so they laid Gino back on the bed to put on his shoes. The blue gown stayed on for a shirt; Gino's T-shirt hadn't made the ambulance. Joe helped Gino through the checkout process while Tony got the car.

Gino sat in the back. Joe called the captain to have the trainers and their bags ready to ride to Raleigh. No extended good-byes.

It was nine. Joe crossed himself and dialed his sister. He put her on speaker so Tony and Gino could feel the assault. After taking his licks from his sibling, Joe took Gino back to the boat with Tony.

〉〉〉

ASHLEY AND HER friends were in Cale's Land Cruiser with Barry behind the wheel. Ashley used her phone for directions to find the marina. The Jersey guys pulled out as they pulled in. Solemn looks alone were exchanged in the passing. Joe and Tony stood on the covered aft deck, drinking coffee, and the captain adjusted the dock fenders in the rain.

When they made eye contact, Tony whistled, Joe smiled, and Ashley felt better. She wondered whether they were evacuating. Were Joe and Tony staying on the boat or heading inland? Chief said that when a hurricane came ashore, they took the boats to deep water. Did boats like this do that, or just big navy ships?

Deckhands in rain slickers tidied the marina, putting hoses in lockers, disconnecting shore power feeds, and clamping lockers shut. Cushions went below decks, Bimini tops were removed, rain dodgers were zipped, and yardarms and fighting chairs were stored. Everybody was in a really good mood. Ashley expected the ominous foreboding of a coming storm but instead found the air had a very communal feeling. The gunslinger brings the ranchers together.

"Joe, do we stay on the boat?"

"Captain says it's OK. The wind is gusty, but not too bad. Just rain all day. Some cruise you signed up for, huh?"

"Sunny and Gino versus rainy and no Gino. That's a tough call."

She'd expected Joe to laugh. He forced a smile.

"Here's your money back. I'm sorry I even took it. I was just so . . . What's the right word? . . . confused . . . with all the action. I can't believe I'm admitting this, but I was happy you took charge and told me what to do. Until you got there, all I had my mind on was hitting Gino as hard as I could. Oh, and we didn't need it. The money, that is. The bachelor party guys let us crash with them."

》》》

SHE HAD HIS attention. He was jealous. Green, mean jealous. *Crash*? What did that mean?

Simmer down. She wasn't his girlfriend. She wasn't his daughter. And *daughter* was more realistic; if his kids had kids the same age he had 'em, *granddaughter* wasn't too far off. OK. Feel jealous, just don't let her see you're jealous. Joe felt the darkness in him take firmer hold.

〉〉〉

JOE'S AWKWARD PAUSE made Ashley keep talking. "Cale. The guy who was right in Gino's face. He owns this really neat little house out on the water. Not on the beach but on the . . . what do you call it?"

"The Intracoastal Waterway?"

"Yeah. The Intracoastal. It's really old. Huge front and back yards. Perfect view down to the water."

"Could you find the house again? Do you have his phone number?"

"Sure. I have his address in my phone. I didn't get his phone number. Why?"

"I think I need to talk with him about Gino."

Joe wrote down the address, and the conversation concluded awkwardly.

Ashley went to her cabin to shower, scurrying through the rain. The cabin door opened upward. To get in, she descended a ladder. By the time the door shut, the floor was soaked. She stripped out of her damp dress, then used it to mop the floor. She hung her dress on a hook and hopped in the shower.

〉〉〉

JOE ASKED THE captain to borrow a car for him. He unlocked his safe and put his pistol in the pocket of his rain slicker. He couldn't find Tony and thought it best to go without him anyway to keep him out of whatever trouble Joe ended up causing.

The captain returned with an entry-level pickup—rear two-wheel drive only, vinyl bench seats, roll-up windows. Joe was surprised you could still find roll-up windows. It was one less electronic component to break down. The truck had a four-speed manual transmission. It had been a long time since he'd driven a manual. Or a four-speed. The cell phone had killed the manual transmission. Who wanted to shift gears when you had to hold a phone to your ear? Maybe new hands-free phone technology would bring it back.

He sat behind the steering wheel and wrote the directions from his phone onto paper. More miles than turns. More miles by land than by water. He started the Mitsubishi, checked the windshield wipers, and set off.

The flat roads puddled at any asphalt dip, poor grading, raised side yard, or clogged drainage ditch. More than once, water sloshed through the bottom of the door onto the rubber floors. There was very little traffic; the tourists were gone and the residents were holed up in their homes. He went slow. He turned off the collector road onto a neighborhood road with houses on each side. There was no consistency in the houses—old, new, big, small, lots of land, almost no land. He found the street and turned onto a ribbon-paved road no wider than sixteen feet.

Trees lined both sides of the road, broken by mailboxes and gravel driveways leading to houses he couldn't see in the rain. He pulled over to let an SUV pass. As it pulled past him, and the headlights no longer shone in his eyes, he saw it was the same old Toyota that had dropped the nurses off, now filled with guys. He figured that was the party leaving town, and he was too late, but he was close enough that he'd find out for sure.

He found the driveway. The mailbox said "Coleman" on top. The street number was on the box itself. Below the box were some decorative crabs in a net, and at the base of the six-by-six post was a cactus in a bed of oyster shells.

He pulled off the street and sat in the truck with the engine running, the lights and windshield wipers on. Joe's thoughts shifted between fury over his nephew and jealousy over Ashley. What happened with Ashley here last night? He should have kicked the trainers off the boat, not the girls. The darkness grew. He felt himself hoping Gino told the truth. He put his right hand on his rain slicker's pocket and felt the danger of the pistol.

»»» 16

HALLELUJAH! THE FRIENDS were gone, the house empty. Cale loved seeing his friends, but you know what Ben Franklin said about fish and visitors.

He checked his phone. A missed call from a 703 area code that he didn't recognize but—surprise—no messages from his daughters. He told himself not to be a grumpy old man. He would go to Facebook to see if they had any updates. There was something about the end of a guys' weekend that made you want to hug your family. The girls had both uploaded new pictures of the little ones—on swings, being held in the pool, asleep in the car seat in a bathing suit.

Cale scanned his other "friends'" posts. Oh no. A former coworker, Jim Radcliffe, died in a fire in an office building. The funeral was scheduled for Thursday.

Toggling out of Facebook, Cale Googled articles on the fire. Cause unknown. Started in an area with construction material. The deceased's remains were too damaged to perform an autopsy. Worry crept into Cale's chest.

His mind wandered. Despite the Facebook connection, he and Jim weren't truly friends, but they were bonded. Every time they worked together, except one, Jim jumped out of the helicopter, and Cale stayed in it. But there was that time in Colombia. (Wow, two times in twenty-four hours thinking about Colombia.) They'd survived. A pair of better men hadn't.

Was it coincidence that this happened to Jim right after the new treaty? After Colombia, whenever the two men crossed paths, they joked that if one died in a strange car wreck, it was time the other stopped driving. Even since both men left the DEA, they'd occasionally sent each other emails with titles like "Still driving?" Such were the type of looking-over-your-shoulder worries the drug runners in Colombia inspired.

Feeling a touch of paranoia, he dialed Sheila, a former boss of both Cale and Jim. Sheila started with the DEA in 1984, fresh out of Vanderbilt Law School. The DEA was pretty fresh at the time too. Cale started half a decade later, right in the middle of the South American campaign of the War on Drugs. Four years before Pablo Escobar met his demise.

It still amazed him that Pablo Escobar had controlled eighty percent of the cocaine trade entering the United States. The loyalty he built through soccer clubs, hospitals, and terror kept him protected for over twenty years in the world's deadliest profession. An obscene amount of time for so risky a venture. *Forbes* magazine listed him as the seventh-richest man in the world. He spent a year in a country club prison he built for himself so he could sleep soundly while his men assassinated his enemies. He openly assassinated three Colombian presidential candidates who were not to his satisfaction. He was finally killed by police officers acting against their own orders but in the interest of their country. The truth behind it all was that the team hunting down Pablo was directed by the DEA's human assets and Delta Forces' soldiers and technology.

Even if Sheila and Cale had started on the same date, they would have been on different career tracks. Her destiny was to be a manager and his a skilled worker. A producer, not a leader. He valued the skill sets of leadership and diplomacy—setting a vision, tact, standing down. He just didn't possess them. Sheila did. She held as high a position in the agency as an non-appointed employee could obtain. If she had a husband instead of a partner, she'd likely have an appointed position by now.

The call went to her office voice mail in DC, where Cale left a brief message as instructed after the beep. He returned to reading about the fire. His phone started bouncing on the desk. The same area code 703 number he'd missed earlier.

"This is Cale."

"Hey, Cale. It's Sheila."

"That was quick. You must have checked your voice mail right after I called."

"I'm in the office. I just couldn't switch over in time."

He started to ask whether he'd missed a call from her earlier and why the number wasn't from a 202 area code, but let it pass. They kibitzed, commiserated about Jim. Cale asked, "What is the agency's feeling about this peace treaty in Colombia?"

"On the surface, it's OK. The rebels agree that their lands will pay homage to the capital in exchange for being able to largely self-govern. As you know, that's no different from the way the warlords, sheiks, chiefs, and patrons divide up most countries. The quality of life in those areas is a crapshoot. When you have the rule of man over the rule of law, it's the man that matters."

"So we learn, over and over. What's below the surface?"

"This was a three-way treaty. The actions of the rebels were codified as part of a war. All participants are covered by the Geneva Convention rules."

Cale sat quietly, letting the news sink in. It wasn't getting very deep. "I'm sorry; I need you to draw the line for me. My knowledge of the Geneva Convention doesn't extend past not torturing POWs. Or, as Bush adjusted it, to uniformed POWs."

"I don't know if W got that change ratified. Do you remember when El Capo wanted Colombia to end the Colombian-American Extradition Treaty of 1979, when part of the deal would have been international pardons for past crimes?"

"Of course."

"Remember what that would have meant?"

"Very well."

"Now multiply it maybe five times, and you'll get a feel for what we've entered into. Do you still need me to draw the line?"

"No, I think I drew it. So we not only drop all prior charges and convictions in absentia but also any travel restrictions against the rebels?"

"Yup. Our consulate in Bogotá has been monitoring the issuing of new passports to our former most-wanted-list folks. The list is getting quite long."

"So these groups can now travel to the US? Folks that we really don't want traveling here? Folks that are narcotraffickers first and guerillas a distant second?" Cale wondered why he was both belaboring the issue and not using names. The point was moot; she knew to whom he was referring.

"I'm afraid so. It seems we have a very short institutional memory."

His brain speed picked up, and Cale began making connections. "Sheila, are there federal investigators in Florida looking into that fire?"

She let the question hang for a moment. "Yes. I'll have someone contact you to let you know what they find. Should be within a week. I'm sure it's just odd timing, but it makes me feel a little uneasy, so be careful until we can rule out foul play."

"Thanks."

"Oh, and before you ask, we already looked it up. Pablo's favorite nephew, who has a quick trigger finger and a long memory, Francisco Escobar, is in the States. It was his brother at the villa." Now she was the one who didn't need to belabor the point. These details were etched in stone in his memory. "Francisco took a flight from Bogotá to Miami. He is scheduled to fly back to Bogotá on Sunday."

"What has he been doing in Miami so far?"

"Were not even sure he's still in Miami."

Cale couldn't believe they weren't tracking him, but she had no obvious reason to lie about it. Cale grunted, "Well, maybe it will be fun to look over my shoulder for the rest of my life, be that forty years or a week."

She laughed because his delivery was funny even though he was being a smartass. Well, maybe she laughed to be polite. Depending on what information was out there, she had more reason to look over her shoulder than a simple pilot like himself did.

Could you feel the spin? *Simple pilot.* He was already rehearsing the lines for his future captors.

Having psychopathic billionaires mad at you was just not a great position to be in. Billionaires, by definition, had significant resources to accomplish what they wanted. Cale reminded himself why he took his pension and ran. The problem pawns faced was that the guys who played chess were at peace with sacrificing a few of them. You could say "chess masters" instead of "guys who play chess," but Cale's experience dictated that was too high a praise.

When the call ended, Cale stepped outside on the front porch for some fresh air. The temperature had dropped twenty degrees since midnight. The air felt different, purer. Perhaps this was the barometric pressure dropping. Deep, low storm clouds and thick rain made charcoal-gray light.

He stepped inside and shut the storm door but left the six-panel door open. The house was dark except for the gray light through the storm door and the LED bulbs burning in the foyer and living room. The closed storm shutters blackened most of the house. It was a good day to sleep on the couch and dream about Colombians sharpening their knives. Maybe they'd dull their knives instead to make it more painful. He couldn't count five postcollege days he'd slept an afternoon away. Forget the Colombians. Thank you, Arlene.

Before he stepped away from the doorway, a truck pulled into the tip of the driveway. Someone lost in the rain? Trying to make a call and needing a safe spot to dial? Speaking of which, Cale pulled out his phone. The battery was in the red. He turned it off and found a charger to rejuice it. It was hard to believe that for the first thirty-five years of his life, he'd had a house phone connected to a wall. Now, for the last ten plus, he'd just kept one of these handy little guys in his pocket and took his phone into anybody's house.

The house was storm ready but needed to become post-bachelor-party ready. Cale put linens in one washing machine and the first load of dirty towels in the second. He thought everyone should have two washers and dryers. Batch processing was a small luxury Maggie inserted into their lives. He dumped the rest of the towels on the laundry room floor to wait their turn.

He felt pretty good . . . considering. The bachelor party was over. There were no more debacles on the horizon. He had done nothing Maggie wouldn't approve of. (In reality, he wouldn't have told her about Blake's adventures, so in the fantasy, she didn't know about that either.) Maybe there were a few thoughts and daydreams she wouldn't have cared for, but those were only daydreams. Nothing happened. You couldn't hold a daydream against a guy. It's actions that mattered. Or was it intent? No, actions. The road to hell was paved with a thousand good intentions. So wait, did that mean it was intent or actions that mattered? His thoughts should make sense by Thursday.

Walking back past the front door, Cale noticed the pickup edging down the driveway. He stopped to watch. It parked. He didn't recognize the vehicle. The lights turned off, then the engine. Who was this? The rain was too heavy to see a face. A yellow rain hood was slipped over the driver's head. Apparently, the driver was getting out. The driver must see Cale clearly, backlit in the doorway. This ruled out a storm looter.

Fatigue-induced brain synapses misfired and made Cale a touch jumpy. Too little sleep and too much booze. His aching hand wouldn't let him forget yesterday's silly altercation. He should have just pushed the meathead into the water and moved on. The choice to go brutal unexpectedly draped him with disappointment. Now was the first time he'd even considered just pushing him off the dock. He thought to himself his own mini-Eisenhower warning about "the military industrial complex." A country—or person in this case—with great power naturally looked for opportunities to display that power. He probed his memory, trying to make sure he hadn't secretly been excited to feel that big bull step on the dock.

Cale flipped on the floodlights and stepped outside. He hoped this wasn't a Colombian. If you were going to be hunted, for both hunter and quarry, it should be a little sporting (even dove farms don't tie strings to the birds' legs). No need to be such an easy target as to step backlit onto the porch unarmed. If the doorway had markings like convenience store doors did identifying height, it might make it slightly easier for them to shoot from farther away.

The visitor seemed in no rush to pull the figurative or literal trigger. Cale waited under the porch's metal roof. Curious. A part of him, despite last night's prudery, hoped it was Ashley, and that's admittedly why he stepped out to meet his doom so quickly. But he could now tell it was definitely a dude. Cale reckoned he should go grab his sidearm but didn't feel up to the effort and would feel mighty silly about it if it turned out to be a buddy.

The sound of rain on copper roofing pushed ninety decibels. A cold shiver fast-tracked across his body. His hands in his pockets, arms straight, elbows tucked into his body, he waited and wished he'd worn a sweatshirt instead of a T-shirt, boots instead of Rainbows.

Would his visitor mind waiting outside in the hurricane for a couple minutes while he went inside to change—or, better yet, started his nap? *Oh yeah. Sorry to keep you standing in the forty-mile-an-hour wind and inch-per-minute rain, but I suddenly fell asleep. No, I didn't notice you drive up. This rain on the metal roof is so darn loud I didn't hear the doorbell. I hope you won't hold it against me. Oh, you're here to give me a Colombian necktie. Thank you, but I rarely dress up.*

》》》

JOE SAW THE tall man waiting. He debated leaving the pistol in the car but kept it in his pocket. He set his phone on the passenger seat to keep dry. Should he run through the rain? Walk calmly and collect-edly? Why worry over these types of details? Details were important to a carpenter. To a developer too. Both presumed a plan, and that was the one thing Joe didn't have.

He found this lack of focus confusing. His mind shifted between fury over his nephew and jealousy over Ashley. What happened with Ashley here last night? He wanted right on his side, justice for Gino—if Gino wasn't full of it. But he also wanted to remove this competitor for Ashley's affections.

He stepped out of the car. Besides the rain slicker, he wore river sandals with shorts. He didn't sidestep puddles. With the hood low and his head ducked forward, he kept the water out of his eyes.

》》》

THE VISITOR HURRIED through the elements. He tried to take the steps quickly but his sandal caught, and he stumbled forward. Cale stepped back slightly as the visitor regained his balance. The good news was that if the visitor knew he wanted to shoot Cale full of holes—a Colombian narcotrafficker, for instance, would already know—this would be behind them. If it was hand-to-hand combat, even worn out, Cale liked his odds.

The hood flipped up. Well, this he should have seen coming.

Ashley said this guy was great, but he wasn't feeling it. She had forty-eight hours on a boat with him. Anybody could behave for forty-eight hours. He seemed pseudo-Mafia: He was overtly Italian, carried rolled cash, owned an expensive boat. He oozed New York or New Jersey; Cale couldn't really tell the difference between the two, but he could tell those two from anywhere else.

Was this guy out to avenge his muscle man? Was he looking for blood? If so, Cale'd just tell him, "Hold on one minute, buckaroo. There is a line of very mean Latin men who have already requested the pleasure of spilling my blood." This guy wasn't holding anything in his hands. Was he starting a lawsuit? Did the kid die? Almost unconsciously, Cale split his stance. His knees bent slightly, his hands slipped out of his pockets, and he placed his left hand flat on the front of his left leg, the other thumb resting lightly on the top lip of his hip pocket. The increased attention stopped his shivering and his belated survival mode clicked in.

>>>

HIS STUMBLING ENTRANCE threw Joe's focus. He felt like an old dog whose nails on his hind legs dragged when he walked uphill. He didn't like the terrain. He was Pickett below the hill, Custer in the valley. His physical mistake stoked his anger, but he wasn't ready to lose his decorum. He was the caller, so he'd start the conversation. He'd begin at the beginning, say what he wanted to say.

"I understand you're Cale. From the mailbox, I take it your last name is Coleman. I'm Joe Pascarella." He extended his right hand. His face was neither smile nor snarl. "We met briefly last night in the parking lot."

>>>

PINGS ON COPPER and wind muffled the words. Cale turned his head to hear better and stepped forward. He took the offered hand. Cale cupped his left ear with his hand, gave an expression that said *repeat*.

The men leaned together, their right hands clasped. Their left hands moved to each other's right shoulders. Joe's hand felt solid, and he applied firm downward pressure on Cale's shoulder. Joe repeated the introduction.

"What can I do for you, Joe?" Cale responded as they stayed locked together, any conversation more than a foot apart lost in the wind.

"My nephew, Gino. The youngster you had the staring contest with in the bar. He turned up in the hospital last night. Says you hit him from behind with a tire iron. Put it right on the police report. Is that what happened, *paesano*?"

>>>

JOE'S FACE WAS too close to Cale's ear to see his eyes. Bad terrain. He should have watched the man's face. With that mistake, Joe felt another surge of anger sweep through him. He rushed the confrontation without the slightest idea of how it was received. Did a toe stub wipe out his experience? Did his stumble erase the knowledge gained from a lifetime of altercations, negotiations, managing employees, vendors, and bankers? Could a couple of years of not caring about the results completely change a man? Could he get himself back?

In general, Joe categorized people as worshipers or complainers. You found something to praise, or you found something to bemoan. You could pick either in every situation. Not a hard choice for where to live your life. He checked back into the first camp and tried to cool his temper as he returned to the reason for his visit.

>>>

CALE GENTLY SLIPPED his left hand down from Joe's shoulder onto Joe's right triceps, where he could more quickly control the older man's arm once they released hands. Cale was playing the odds that Joe was right handed. Joe was solidly built, but Cale didn't anticipate any issues in a conflict where he could see both hands. Nobody was in the cab of the small truck, and nobody would have ridden lying down in the bed on a day like today unless they had a snorkel. That made the going premise that Joe was truly alone.

Was this guy Mafia? He fit the old agency profile. If so, did he believe his nephew's story? Did it matter to him if it was true or not? If you hurt one of his, would there then simply be repercussions? Cale admitted hearing that the boy was alive blew out the lingering fear clouds he'd filed away in the to-worry-about-later department; this conveniently freed up desk space for relations with domestic and international crime syndicates to fill.

The old saying, *denial ain't just a river in Egypt*, ran through Cale's mind, but lying wasn't his natural state. He didn't think he could bluff this away anyway. Inadvertently, a laugh bubbled up as he thought about why and how Gino came up with this story, and said, "That boy isn't hurt enough to not protect his pride, I guess."

Cale was an optimist by nature but recovered from his laugh and prepared for the worst. He wanted to try and talk this through, but the noise on the porch roof was too much of a hindrance.

"Joe, can you step inside to talk so we can get out of the wind and racket?"

〉〉〉

JOE PAUSED BRIEFLY before accepting the invitation inside the house. The laugh took him off guard. Coleman had the feel of a good guy, but so did Ted Bundy and every con artist he had ever known. With caution, he motioned for Coleman to lead the way into the house. Joe slipped his hand into his slicker's pocket and cradled the pistol as he entered behind Coleman.

Inside, Cale asked, "So what are his injuries?"

"Broken arm and busted face."

"Any big dents that look like what a tire iron would do' if I was swinging it at somebody's head?"

Cale demonstrated the speed and power of what his swing would look like, pivoting his hips and chopping his arm down and across.

Seeing his startling speed, Joe paused again, reassessing the hidden size and roped muscles of the man in front of him. He felt vulnerable watching this demonstration. He wondered if intimidation was the intent. He gripped the pistol in his pocket more firmly and slid his finger onto the trigger.

He answered, "Friend, I'm not sure what kind of mark a tire iron across the face or arm should leave. But my nephew was beaten into a lumpy mess."

》》》

CALE WASN'T PLEASED with himself. He'd lost enough contact with Joe to allow Joe's hand to find his pocket. Who puts their right hand in a rain slicker pocket for comfort? *Nobody* was the answer. You did that if you were reaching for something. Cale kept himself positioned to look through the front door to see if anybody else was pulling into the driveway. He wanted to make sure what his visitor was doing in his pocket wasn't signaling somebody else to come over.

Joe tightened up when Cale made his demonstration. Showing how easily he could hurt somebody wasn't exactly lighting a peace pipe. The conversation had taken a turn for the worse, so Cale slowed down and tried to correct.

"Joe," he said, taking a deep slow breath before continuing, "I was looking at a trimaran based out of Bermuda when I looked up and saw your nephew walking toward me. He took his shirt off, poured his PBR out but kept the bottle in his hand. He made some comment about beating me into barnacles."

Cale paused, looking at Joe to make sure he was listening to the story before he continued. "So I waited for him. I wanted to give him the chance to back out, like an elephant doing a false charge. But he didn't, so I whooped his ass—plain and simple. Then I called the ambulance for him and went back to my friends. Thinking about it now, I should have just pushed him into the water. But at the time, the thought didn't occur to me."

〉〉〉

GINO WITH HIS shirt off. The PBR bottle in his hand. Even the barnacle comment. It all sounded like Gino. Somewhere between proud, a cowardly bully, and a blowhard. Analytically, the story made sense to Joe. Emotionally, he wasn't cooling down. He did feel his fear slipping and pulled his finger off the trigger, but his temper was pulsing in a way it hadn't in years.

"So you beat him senseless and left him there? Aren't you pushing the age envelope for this kind of hooliganism?" Joe looked at Cale's left hand and then, before Cale could respond to the first set of inquiries, asked another set, "What did you tell your wife about this? Wait, more to the point, what did you tell her about having three young women spend the night with you?"

Cale's eyes looked dazed, like he had been brained with a two-by-four. He quietly repeated the last question, "What did I tell my wife?"

The sad tone in Cale's response began to take the edge off Joe's temper. He felt a twinge of embarrassment at the tack he'd taken with the conversation but, with less heart in it, kept pushing forward. "Yeah, that question, it seems to speak to me. Bringing a beautiful woman and her friends back to your home while your wife is away. I think that behavior says a lot about a man's honor, his trustworthiness." Belatedly, without conviction, he added, "The kind of man who'd do that might be the kind of man who'd sneak up on somebody and whack them from behind." Joe knew the connection between being a philanderer and a batterer was tenuous at best before the words even left his mouth.

Despite Joe's last throwaway comment, both he and Cale realized the shift the conversation had taken. It no longer focused on Gino. It wasn't even the girls as a group. It was Ashley.

>>>

WHAT WOULD I *tell Maggie?* Cale rolled the question around in his brain. He decided he was good with the truth, which was a cleansing confirmation. He confessed to himself first, then Maggie, that he was truly interested in Ashley but wasn't going to track her down. Basically, his plan of non-attack was driven by the fact that he wouldn't want a middle-aged guy chasing his daughters.

Cale returned his attention to the man standing in front of him. "Joe, I understand you've only known Ashley for a couple days, so is the concern for her or my soul?"

"Ashley was put in this situation because of my decision."

It was good they weren't talking about souls. Cale no longer worried this would be a violent situation. Without the adrenaline, fatigue crept back in. It was time for his visitor to be shown out.

"Joe, I don't think Ashley felt too put out by the situation. Her friend, unfortunately, was romantically inclined toward one of the guys. Ashley helped me prepare the house for the storm, which I appreciated. We spent a couple of enjoyable hours talking while the others squeezed the rest of the life out of the party. When I came out of my room this morning, she was asleep on the couch."

Joe nodded his head. The extra blood in his cheeks was draining back to a normal state. He said, "OK."

In unison, the two men nodded their heads slightly toward each other. Joe turned and started to leave. As he reached the door, Cale remembered the original purpose of the visit. "Did you have any other questions about what happened with your nephew? I really wish I'd just pushed him in the water."

Joe turned back around. "He had his two friends back at the bar. If you pushed him in the water, it could have taken a turn for the worse."

"Thanks. Still, I wish I hadn't hurt him so badly."

They uneasily shook hands. Without parting words, Joe returned to the rain and the four-speed.

»»» 17

THE GULFSTREAM DEPOSITED the three men at the North Carolina coast, then flew inland to avoid the approaching hurricane. Francisco and his men checked into a hotel built inside an upscale outdoor mall. Issued by a Swiss bank, his credit card's digital information did not reveal his name. It would be very difficult for the United States government to get the bank to release the identity of the cardholder.

The men rested during the worst part of the storm in the living room of Francisco's suite.

"Alberto, do we know Mr. Coleman's home address?"

"*Sí*. I beg your pardon. Yes. Let me get it for you. Do you want the little computer too, Mr. Escobar?"

"Yes. Thank you."

Francisco flicked on his new tablet. He typed in the address. He clicked through various screens and looked at an aerial photo of the house. He noticed the distance between Coleman's address and the neighboring homes. He saw the water and registered the massive size difference of the houses across the water from Coleman's own home. He changed the view to look at the house from the street level. He drove up and down the street using his finger on the screen and then went back to the aerial view. He looked at routes for quick getaways. He also looked for hiding spots within a mile of the house. He found a long driveway cut-in where no home was ever built.

"Alberto?"

"Yes, Mr. Escobar?"

"Please review the plan with me."

"We are told Mr. Coleman's wife is dead and his children have moved out of the house. We should drive up to his home. He has no reason to think we are anything but someone he knows or someone who is lost. When he comes to the door, we will grab him. Then the Cuban and I will take him inside and tie him with wire until you are done."

"How will we dispose of his body, Alberto?"

"However you wish."

"What would you suggest?"

"We weight his body and drop it in the water behind his house."

Francisco didn't respond. The half-thought-out answer showed why Alberto never rose above loyal and brutal guard. There would be blood and other evidence to indicate a crime had occurred even if there was no visible body. Francisco and Alberto had spent their lives in villas filled with servants who cleaned where they stepped; neither of them knew how or had any desire to clean. Why spend such effort on something for which they could not succeed? Francisco, just as Pablo would have done, was going to leave the mutilated body wired to the chair. It might be a day or a month before it was found. Either way, Francisco would be gone.

Sadly for Francisco, Alberto never fully blossomed. Too many of his men were that way. They were powerful canopy trees casting long shadows, but they were not a forest. They had never nurtured the beauty and produce of the understory trees that flowered with fruit. They lacked the bushes near the ground, where coffee and chocolate flourished. Could they have become a forest yielding much more value to its owner? Francisco assumed so but did not take responsibility for their half-fulfilled potential because they were El Capo's men, more than twenty years his senior. But he did take responsibility for the many undeveloped young men in his own employ. No one in

Francisco's orbit had dared tell him he had failed these men so far, but he understood that he had. And he understood that this failing limited his family's operation at this moment of its greatest opportunity. He looked to the Cuban, "What do you think we should do to the body?"

"I would leave it. Nobody knows we are here. We will be gone by the time it is found. If you want, when we are gone, I can have the house robbed."

The Cuban's suggestions resonated with Francisco, who nodded silently.

He suddenly needed to understand what had stopped him from further developing his men. Had it been the setbacks from energy invested in so many men who were killed by the *norteamericanos* or the civil war? Was it because he purposely avoided the world's largest market for his products and could thereby survive with men who were only half-realized? He had not even begun to groom a successor. Surely, one of his many nephews or cousins could be groomed to be the next boss. But each had grown up so wealthy and felt entitled to their wealth. Would they accept a leader rising among them, or would an outsider be easier? He would keep the Cuban close to him to see what role he could play.

Just as each Argentinean opera star competed to play the lead role in an opera's first production, so they could define how that role would be played for the opera's life, be it one season or five hundred, Francisco thought he might be playing his role as Pablo defined it. Yes, he had his men's love and fear more than El Capo ever did. But what had he done with that love and that fear? He had let too much time go by without building the skill sets that the present opportunity demanded they have. He had neglected something as simple as cultivating the ability to speak good English in his circle of bodyguards.

To realize the change he needed to see in his men, Francisco needed to change how he ran his business. He needed to identify rising stars. Why did he keep coming back to the Cuban? He needed to stop spending his time on those who wilted in the heat and replace them with those who thrived in the sunlight. He would spend his time, as Pablo had done for him, teaching both the broad game and the small skills to let them succeed and grow the family's operations.

He would have to indulge himself less. Fewer starlets and car races. The new jet and Estella seemed suitable replacements that would fit into the flow of his new work life. He wished she'd stayed behind when the jet flew inland. Now would be a good time to send Alberto and the Cuban to their rooms and use the enjoyment of her treasures to stop the barrage of ideas bouncing around his brain.

But Estella was not here, the wind and rain pounded outside, and his brain had no diversions to escape to. So he tried to target his thoughts on the big conquests to achieve.

First, to grow the powder trade to exceed the global dominance it once held, he needed to identify and proceed with the new alliances he so feared. Past this fear was growth, where the pain and pleasure trade-offs lay. This was where the men in his family could reach out and begin to rely on each other as brothers-in-arms instead of looking at each other as adversaries competing for the rare promotion or infrequent new project. Without the distraction of the Colombian civil war, Francisco could sense that their destiny would be adversarial if they remained stagnant.

To succeed, he needed more fully developed men—more forests than trees. He would invest his energy in developing his men to have complete skill sets, not just in enforcement or distribution or procurement. He would make his strongest men work in each of these areas and in different parts of the world. He would teach them the skills he himself possessed to keep them from making mistakes that, more than merely costing him money, could cost the men their lives and could cost him good manpower and large amounts of energy.

Finally, he needed to put his fortune meaningfully into the world's legitimate economy. This might prove the hardest and the most rewarding step. It was certainly the one he knew the least about. He had no knowledge of the stock and debt markets. He had never purchased operating businesses, but saw the value in owning them. Buying a chain of hotels like the one he now stayed in made sense to him—perhaps hotels with casinos attached. There was always profit in vice. He had never used a bank to borrow money but understood that when buying legitimate businesses, banks were willing to give the purchasers eighty percent of the money required to purchase the business. So if he put two hundred million into a business, a bank would give him eight hundred million more to use? There had to be an opportunity to simply pocket the eight hundred million or to split it with the owner of the business he would be buying. Would a banker have the courage to pursue him when the money disappeared? Yes, learning how to use legal money to grow his own was perhaps the biggest and scariest conquest Francisco saw for himself.

Francisco was ready to be done with this trip's myth-building and to turn to the task of capturing kings. It would take a year, perhaps even two or three. He tried not to let the long work period tire him out before it began. Could he stay focused for that long? He needed to transform himself again. He had transformed himself once twenty years before, going from enforcer and confidant to boss. He would succeed in transforming himself again.

HE FELT MORE old goat than old fool, and that was good. How many septuagenarians drove through a hurricane and accused a beast of throwing a sucker punch? Not too many. He liked the Ashley daydream he'd tried to deny he was having too.

She had no idea the power she had. Her dancing—moving slightly, confidently, matching the beat's rhythm. That flower tucked behind her ear yesterday. Her big smile. Most importantly, the smile. The smile that was always just below the surface. It was a gift opening when you caught her eyes. This stuff made men write poetry, fight wars. He should give it a shot. Not a war or poetry, but advancing the front with Ashley. Still, he didn't know the best approach, what drove her.

Pajama Hefner in his silk wardrobe knew what drove a class of women. Were the rest much different? Were men different? A middle-class widow he knew, pushing seventy, was hot and heavy with a thirty-year-old man. How did that fit with what the psychologists called a "hierarchy of needs?"

As he played with the daydream and pondered it more, he suddenly fell back into reality. He dove into the math. There was a fifty-year age difference, give or take. That meant he'd lived 200 percent longer than she had. No, this was not a relationship likely to happen. But as that daydream died its sweet, sad death, he realized that he needed to thank Ashley. She rekindled the fire in his belly. There was a lot of life to live beyond being a grandfather and a reluctant boater. Life held a full range of emotions, and there was no reason for him to neglect half of them for the final twenty years of his life.

As he eased down the road, an AM station played Chuck Berry, complete with 1950s static from the weather. A roadside bar's neon lights blinked *Open*. The parking lot was busy. A hurricane party was in full swing. A lifetime ago, he'd caught a hurricane party on DeVaule Street. The bridge had been closed. A bar in town was as safe as the waterfront drive-in motel, so they had stopped in at Captain Tony's. An hour into the afternoon, his wife had won a Hula-Hooping contest. Joe had won the arm wrestling contest. He'd heard their tattered Polaroid was still on the wall by the bar.

Why not stop for a quick one? A chain looped through wooden posts split the gravel into parking aisles. Joe backed the small truck between an F350 and a Suburban. He flipped up the rain slicker's hood and stepped into the elements. A non-native palm beside the walkway was bent forty-five degrees by the wind. An empty plastic bag blew past. He splashed through puddles, making his feet feel oily and sandy.

The wood steps of the bar sagged between the stringers. The gray handrail was a pine two-by-six face-nailed onto four-by-four posts. Even in the rain, Joe could see the sun's work on the board's grain. They probably changed the boards every spring too. He avoided the splinters and took the steps without assistance. Stumble free—attaboy! One of the double doors was propped open, and he stepped inside.

The hurricane suspended the no smoking ordinance. Joe's nose registered the smell of stale beer and fresh cigarettes. The ceiling fan light kits and neon beer signs contrasted sharply with the gray storm light outside. A chalkboard stated today's special: One-dollar Miller High Lifes. All carpenters drink dollar beers on rainy afternoons, at least before they become foremen. He thought to call Tony and remembered his phone was in the truck.

Two uniformed police officers entered the room, brushing past Joe. Their baseball caps and clear rain ponchos shed water as they walked to the bar. The bartender poured two mugs of coffee. Joe guessed that Krispy Kreme was closed for the storm. Nobody at the bar appeared to have any intention of leaving. The officers faded into the background, checking their phones and talking to each other.

Joe acknowledged a group of dockhands he'd seen at the marina— young guys delaying school, families, and careers, and middle-aged guys who'd tied lines and rinsed boats for twenty years. Most of the young guys would return to the mainstream. The old guys would tie and rinse until alcoholism consumed their meager skills and they had to be chased from the docks before they scared the clients.

The dockhand life looked romantic until it was closely inspected. The cash from tips would be enough for a decent rental house and a nightly bar visit. There was a steady stream of new girls, at least in the early years. It was an easy profession to pick up the gift of gab in, learn a few salty one-liners to impress the weekenders. Eventually, the booze damage accumulated. It kept your mouth from conveying thoughts, or maybe kept your mind from having coherent thoughts, and your mouth accurately relayed the jumble. You'd always have a good suntan until the dark spots and worse took over. Not a bad way to pass a year—if you could stop after a year.

A through-the-wall air conditioner unit blasted Joe. It was cool outside, but the A/C ran to minimize the stickiness inside. But it was hard to stay ahead of 100 percent humidity; the shine on the customers' faces wasn't entirely attributable to alcohol. There were a hundred-plus guys in the bar. There were three women sitting in a group at the bar. They were in their late forties and all some shade of bleached blonde. One wore a wedding ring and had short hair, a sure sign of having given up, in Joe's book, like she was more concerned with other ladies' opinions than her husband's desires. She'd brush off his complaints. "It's so much easier to take care of." Joe didn't buy it. He figured she didn't want to appear to compete with younger or fitter women for her husband's or any man's attention. The logic went *if you don't think you can win, play a different game.* The other two appeared to be single. They fought the good fight: Their hair was below their shoulders, their clothing tailored to their strengths. He moved to an open barstool beside them.

One turned and caught his eye. He leaned toward her and said in a fake whisper, "You three must be absolutely terrified. Let's work out a code for when you need help." He leaned back out and winked.

She laughed and responded, "Are you kidding? At our age, this is our dream come true. You know what cow patties and blondes have in common, don't you?"

Joe's eyebrows responded: *No.*

"The older they get, the easier they are to pick up."

They flirted unabashedly. Joe ordered a second "Champagne of Beers" and bought a round of mixed drinks for the ladies. In a rough, aged manner, he was good-looking in any market. Excluding the aged part, he always had been. In these Southern states—Florida excluded—being an Italian from Brooklyn gave off an extra whiff of the exotic.

He bounced between anecdotes, compliments, and questions. Guys sidled beside the group to buy drinks, but the riptide pulled them out. Joe was on a roll, and it created a strange force, an aura, a power. It soaked up those willing to ride and kicked out those who weren't. But the force was fleeting and vulnerable to the tide's inevitable turn.

A young man, with a flushed face and curly hair half under a trucker hat, stumbled three steps to the right and bumped into the funniest blonde. Her drink spilled, mostly on the young man himself. He dropped his full longneck and scooped it up with surprising agility. His beer started foaming out the neck and down his hand and arm. The blonde apologized. The curly headed young man just shook the beer off his hand, and it sprayed Joe and the ladies. No apology for the bump or the foam bath as he started to walk on.

Joe involuntarily grabbed his wrist. "Friend, don't you think you should be the one apologizing to this woman?"

The boy mumbled. Joe focused on the eyes. He sighed. No use. The kid was too vacant, all booze. Let this one be on his way; wrong time to teach manners. He let go of the boy's wrist and shooed him on with a double flick of the wrist.

Joe returned his attention to the ladies. The spill created a small wet T-shirt event for the blonde. Joe chivalrously helped dry off the important parts with a handful of napkins.

The boy rubbed his wrist, and his head pivoted around. The two friends standing nearby gave him confidence, which slowly morphed into rage. He yelled a witty "Hey, you!"

Joe turned, and the boy swung the bottle. Joe moved like an oak. That is, he didn't move at all, but the swing still missed by a foot. The force twisted the boy's arm across his body. Joe's brain made his feet step forward, and he punched the kid's exposed chin. Connected enough. The boy fell over, from the buzz as much as the punch, which connected like a push. The friends rushed over. The aisle between the bar stools and the tables was narrow, so they were forced to come single file.

Were the young man's friends coming as blue helmets or jihadists? Joe chose self-preservation and punched the first one cleanly before his intent was known. The second got in close and grabbed Joe. They wrestled standing up. Joe got him in a headlock. He pawed at the man's head with his free hand, tried to find a spot that wouldn't hurt his knuckles to punch.

The officers took a shortcut over the far counter, through the bar pit, and over the near counter. A baton to the throat pulled Joe's body up and back. The choking got his attention on a primal level. He threw the man in his arms down and grabbed at the baton. Holding it away from his throat, he whipped his hips and bent forward quickly. The officer flipped over his back and landed on the floor. They now both held the baton with outstretched arms. Realizing he was an officer, Joe let go and stepped back.

The second officer switched his focus from Joe's opponents in time to see his partner on the ground. He reached for his sidearm, but he couldn't get beneath his poncho. Before he hiked it up, his partner regained his footing and stood between him and Joe. The room was quiet except for Kenny Chesney singing about having fun somewhere sunny.

The ladies started to tell the story to the officers, and things calmed down. Then, following protocol, they frisked Joe.

»»» 19

ASHLEY'S FRIENDS WERE suffering from the aftereffects of the previous night's festivities. They closed the curtain on their cabin's small window, curled up under the sheets, and wrestled demons in their semisleep, listening to the wind and rain. Ashley was tired, but she hadn't engaged in the volume of drink or conscience-vexing behavior that her roommates had. Her body wasn't accustomed to the luxury of wasting a rainy day in bed, and despite her best efforts to enjoy not having anything to do, she found herself needing to move around.

She pulled on a pair of jeans, her Rainbows, and a hooded sweatshirt and left the cabin. In the salon, the captain was wiping down the control panels with a cloth. Tony had his feet up on the couch, glasses low on his nose, and his concentration on the newspaper's daily sudoku. He crinkled his forehead and gave her a smile when he saw her come inside. She was amazed at how much warmth and welcome he could project without uttering a word or making a movement. She embraced the familiarity, pushed his feet off the couch, and sat next to him.

Looking up from his puzzle, he said, "Thought you'd be down paying for the wages of sin today."

She ignored the comment. "It's funny to just hear wind and rain and not people's voices."

"We are down three large passengers and a whole lot of bad music."

"Where's Joe?"

"Ah, Gino apparently got into a bit of trouble last night with the skipper of that boat that took youse girls to the bar, and it all ended with Gino in the hospital. I think Gino is pretty glum about it, but his face is so swollen he couldn't frown or smile. Joe wanted to discuss the particulars of what happened with the skipper. His sister gave him quite an earful. Kind of like going into a 1950s time warp listening to her. I could almost see the boys playing stickball on the street and somebody's mom laying into their deadbeat dad on the front stoop. The mom would have curlers in her hair, a satin robe, and house slippers. The dad would be in long pants and a ribbed undershirt with stains."

Tony's semiallegory brought a smile in spite of the information conveyed. "You mean a *wife beater*?"

"No, the guy is a drunk or a cheat or lost his paycheck playing dice. Not an abuser."

"I meant the shirt. They call those *wife beaters*."

"Hmm. Good to know."

Ashley thought over what he'd said about Cale, perplexed by the contrast between what she was hearing and what she experienced last night. Her mind traveled the maps she knew. If a grown man just got in a fight that sent another man to the hospital, you'd think he'd be either emotionally charged up or drained; it wasn't something that happened to a person every day. She'd have expected that he'd need to talk about it or decompress in some selfish manner. But she'd spent three hours picking up his yard and talking with him and sensed nothing amiss.

The only man she'd known to deliver such beatings to other men was her father. She pictured him winding down after he'd battered some troublemaker with his blackjack or pistol handle. He'd sit in his plastic outdoor furniture, drinking cheap bottled beer, occasionally spilling it on his T-shirt or splattered painter pants. An energy radiated from him in those times, saying, *Stay away*. This was the only vision she had for how someone would react to such an act.

"When I saw Cale later in the night, he didn't look like a finger had been laid on him. We talked for a long time, and he never mentioned it."

"Gino says Cale—is that right? Cale?"

She nodded.

"That Cale hit Gino from behind with a tire iron and then pounded him when he was down."

Ashley was quiet. Cale had to know she'd find out about the fight, but he hadn't tried to pre-spin it. Despite her interest, he had snuck off to bed without saying good-night. She couldn't remember a night out she hadn't had to turn men down. She had the unusual feeling of rejection because she wasn't given the opportunity to reject *him* at the end of the night. She'd felt the way he looked at and talked about his family photos. He wasn't walled off. He just must not be interested in her. How did men get so good at handling rejection?

Tony spoke again. "Youse think he is the kind of guy who'd whack somebody from behind?"

"I don't know. Maybe if he needed to. He seems like the type who'd do it out of duty in a second. But was there any duty with Gino? God, I was scared, but to him, it was probably just a quick pushing match. And Gino left humiliated with Joe dragging him away by his ear. I also don't think Cale would need to hit Gino from behind, if you know what I mean."

Tony shook his head in agreement. "Yeah, doesn't come into square. Your new friend had a big crew of guys out having fun that he needed to entertain. He'd just been the hero. And watching him move across that space to Gino, I agree: I don't think he was that worried about what would happen if it came to fisticuffs."

A relevant thought came to Ashley's mind. "Oh, Tony. You should know this too: Cale is retired from the DEA."

"Retired? I should have worked for the government. How old can he be? Not old enough to be retired from anything, I'd think."

Ashley thought he'd missed her point, but he came back around.

"If he worked for the DEA, does that make him more or less likely to hit somebody from behind?"

That was a good question. It did make Ashley think he might have seen enough adrenaline to put a fistfight out of mind easily. She could even see how, given the opportunity, that background would help rationalize taking a tire iron to the back of an unsuspecting bully.

JOE WONDERED WHETHER the squad car's backseat was production built and then stripped of door handles, lights, and window controls or whether the vehicle's use was always intended, and it left the assembly line half finished. Probably cheaper to build out and strip. Seemed like a painful waste. He'd done the same thing a hundred times before with buildings, though—just part of the process.

The backseat was utilitarian. No way to escape, not that he was looking. No way to hurt yourself. No way to hurt the officers in front of you. It was a mobile jail cell. Joe's hands were cuffed behind him. Getting inside the vehicle in cuffs, Joe realized his knees wouldn't bend enough to get in the backseat. He sort of tumbled headfirst onto the bench seat and then brought his legs up. It took him several seconds to sit up straight. He sat in the back of the car a long time before the officers returned. At least they hadn't cuffed him to the floorboard bar; that would have kept him bent over. They must not have considered him too dangerous. He didn't even consider himself too dangerous.

Wind drove debris past them as the police cruiser crawled to the booking center.

Up front, one of the officers asked, "Mr. Pascarella, why were you carrying a concealed pistol?"

"I forgot it was in my jacket's pocket when I left my boat."

"And you don't have a permit to carry a concealed weapon in North Carolina?"

"No, I don't have a permit in North Carolina. I do in Florida."

"Did you know it is illegal to take a firearm into a place that serves alcohol?"

"I did."

"Then why did you bring it into the bar?"

"Officer, I forgot the gun was in my pocket."

His current predicament was a bit of a mess, but Joe was feeling pretty good. In a single afternoon, he'd confronted someone who beat up Gino, fought three guys himself, decided to make a move on a twenty-five-year-old knockout, changed his mind about the knock-out, and decided to generally pursue life to the fullest again. Nothing ventured, nothing gained.

The officer continued, "What brings you to our town to begin with?"

"Hurricane insurance."

"No need for smart comments. What made you attack my partner?"

"I thought it was another one of those hoodlums attacking me from behind. As soon as I realized it was an officer, I obviously stopped." Joe wanted to say something like, *after I tossed that boy like a sack of potatoes, I let him go*, but didn't see any reason to gloat. He figured the officer's partner would give him a hard enough time about the septuagenarian smackdown back at the station.

"Why'd you attack those barflies in there?"

The semi-interrogation only lasted a few minutes before the officers lost interest. Bar fights happen. Police get jostled. If it weren't for the loaded nine millimeter in the pocket, they'd have just told the barflies to go home and let Joe carry on with his business.

"Officers, can I ask a question?"

Nodding heads.

"Why wasn't I read my Miranda rights?"

The passenger-seat officer turned around. "Do I need to? We didn't think we were investigating a crime. The DA will decide what charges to bring based on our report. Is there a crime we need to investigate?"

"No. Makes sense."

What is it his kids' teachers had always said about "no question is a dumb question?" In hindsight, Joe thought that was not the best question to ask while they were writing the report.

The booking center's smell was that of distinctly unshowered masses; unlike wine, each year's vintage smelled the same. This scent was somewhere between high school locker room and homeless shelter. Currently, it lacked the masses but retained the fragrance.

Joe signed where needed, rolled his thumbs as directed. He pulled his shoulders back, tucked in his stomach, and smiled for his photos. No sense looking beaten down when you're not. With his belt removed, he appreciated the discreet elastic in his waistband even more.

He was handcuffed to a chair and left to stew. It was a hurricane holiday in the office: few intakes, even less efficiency.

The second shift arrived with wet hair and new vigor. Joe was shown to a cell with twelve bunks. Four new friends sharing accommodations—it seemed a bit like how his kids described the hostels they'd stayed in while backpacking Europe. *Dad, you meet people who are totally different from you, and you share these rooms and experiences together.* Tuna macaroni casserole with stewed apples on the side was served for dinner. He didn't recall being offered a phone call.

Joe chose the bottom bunk farthest from the lidless metal toilet. He'd cross that very public bridge in the morning. There were no handholds to help hovering. Maybe he'd catch a glimpse of how his more experienced bunkmates navigated the system before nature called. Best to turn down the coffee in the morning.

Eight thirty, lights out. The faint buzz of the fluorescent exit lights became noticeable. One of his neighbors said the Protestant version of the Our Father, with its debts and debtors. Joe thought his nearest bunkmate murmured along. Sleep came easily.

»» **21**

TONY RANG JOE five times. Something resembling worry clawed his mind. It felt like evening all day, but now it was night, and Joe should have been aboard. Either his errand or the drive in the rain could have gone badly. The more time that slipped by without a call, the slimmer the chance was that Joe was having fun somewhere.

Tony drove another borrowed car, his knuckles white on the wheel. He drove well below the speed limit. Ashley rode shotgun and called out the GPS directions.

She asked, "What do you think happened?"

"Depends how guilty Joe's sister made him feel. Gino's a grown man. She's living in memories, thinking Joe's the family muscle. That kind of thinking happens when you never leave the block you're born on and your brother pays off your mortgage."

"You think they got in a fight? Or worse?"

"Beats me. No sense worrying about it until we know more."

They drove all the way to Cale's place, but in the rain, they overshot the driveway. They slowly backed up, turned onto the driveway, and proceeded to the house. The house was dark. Tony stayed in the running car. Tony watched Ashley run up to the front porch through the waterfall streaming off the metal roof. She knocked. Waited. Turned and shrugged. Knocked again. Waited. Opened the door. She stuck her head slightly in. "Cale? Joe?" she called and shut the door again.

She turned and shrugged to Tony again. She hopped back through the waterfall, then turned and went around the side of the house.

〉〉〉

WHEN IT WAS above forty degrees, Cale slept best on his back porch. There was a Sunbrella upholstered couch that put him out as soon as he laid down. Normally in August, he'd have a towel under him and trunks on. Today, he was fully dressed under a wool blanket. The couch was sheltered from wind and rain, and the wool blanket kept what mist found its way in off of him. As always, Jimmy slept on the floor beside him, unfazed by the weather.

"Cale. Wake up. Hey, get up."

His eyes didn't want to open. His mouth worked first. "Who is it?"

"It's Ashley."

Ah, well, if it was destiny, then resistance was futile. It was amazing she had the willpower to stay away this long. Her folks will be happy as a clam to meet him, Cale thought. *My favorite band in college was Guns N' Roses, too!* He was ready to group Skype his girls now and tell them the good news. *So, girls, you know how you've been pushing me to dip my toe back into a relationship? Well, let me introduce Ashley. I think she is only two years younger than y'all, so you should have plenty in common besides me.*

"What's up, Ashley?" His eyes working now, Cale sat up, not sure how long he'd been asleep. Not sure if halitosis crept in. If this visit was designed for more than a forgotten shoe, Cale would need to sneak some Listerine.

"Have you seen Joe?" she asked.

"I have. He stopped by. Why?"

"Do you know where he is?"

This visit wasn't destiny after all. A missing Joe instead of a missing shoe. This old life kept on forcing you to learn to live with large and small disappointments.

The two of them went inside. Bahama number two walked in the front door uninvited. Ashley introduced him as Tony. The men nodded from a distance. Tony kept his cell phone in his hand, and Cale noticed he wasn't looking too trusting of him.

As requested, Cale retold the story with Gino on the dock. He convinced Tony and Ashley that Joe wasn't buried in the marsh with a small pickup on top of him. Cale's car was on the other side of the state, so they got in Tony's borrowed car to continue the search. His nap over, Cale found no reason to wait around for Rodrigo, Carlos, José, and Pepe to pay a visit. Radcliffe, the treaty, and Escobar in Georgia were surely just a set of unrelated coincidences. *Stop being a ninny*, he told himself.

They drove the most likely route toward the marina and plugged a spotlight into what predecessor models labeled the "cigarette lighter." Cale remembered station wagons without cup holders but with front and back ashtrays. The front—OK, that made sense. I mean, Mom needed her little helper. But young Johnny rolling around the backseat?

Cale clipped the spotlight onto the passenger window and lit up drainage ditches as they passed. No small trucks in view, but there were a few deer undeterred by the weather conditions. The deer froze when the light hit them.

Ashley asked, "Why do you have a spotlight that plugs into a car?"

Cale pretended not to hear the question, because he didn't want to share the answer. He knew she wanted to hear it wasn't for spotlighting and shooting deer. She asked again. The movie *Bambi* did society a great disservice. What was so sweet about deer? Besides their hind shanks slow-cooked in a vinegar-based barbecue sauce. For goodness sakes, they carried Lyme disease, ate your azaleas, and wrecked your car. If you get a case of Rocky Mountain spotted fever, with a headache that blurs your vision, don't blame the tick, blame the deer that dropped the tick in your yard.

But since she kept pressing, he provided a nonanswer answer. "I had credit card points expiring, and the merchandise options were pretty limited." Inane answers could get the most interesting topic dropped. Of course, inane answers wouldn't enhance his value proposition with Ashley.

They made the main road without luck. They travelled slowly, circling every parking lot with cars. At a roadhouse bar that frequently changed names but neither employees nor owners, they found several possibilities. Cale assumed the name-changing was to skirt alcohol violations or lawsuits.

Their search was stymied by the fact no one knew exactly what the truck looked like. Cale was the only one who'd even seen it. Tony left a couple of voicemails, trying to get the plate number. They pulled up close to a little truck and shined the light in.

First one head, then a second came into sight. Tony said to the windshield, "Oh, excuse me, sir. Oh, and ma'am. I didn't mean to interrupt you. . . . Oh, I mean and other sir. I really . . . we'll just get going. . . . Carry on."

They tried another. Maybe. And another. Could be. They shined the spotlight into a fourth and saw a phone in the front seat. Tony dialed Joe's number. The phone lit up. Aha! Mystery solved. Look at the big brain on Tony.

Who should run in and get him? Well, with not a lot on the evening's agenda, it couldn't hurt for the whole gang to have a celebratory one. Personally, Cale was curious to see what was inside that held Joe's interest for so long. They parked and splashed inside.

Business was booming. To paraphrase Twain, a storm was one of life's greatest luxuries, as long as it wasn't too severe and didn't stay too long. The guy-to-girl ratio, however, was more favorable on an aircraft carrier. Maybe the fairer sex didn't appreciate the luxury fully.

Who cared? thought Cale. He was in the bar with the best-looking twenty-something he knew this side of his own children. (Man, how did he let that thought slip in?) He got Tony's and Ashley's orders and headed to the bar while they scouted for Joe.

Alone, Cale leaned against the bar with three drinks. He scanned the room, looking for Joe but inadvertently doing a double-take on anyone resembling an Escobar. After a couple of minutes, he locked eyes with Tony and Ashley and got the *I dunno* look from both of them. So he asked the barkeep, "You seen an older guy named Joe? Yellow rain jacket. Dark hair. Dark skin. Probably got here midafternoon? New York accent."

"Look straight out of central casting for *The Sopranos*?"

"Yes." The comparison was off, but Cale couldn't find the appropriate analogy in his memory bank. More Brando than Gandolfini. But not exactly Brando either.

Fortunately, the barkeep continued, "He got in a fight with a couple of deckhands. Left with the police, cuffed." He wrinkled his forehead, saying *cuffed* as though that conveyed extra significance.

"For *his* protection or the deckhands'?"

The bartender leaned close and whispered, very conspiratorially, "Look, don't repeat this. I don't want the girls in here freaking out. But the police pulled a gun off him."

The comment about the girls distracted Cale, because there were . . . uh, so few. He wondered how much of his own product the bartender had sampled today. Then the heavy thought: *This dude, Joe, just came to his house with a gun!* Tony and Ashley didn't mention that. So he wasn't crazy; Colombians and Italians were both on the hunt. Maybe their conversation went better than he had thought.

He waved Tony and Ashley over. Having spent his first career in law enforcement, he knew how to handle the situation. Granted, he'd never arrested or interrogated anybody, but he'd surely picked up something via osmosis. So he decided to start on Tony with a deft feint—a light touch, build rapport, work his way to the question at hand.

"Tony, why the fuck was Joe packing heat when he came to see me?"

A feather tickling. To enhance the subtlety, he slammed the side of his fist on the bar hard enough that several folks stepped back, and the bartender gave a warning look.

Tony didn't know. Well, Cale thought he could tell Tony was telling the truth, but there were plenty of good actors out there.

Cale's mind drifted down an alley on the actor thought. Why did actors get paid so much if so many folks could do it? Didn't that violate both the law of supply and demand and the correlation between risk and reward?

Back to the moment. He liked Tony's response: "Why do you *think* he was packing heat? If you were a seventy-three-year-old going to confront the man who just put Hercules in the hospital, what would you take with you? Me, I'd take the cavalry."

Yes, Tony, investigate these almost superhuman achievements further. The big oaf did flatter Hercules, didn't he? Mere mortals should fear me if half-gods can't handle me, thought Cale.

After Cale relayed the barkeep's story, Tony left to make phone calls. Ashley wedged herself next to Cale at the bar.

"Do you think he'll be OK in prison? Do they separate prisoners by age? Or race? I hear in prison, gangs are all race based. Do you think there is an Italian gang in prison like in that old movie *Goodfellas*?"

Goodfellas. That was closer. Not sure what she meant by "old movie." It wasn't black and white. Was she born when *Goodfellas* was made? Joe was sort of Ray Liotta with a clearer complexion.

"I guess there are Italian gangs in prison. But Joe is in the drunk tank, not prison. The door shuts heavier in prison. He might deal with some aggressive flatulence and sleep apnea–induced snoring, but that's about it. If the storm doesn't keep the courts closed, he'll make bail by noon, and y'all can sail by one."

They settled into their drinks facing the bar. This had been a long weekend, with more drinking than Cale was used to. Oh well, one more couldn't hurt . . . much. The first sip felt like drinking a bag of rusty nails. Weren't the aftereffects of bachelor parties grand? Cale forced a second sip. It improved to drinking chipped glass. A third. Not too shabby. His right foot dug into the stirrup as he threw his left leg over the saddle.

Tony returned nearly an hour later, and although he was a like-able fellow, Cale hadn't missed him. He'd taken in enough talking with Ashley that he forgot why they were there. *I think she digs me*, he thought. *What do you think, Maggie?*

Tony said, "You were right. Joe's in jail. The charges are carrying a concealed weapon without a permit and carrying in a place that serves alcohol. I was able to get ahold of his personal attorney. He got me in touch with a criminal defense attorney who got me in touch with a local criminal defense attorney."

How important was Joe for Tony to get the attention of three attorneys on a Sunday night? Cale was glad they weren't referred to as *consiglieres*.

"What'd they say?"

"A lot. They bill in six-minute intervals, you know. But here are the main points: The local guy said that, normally, a magistrate would set bail tonight, but the storm has things stirred up. So he put me on hold and talked to the DA. Comes back on the line and says he'll make bail in the morning for $10,000. Says if Joe was local, he'd only have to put up ten percent, but since he's from out of state, he'll have to put up the whole ten grand. I tell him no problem; Joe's cleaning lady finds that much cash in the washing machine each week."

Was that a Mafia joke on money laundering? Or was Cale just being sensitive because Uncle Sam was letting a billionaire psychopath hunt him for sport? Why did he even think Francisco knew he existed? Well, there was one burning reason. (Was that a pun on Jim's death? Lovely.) But if the Escobars wanted to know about Jim and Cale, they had to be capable of finding out. Given that he'd seen on the Internet what the secretary of state thought about the Russian prime minister's breath, Francisco could find out who killed his brother. Were the documents recording those days still classified? Could they be released with a simple Freedom of Information Act request? If so, were the names redacted?

Tony continued, "So our guy and the DA get back on the phone and broker the charges down to misdemeanors, plus a fine. Conveniently, the fine amount matches the bail bond amount. Kind of like a speeding ticket—profiting off the tourist. It'll cost Joe ten times what it would cost a local boy."

Ashley asked, "So what can we do to help?"

"I'll meet our guy at the courthouse at nine forty-five. The judge will bump Joe to the top of the docket starting at ten. He officially sets the bail-slash-fine amount. I give the clerk of court the $10K. They'll check Joe out. We go down to the jail magistrate's office from there, and they hand him back all his stuff. Oddly enough, including the pistol."

It worked the same for any inner-city youth assigned a public defender. Two felonies reduced to misdemeanors, bail, and fine set on Sunday night. Cale pictured the judge with a pipe, a smoking jacket, and slippers conducting his business in a wood-paneled study, a fine bourbon in a decanter on the right upper corner of his desk. In any event, for the three of them, it was like the aircraft carrier banner said: *Mission Accomplished.*

Tony kept the group entertained for a few minutes. He ordered everyone another round before Cale finished the one in front of him. Tony took his refill and walked the room, and Ashley and Cale returned to their banter. Was he smiling more than normal? Slightly more animated? She twice flipped her hair to the other side of her neck. Not that he was looking for signs. Or counting them. But that was a good sign—two, actually.

Before he could order a fourth round, nature called. Cale excused himself. On his return, three guys surrounded Ashley at the bar. Where had he seen this before? Did his jaws just clench? She saw Cale coming, hopped up, and grabbed his hand. She led him to the small dance floor. A preemptive strike? That was the Bush Doctrine. And how did that work as foreign policy? No matter; it worked well domestically tonight.

Because of the lack of women and the men's apparent disinterest in dancing with each other, they had the floor to themselves. Cale was sober-ish, and there was no crowd to hide in. Fortunately, Ashley's dancing was lovely, just like she was. So he said, "Mademoiselle, your beauty is only outshone by the beauty with which you move." Of course, he didn't actually say that. He was concentrating too hard on not putting his teeth on his lower lip. He supposed that if he said that, it would have felt a bit old-fashioned. Like a wallpapered kitchen. Old-fashioned was not the feeling he wanted to convey. Should he mention all the daddy–daughter dances he'd attended?

They danced; Cale stayed on beat, moved smoothly, and smiled. The smile was important. Ashley led. There was even a song that required clapping on the two and the four beats. He congratulated himself on ignoring his natural Caucasian male instincts to clap on the one and the three for the whole song.

They were alone for three dances. Somehow—perhaps a few spare ribs were involved—a smattering of women appeared. Partners joined them. Tony was doing the hustle—*dunt dunt dunt da dunt da da dunt dunt*—and his partner seemed pleased. With the extra dancers, the space tightened. They danced closer, more hand holding. More elbows above the shoulders. More body contact. It was incidental on Cale's end, of course. He figured she did it intentionally. They sweated. Smiled.

»» 22

THAT NIGHT, THE rain continued but the wind lessened, and they began their hunt. The three men took the black Suburban to Mr. Coleman's house. He was not home, but they knew he was nearby. In fact, Alberto had chartered Coleman's plane under an alias and made a deposit for Tuesday morning. Francisco found this a small expense to ensure the trip bore fruit.

Francisco had recognized Coleman's twin turbo prop's call sign at the FBO when his G5 landed. If he did not so strongly wish to personally watch Mr. Coleman suffer and also realize his physical presence at the man's death would add to his legacy, he'd have rigged an explosive to the plane. Instead, he would avenge his brother directly, and in a spiritual manner, he would avenge his mentor, Tío Pablo, too. But most important, Francisco was building the legend of timeless vengeance to right wrongs. When his tale was told around the law enforcement water coolers, would this change the *norteamericanos'* behavior? He was not sure, but he was sure it would be reinforced in the minds of any new strategic partners.

In person, Mr. Coleman house's was as suitable a location for the end of the man's life as it had appeared on the tablet. The significant physical separation from his neighbors was privacy he must normally enjoy; on a windy day, no noise, even that from a gunshot, would reach his neighbors' ears. Coleman would be surrounded by things he loved, providing him no comfort in his darkest hour, thought Francisco.

The three men entered the back screen door. Alberto prepared to kick open the back door, but the Cuban turned the unlocked handle first. Alberto stepped in and jumped back, quickly shutting the door. "*Dios mío*," he gasped.

A dog the size of a burro padded across the room, silent except for its footfalls. The dog stood on its hind legs. Its steady, unhurried growl competed with the rain splashing. The dog's eyes narrowed as it looked directly into the men's eyes through the glass of the half-light door. The low growl vibrated the door's window where Alberto's hand rested.

Alberto pulled his hand from the window and drew his Glock. The dog would be little trouble. He started to turn the knob. The dog felt the door knob turn, hopped down, and got in position to come out the door. Francisco put a hand on Alberto's arm.

The Cuban asked, "Alberto, what happens after we shoot the dog?"

Alberto answered, "We will go inside as we planned."

Francisco was embarrassed to have to finish teaching Alberto what the young man, relatively new to his employ, knew intuitively. If they shot the dog, they would have to stay and wait for Mr. Coleman; otherwise, he would come home to find his dog dead and be forewarned. If they let the dog live, they could return at a time of their choosing.

This was a lesson Francisco learned from the *norteamericanos* of Delta Force when they hunted El Capo. The Delta Force officers coordinated the hunt for El Capo while Colonel Hugo Martinez coordinated the Colombian military police effort. Colonel Martinez showed no desire for wealth or a fear of death. Some called him a patriot, but more called him an errand boy for the *norteamericanos*. He led his men in the hunt even after his more pliable superiors ordered his replacement. Delta Force showed patience, knowing that when you find a place where your quarry will return, you leave them every reason to return to it.

For El Capo, it was family to which he always returned. Even after buying his wife and children's asylum in Germany, there was still family like Francisco to visit.

For Mr. Coleman, perhaps the dog and the house would do for a lure. If not, Francisco was sure, like the *norteamericanos* had done with Pablo, he could move to Coleman's family.

Francisco looked through the glass past the dog. He disliked the interior's finishes. Wood floors. No marble. Not enough ceiling height for a dramatic chandelier. Photographs instead of paintings on the walls. But the utilitarian house would work for the utilitarian purpose Francisco intended.

The men walked through the rain across Coleman's backyard to the water's edge, where the wind still gusted. They noted the boat raised on the lift and poked their heads into a small shed filled with surfboards and fishing rods. With nothing more to learn, they left.

Francisco told Alberto to call their pilot. Have the plane arrive in the morning. They would return to the house at dawn. It was always easiest to catch them asleep. How many judges were dragged out of their homes, screaming, as their bleary-eyed families slowly awoke? There was something about taking a victim away in front of his family that both excited and nauseated Francisco.

He wished he had timed his visit for when Mr. Coleman's family was in town. The brutal death of innocent family members was particularly useful in instilling fear into allies and enemies alike. In his life's equation, scared allies and enemies saved his men's lives. But Francisco had decided to focus on kings. The killing of more innocents was focusing on pawns. He would not spend the time tracking down the remaining family members unless he needed them to catch Mr. Coleman.

Leaving the premises, Francisco decided that, at dawn, if Mr. Coleman was not there, they would wait in the house for him.

23

TONY DROVE HUNCHED forward to see through the rain, Ashley rode shotgun, and Cale sat at an angle in the backseat with his feet behind Tony and his body behind Ashley. There was a test of the emergency broadcast system that silenced their chatter for a moment. Funny that they went forward with this scheduled test even when an actual hurricane was in town. Ah, regulators. You had to love 'em.

During the beep, Cale's mind wandered to his abbreviated time in college. The best class he ever took was dance.

It wasn't dance theory. Or dance history. It was actual dancing. He signed up, thinking, rightfully, that it would fulfill his physical education requirement and that he'd meet chicks. He met Maggie there. In the class, it was fortunate that the guys didn't wear leotards; it was unfortunate that the girls didn't. The end of the acid wash and the start of the grunge era was the least optimal college clothing era for displaying young bodies in fifty years. OK, maybe the shoulder pad era was worse, but not by much. Of course, it was a class that started in January in the upper Midwest, so most of the students weren't exactly in fighting shape. But if leotards were required, would he have shown his boys off? Would he have resorted to a confidence prop? Not that he needed a prop. Or help with his confidence.

Thinking of props, an old joke ran through his mind. It was just the three of them, so he went ahead with it.

"So two friends," he said aloud, "a Frenchman and a Pole, visit the beach. The first day, the Frenchman puts on his Speedo and struts around the beach. He meets two girls and takes them back to the hotel. The Pole is very impressed. The next day, the Frenchman does the same thing again. So on the third day, the Pole asks, 'My friend, how do you do it?'

"The Frenchman replies, 'Mon ami, after I put on my Speedo, I put a potato in it. The potato is what gets the ladies' attention.'

"The Pole thanks his friend for the advice. He goes and buys a Speedo. He goes and buys a potato. He puts the potato in his Speedo. He walks the beach. That afternoon, he walks up from the beach in his Speedo by himself and sees the Frenchman. The Pole is very upset.

"'My friend,' he says, 'why have you tricked me? I put the potato in my Speedo, and instead of meeting women, people have run away from me.'

"The Frenchman looks at his friend and says, 'Mon ami, do it again tomorrow. But this time put the potato in front.'"

The joke received a polite laugh.

Tony jumped in. "A Frenchman, an Englishman, and an Irishman walk into a bar, sit down, and order three beers. At the exact same moment, a fly drops into each of their beers. The Frenchman says not a word, but pushes the beer away with a look of disgust. The Englishman takes the fly out of the beer, tosses it to the side, and then takes a sip. The Irishman picks up the fly, holds it by its wings, and yells, 'Spit it out, ya bastard!'"

Cale laughed a little more than the joke warranted. It felt good, and the laugh came easy. They had become a comfortable group.

Ashley started another. "So this guy and girl went parking. The guy looks at the girl and says, 'Do you want to get in the backseat?'

"She looks at him, a little puzzled, and says, 'No. I'd rather stay up here with you.'"

Cale laughed a lot more than the joke deserved. Well, it was cute, reminded him of one his kids said no less than a thousand times.

Daddy, why didn't the pony sing? Because it was a little horse. He left that
one unsaid; they weren't that comfortable a group.

Cale's thoughts returned to where they were before the jokes:
Dance class. He learned shag, salsa, and the Electric Slide. How many
times had he used that knowledge? Now *that* was a liberal arts education. How many times had he used what he learned in biology? So the
mitochondria were the powerhouse of the cell, but what did that mean?
Tonight, he was again pleased with that dance class. There was no salsa
music, but the basics transferred; he'd held his own with Ashley.

It was after midnight and Cale was bone tired, but the night possessed unasked questions. Should he invite them in for a nightcap?
Should he invite just Ashley? Would she say yes?

Ashley beat him to the punch. When Tony pulled into the driveway, she read a text from her friends. They asked her to pick them
up. No cabs were running tonight, and they needed a lift to the boat.

Ashley said she'd call Cale tomorrow when Joe was free. Since he
was without a car, Cale agreed to take the water route and meet them
to celebrate the restoration of liberty. He was gambling that the wind
and rain would slacken enough by then. What was the plan to get his
car back? Oh yeah, Barry was driving back Friday and leaving it at the
FBO. After tomorrow, he had a charter that would have him out of
town until then anyway.

Cale scuttled in the front door and rubbed Jimmy's head. The two
housemates walked through the quiet rooms to the back door. Cale
flipped on the back porch light and froze.

There were puddles of water. They tracked from the screen door
to the back door. Someone there? He flipped the light off. From the
volume of water, it looked like several pairs of shoes or multiple trips
in and out.

Nobody came inside. Jimmy would have demanded a fight. Cale
checked him for injuries. He felt fine. Cale used his phone's flashlight
app to spotlight the kitchen floor. No water. He shined it around the

doorframe. Two big paw prints were on the glass door. Good boy, Jimmy. Cale rubbed his head again.

Who visited? Friends on boats used the back door. Friends in cars used the front. Nobody was on the water tonight, so this wasn't a friend. A burglar not willing to mess with a 120-pound dog? A Colombian with a fillet knife?

Cale left the house lights off. He unlocked his safe, withdrew the Beretta, nestled it in the small of his back, and pulled a fleece on to conceal the weapon and keep warm. He hit the head, brushed his teeth, gurgled Listerine.

He sat on his bed to think. Jimmy laid across his feet, creating a less-than-optimal ready position. He envisioned trying to run with one foot asleep, dragging behind him. The more adrenaline Cale had running through his veins, the more he joked.

He had killed three men while at the DEA. The agency's psychologists said most folks were torn up by these incidents. A few accepted them and moved on. Most of those remaining were sociopaths. Cale was definitely in the second group and hoped not the third. Three kills was a huge number for any law enforcement official. For a soldier after a decade of war in the Middle East, maybe not so much, but it was unheard of in the DEA for someone who wasn't actually an arresting agent. Most SWAT team snipers have never killed, much less pilots.

The first kill was outside Tijuana, in a hamlet referred to by locals as San Diego. He was at an airport, at a small FBO. The agency normally operated from the commercial airport, but this was a clandestine operation, so the fewer eyes—even those of their own team—the better. For this operation, Cale was flying an agent posing as a buyer into Jalisco.

The intent was to buy, load, and fly back a hundred kilos. He would have two hundred and fifty packets of one hundred-dollar bills in a gym bag behind his seat. They would turn the powder over when they landed back in the US. It would be tested, then burned.

Cale was disgusted by the idea that $2.5 million dollars in tax money was paid to drug smugglers. Better to drop the cocaine on Iranian Revolutionary Guard military bases than burn it. But this $2.5 million was a small chip in a no-limit Texas Hold'em tournament for the brass.

The transaction took months to materialize. The buyer's deep cover was as a dance club promoter; the poor guy spent eighteen months partying until four in the morning, Thursday to Saturday each week. He cultivated a reputation as someone with significant distribution ability for blow, constantly making it known that he needed larger supply sources. The demand, he maintained, outstripped the supply. He convinced the seller's eyes and ears in San Diego and secured an introduction. They performed several domestic transactions. A kilo here, a kilo there.

The buyer made the case to buy in Mexico, where the upfront cost would be lower, and he could transport it himself. This was the first international buy. It would build confidence and enhance the working relationship. They would then progress upstream to meet bigger fish. This was standard practice. It looked good on paper—if you played the long game of no-limit Hold'em. If you were flush with other people's money.

Cale prepared the unmarked chopper for departure. Its black bottom and dark gray sides made it a tough bird to see from the ground at night. Cale stowed the money bag and proceeded with his preflight exterior inspection.

Two men in suits approached the bird next to him. They pulled wheeled luggage, which jostled on the pavement as if it were empty. They raised their voices enough to be overheard. One of the men was loud and indignant while the other man nodded in support. The first ranted about their upcoming flight, their pilot's tardiness. How they now had thirty minutes to kill on the tarmac.

This didn't fit, but maybe it was an innocent mistake. Did they walk to the wrong bird? This area had been closed off to civilians;

the only door keys to the helicopters in this section jingled in Cale's pocket. That helicopter wasn't going anywhere. His internal radar pinged. He tugged the back hem of his nylon jacket. His hand grazed the hidden Ruger.

He continued the preflight inspection, never turning his back on the two men. When he wasn't battling through the booze, Cale's survival instincts were highly developed—so developed it bordered on cowardice. He constantly envisioned the possible outcomes of so many events that never materialized. Half his life was spent on mental exercises for events that never happened. This was why, in a confrontation, he was disproportionately brutal.

Eventually, the animated man initiated a conversation with Cale. "Excuse me, partner, are you the pilot for that helicopter?"

Underneath the colloquial use of "partner," he heard a faint accent. He replied simply, "Yes, sir."

"Are you looking to take on extra charter work?"

"No, sir."

"That's too bad. Between you and me, partner, we are having an issue with our pilot. I think I'm going to need to interview backups. How do you like flying this helicopter? Do you have the range to reach Las Vegas from here?"

"It's a good job. With the right conditions, this helicopter can make it to Las Vegas."

The men used the opportunity to approach. Their bags bounced behind them—definitely empty. The same man continued, "Let me give you a business card, in case you change your mind or know of someone." Cale realized he'd never heard the other man speak. Perhaps because he only spoke Spanish?

They were too close now. The Ruger was inaccessible. But Cale knew he still had an opportunity. If he was right—and not shit-can crazy paranoid because he was getting ready to fly to Mexico to buy two and a half million dollars' worth of coke on the side of a dirt road from ten guys with machine guns—these guys needed silence and would come with a knife or a rope.

The one talking extended a card and gave a formal introduction with a made-up gringo name. The silent one approached to Cale's right. Cale changed his footing to reach for the card with his left hand. The adjustment created a brief pause, then the silent one went for it anyway, a knife in hand.

He lunged for Cale's throat. Cale pushed the man's arm up with his right hand while his left fist broke the man's exposed ribs. The man buckled slightly. Cale dragged the man between him and the speaker while his right arm slid to the man's hand. He twisted the thumb up until the wrist cracked. The man released the knife, and the falling blade got caught between his belt and pants. Cale grabbed the hilt and brought the blade tip swiftly up into the soft part of the man's chin, driving the blade through the tongue and into the top of the mouth. Cale pulled it back out and drove it through the man's trachea and into his spine. He pushed the corpse into the speaker.

The speaker dodged his dead partner, now holding his own knife. He sized Cale up then turned and ran. Cale caught and tackled him violently, whipping the man's head face-first into the asphalt. Cale braced his forearm on the base of the man's skull, pushing his face into the tarmac. Cale hit the man's half-exposed face with his free hand until well after the man was unconscious.

When internal affairs released him from questioning, he and Maggie stayed up talking all night. He'd heard so many stories of tough men breaking apart after a kill that he expected awful emotional waves. After a few weeks without any mental tsunamis, he tried to encourage them to come on so he could hurry up and deal with them. He humanized the victim, opined maybe the guy had a bad childhood, delivered Meals on Wheels to elderly shut-ins, or was, at a minimum, somebody's son. He tried to make himself believe he'd enjoyed the feel of the knife entering the body. But the attempts at guilt didn't stick. Reality was too clear. The victim was trying to kill him. Cale hadn't enjoyed killing him instead, but he had too much to live for not to fight. It happened and was done with. He lost only that one night of sleep with Maggie.

His other two kills were in Colombia—another clandestine operation; he couldn't understand now why he'd agreed to so many of those. The first guy was a bodyguard that ran his vehicle through Cale's chopper. Cale killed him as the man was setting up to shoot one of Cale's teammates. The last was the prodigal nephew in the Escobar drug cartel. Cale shot him with his bodyguard's pistol.

That mission, specifically that shot, was why he sat thinking while Jimmy put his feet to sleep. He made his decision, stood up, armed the alarm, and walked into the rain. There were no "protected by" signs at his house. Except when his grandchildren visited, he never set the alarm. Theft wasn't a concern, nor were local hooligans. The house's physical boundaries were a deterrent. Jimmy was a deterrent. The small armory of weapons he owned was a deterrent. Cale, himself, was a deterrent. So he never used the alarm.

Oliver North had convinced Cale to install the alarm. Not personally, of course. Cale was a teenager listening to the Iran–Contra hearings, where Ollie testified on why his $200,000 house needed a $100,000 alarm system. If memory served, it was because of some guys in the Middle East—guys eventually called jihadists. Nobody believed him. *Here? Thousands of miles from the bad guys in the mud huts? Impossible! Go figure.* In Cale's possibly faulty memory, North even mentioned bin Laden by name, who was waist deep in US-provided Stinger antiaircraft missiles at the time.

Cale worked with the alarm company to customize the install; if the alarm was set, he needed to count on it not being outsmarted. The alarm's door contacts were on the hinge side, rather than the usual placement on the top. Casually checking for contacts, nobody would notice them near the hinges. The alarm sound was a loud recording of Jimmy barking at a bobcat in a tree. It scared Cale hearing him bark that way; for anyone who had seen the dog, it was deeply unsettling. In addition, the good folks from the alarm company would call in, projecting from the alarm's speaker system, forcefully demanding that the intruders identify themselves. He had never given them camera access, which felt a little too creepy, but he currently wondered whether he'd been shortsighted.

Cale crossed the yard and pulled a sleeping bag and hammock out of the dock locker, which banged open when it caught the wind. He pulled the lid back shut and took his gear into the shed, out of the elements. He rearranged the surfboards to make room, hung the hammock inside, gathered his compound bow and spear gun. He laid them under the hammock. He wished he hadn't gifted his rifles to his sons-in-law. Cale then prayed that he was going a little insane from paranoia, but then wondered if being hunted might actually be better than being insane.

He hadn't engaged an Escobar in twenty years. Cale felt their family was being a bit petty singling him out for their grievances. Given the arc of violence in their lives, this wasn't much different from holding a grudge against the guy who kissed your prom date after you'd gotten married and raised a family. Cale thought that by his thirtieth-year reunion, he'd definitely be able to talk to that guy or—at a minimum—hit on his wife.

Cale lowered the Whaler to the water, trimmed the engine, and set the key in the ignition. He looped the line such that only one knot needed to be undone to cast off. Hopefully, the worst of the wind was gone; this was not the way they taught you to secure your vessel in a storm. He went back into the shed, taking Jimmy with him, laid in the hammock, and slipped into the unzipped sleeping bag's fold, keeping his shoes on. He found himself thinking about Ashley before holding a brief good-night conversation with Maggie and then falling asleep.

24

TOO EARLY, A low growl woke him. Cale hushed Jimmy with a gentle hand placed on the dog's massive head and rolled out of the sleeping bag. The rain seemed over, and the wind was gone. Brake lights flickered on and off as a large vehicle backed down the driveway. Cale couldn't make out the license plate. The vehicle stopped halfway up the drive. The gear light changed to park.

Three men exited the vehicle. They left it running. *Not very environmentally friendly, señores.* Cale didn't recognize the men, but he knew them. As they approached the house, each slipped on a pair of goggles. Cale recalculated the odds with his opponents having night vision. He mentally realized he was down on numbers, sight, and most likely weaponry.

One of the men, moving lightly and rapidly, split off from the driveway, went in front of the house, and was lost from sight. The light shining around the edges of the house went dark. The rascal had unscrewed the bulb. Cale noted to use a trickier globe next time. It was the little things in home security: Plant a yucca under your windows, keep a hedge of pyracantha at the corners, install deadbolts, dig and spike Burmese tiger traps lightly covered with pine needles.

One man stopped even with the house's side and leaned against a pine. Cale bet that was Escobar and hoped the sap would stain his

Armani windbreaker. More accurately, he hoped an arrow from a compound bow would find its way through the Armani windbreaker. Cale wasn't that good a shot. Maybe if he was in a stand above him, he could do it from this distance. The third man was larger than the other two and moved more stiffly. He entered the screened porch and headed toward the back door.

The alarm sounded. *Woof-woof-woof.*

Jimmy didn't think the recording sounded like himself. To keep him calm, Cale whispered to him, "You sound good, old buddy. Prime of life. Imagine, with balls, you could turn that tenor into a bass." Cale rested one hand on the furry head to keep Jimmy from voicing displeasure at the soundtrack's quality, ducked below the window, and dialed 911 with his other hand.

>>>

FRANCISCO COULDN'T SEE his Swiss watch in the dark. When the house's alarm went off, he reached in his pocket and started the timer on his phone. He would give his men five minutes from the time the alarm went off before leaving. They would not rush, and they would not overstay. They did not even question him on what they would do but continued searching the property.

Each time he checked the timer, briefly exposing himself to light, he moved. He moved from tree to tree. He did this without thinking. He was a predator who never forgot that he, too, could be the prey.

>>>

CALE THOUGHT THAT, to a late night dispatcher, the truth might come off a wee bit fanciful. *Hey, this is Cale Coleman, and it's the darndest thing, but there are three hit men at my house. . . . Yes, hit men. . . . They traveled all the way from Colombia, dadgummit, just to give me a painful death. . . . No,* *not Columbia, South Carolina. Colombia, South America. . . . You think you could send some fellas out to arrest them?*

There was an upside to envisioning every interaction before it occurred. He knew he couldn't wait for the security dispatch to call. The deputy responding would be half asleep, assuming the storm blew a door open. This would shorten the deputy's career trajectory. Cale got his mental story straight for the call.

"9-1-1, what is the nature of your emergency?"

"I need the police." Without pause, he gave and repeated the address.

"Sir, are you whispering? Please speak up. There is a dog barking in the background. It is very hard to hear you. Why do you need the police, sir?"

Why was he whispering? Hadn't this lady had sensitivity training? Unlike his visitors, Cale let bygones be bygones. Slightly louder, he pleasantly continued, "Three men have broken into my house. I am down by the water in my shed. They don't know I'm here. I can see the men. They are carrying guns."

He hadn't seen any guns but assumed they had them. He wanted to convey urgency and caution without resorting to South American hit men stories, which, in fairness, was so 1980s Miami.

The dispatcher dispatched officers. Cale gave her the description of the intruders' car. She typed it in. He mentioned that the alarm company would call dispatch too. "Make sure those officers know this isn't a routine alarm."

She wanted to keep him on the line, the training finally kicking in. "Sir, can you see the perpetrators?"

What percentage of callers knew the word "perpetrator" he wanted to ask, but let it pass.

He picked his head back up, looked through the window, and saw the larger and smaller men gathered by the back door gesticulating. Escobar was now somewhere out of sight. Cale heard the security company demand the intruders identify themselves. The larger man responded by pulling out a pistol and firing a bullet into the speaker, giving the alarm an echoing quality. He then fired another into the back door's window, which was just plumb mean. Did he have any idea how hard it was to get glass cut the day after a hurricane?

"Sir, are those gunshots I hear? Sir?"

"Shhh. Yes, those are gunshots."

The men swiveled around, hoping to see Cale hiding or fleeing. He mentally suggested they run their hands through the pyracanthas and make sure he wasn't hiding in the bushes.

The larger man entered the house. The smaller, quicker one who'd unscrewed the light bulb started into the backyard. He moved forward in quick, uneven steps. Three quick steps then a crouch. Two quick steps, crouched low, then he stood up, and moved sideways. The man didn't follow the stepping stones, but moved on and off them, soaking his shoes. The uneven cadence made him a difficult target.

The smaller man briefly moved out of sight as he went behind the hedge. Cale saw him emerge in the outdoor kitchen. The man briefly grabbed a large filleting knife before setting it down on the counter. He then looked to the dock and shed. He began his approach, again moving in spurts that betrayed no pattern as to his next movement.

Cale told the dispatcher, "I need to set the phone down. Please don't make a sound until I come back on, as they are coming closer to me now."

He set the phone down. Without taking his eyes off the approaching visitor, he reached down for the compound bow with his right arm and fumbled for the arrow beside it with his left. For the first shot, he thought the bow would be better. The other two guys wouldn't see the flash of flame that would reveal his location. It also felt more primeval, more fear inducing than the gunfire they were so used to. He knew the larger man was in the house. He wished he'd kept track of Escobar.

>>>

ALBERTO REAPPEARED FROM the front of the house. He held a few keepsakes in his hands, and, by his mannerisms, Francisco could tell Coleman had not been in the house.

Everything indicated Coleman had been home recently. Perhaps he was still nearby.

>>>

CALE BROUGHT BOTH the bow and the arrow up to his shoulder. He notched the arrow and broke the bow back into an armed position. If the man approaching got within twenty-five feet, he would release. Cale found the spot in the path the man was roughly following that he judged to be twenty-five feet, so he wouldn't pull too early. He didn't think the single-pane window would alter the arrow's flight, but he'd never tested that theory before.

Given his target's unpredictable path, he needed a close shot that would not miss. This man was either formally trained or had lived a very dangerous life—a worthy adversary to ambush, although Cale would have preferred a buffoon in case he missed.

Consciously, Cale slowed his breath and felt something like contentment wash over him. He followed the man's progress, looking for a rhythm to the movement, but found none. The moment was at hand.

>>>

FRANCISCO TRIED TO scan the property but found the post-rain humidity was making his goggles difficult to see through. He pulled them down, and it took his eyes a moment to adjust to the darkness.

He looked for Alberto, who was in the driveway facing the front yard—still doing his job but clearly ready to leave.

He looked at the Cuban making his way toward the water. His night vision goggles now hung around his neck as well. The Cuban's movements were both stealthy and fearless. He had not yet pulled his gun from his pocket. Francisco was not certain where he carried it. Something about the Cuban's competence made Francisco want to join him in the hunt. He took two steps forward before feeling his left hand vibrate: their five minutes were up.

》》》

WHEN THE MAN was still fifty feet off, Cale heard Escobar's whistle. The approaching man instinctively took a few steps backward but continued facing forward before taking a quick glance toward the whistle. Cale envisioned Escobar motioning for him to return. Cale watched the small man's eyes do a double take on the boat floating in the water. He then took a series of rapid crouched steps forward again. Cale heard a second whistle. This time the man followed the command, changed direction, and headed to the driveway. Cale watched the three men load and depart in the vehicle without turning on the headlights.

Cale put the weapon down, picked up the phone, and in a normal voice said, "OK, they are in the car and just turned south out of my driveway. If your guys see a black Suburban, please don't stop them. Just trail them until you get backup, and be very careful."

Should he mention they all spoke Spanish? This could help them know they had the right black Suburban at a stop, but it might confuse the situation. How would he explain how he knew they spoke Spanish?

Decompressing from the adrenaline rush, he realized how much he wished they'd come to the shed and gotten it over with one way or the other. As long as they were in the United States, would he wince every time he started his car? Feel compelled to hide? It was hard to run a business that way. Would the Feds put him in witness protection? His kids, grandkids, and sons-in-law couldn't all go underground.

If the police caught them, what would happen? At best, they'd have them on breaking and entering and a little destruction of property— probably not enough to get their passports confiscated. Maybe if they were caught with their firearms.

County deputies showed up with lights and sirens. Cale filed a report. They inspected the damage. It was minimal. Annoying. They hadn't caught them. If they hadn't yet, they wouldn't. The search was over. No reason to bring up his suspicion that these were infamous international narcotraffickers. The guys at the sheriff's office got that all the time.

››› 25

MORNING CONTINUED THE dream. Joe looked through the bars on the elevated windows. The rain was over, the clouds knitted tight. The fluorescent lights came on at six thirty. "Just another Monday morning. Strap on your nail pouch," Joe said aloud. He heard mumbled assent.

His roommates led the breakfast shuffle. They went to a larger holding tank. They each got a tray of grits, boiled eggs, and a school kid's carton of milk. Joe sat on a bench with his breakfast tray on his knees. Someone slipped onto the bench next to him.

"Hey, man. You want those grits?"

Joe looked at his peer. Black ashy skin; nappy, matted hair; jaundiced eyes. But he had surprisingly long, clean fingernails. One thumbnail was long and hooked like a spoon. He looked hollowed out and smelled like his clothes were put away wet. Joe considered trading the grits for the hard-boiled egg. Then he remembered he missed his morning Prevacid and thought two eggs would feel less than great.

"No, friend. I don't want them. You can have them, but you need to take my tray up."

The neighbor's eyes showed he wasn't used to being called *friend*. The unfamiliar greeting made him hesitate in accepting the terms. In the end, hunger won out, and he scraped the grits onto his own tray before putting Joe's tray underneath. He ate the grits and moved on. Joe realized he still had the little milk carton. He needed to get up anyway.

Joe noticed the prisoners had different-colored wristbands. He asked the next guy who sat down near him what they meant and learned that they identified the severity of the inmate's charges. Joe noticed that, largely, folks with like wristbands were grouped together. Actually, by race first, wristband second. Did people bond into groups that arbitrarily? Joe was in on a weapon-related felony. His wristband was red, a good jailhouse status color.

Everyone sat; a few, like Joe, on bolted-down metal benches. He noticed red wristbands dominating the benches. Most inmates sat on the floor. They leaned against walls or bars. A few talked. Friends from the outside or friends from the inside? Many held their heads in their hands. What was the Twain quote comparing boats and prison again? Boats smell better. Boats serve drinks. Women like boats too. Joe always thought Twain was sharp before. He'd take his chances on drowning and choose a boat.

His fellow inmates appeared to be engaged in introspection— mostly the red wristband crowd. Some were probably facing extended time away from home.

Green wristbands signified alcohol-related misdemeanors. The liver did its job overnight and processed the malt liquor while they slept. Now the green-wristband crowd sat quietly on the floor.

Joe decided jail was boring and uncomfortable. His bed was hard, and there was no pillow. He had to sit on a metal bench, or a concrete floor, lean against a concrete block wall. He had no belt, and his pants sagged despite the secret elastic waistband. No books, TV, playing cards, or music. He used the boredom to think more about how he wanted to live the final years of his life. He reaffirmed to himself that the pursuit of another mate wouldn't lessen the relationship he'd had with his wife. He grew a little philosophical, thinking about how his mind could stretch if he started dating people who had never lived in Brooklyn. Maybe he'd make a rule not to date anyone younger than his youngest daughter-in-law. That sounded about right. He smiled, thinking his jailors would be proud of how he'd used his time in the clink.

At nine thirty, the jailors collected the inmates; Joe was called last on the first docket. He was the only red wristband called; everyone else had green wristbands. He took that as a good sign that Tony was on the job. Joe wondered when he'd get to phone out. He'd gotten Tony out of the pokey before; Joe was sure he enjoyed returning the favor.

The inmates took a service elevator to the basement and into a hallway. The hallway must have tunneled under the street, because Joe could hear traffic overhead. Another service elevator took them up into the courthouse, where the guard led them into the court-room. They were seated in rows to the right of the judge's elevated throne. Height, robes, gavels—a lot of ceremony to provide power to the justice institution. The process made the judge himself a bit more than mortal.

The bailiff called out, "All rise for the Honorable Judge Has-sell." More transfer of power, making everyone stand until the judge deemed them worthy of sitting.

Joe was called first. He walked to the defense table, met his attor-ney. He smiled and winked at Tony in the sparse crowd. Tony grinned ear to ear. The attorney whispered the arrangement in Joe's ear. Ten large, bonded and done. Was he OK with it? Sure, he was OK with it.

The charge was read into the record, then the plea agreement, and the attorney's conference with the judge. Complete in five minutes. Joe and his attorney shook hands and walked out of the courtroom.

Tony greeted them, bobbing and weaving, shadow boxing the air. "And in this corner, from Brooklyn, New York, The Great White Dope, Joseph 'The Carpenter' Pas-ca-rel-laaaaaaa."

"Well, at least I have a good cornerman. How'd you know I got pinched?"

"Bartender."

"You found what bar I went to? You call my credit card company for the last charge?"

"Didn't think of that one. No, we found your loaner car. Nice of you to leave the cell phone in it for confirmation."

"Who's we?"

"Ashley, Cale, and me. Speaking of which, why didn't you take me with you to go see Cale? Gino could have been telling the truth."

"I don't know, Tony. Age isn't all wisdom. And Tony, you know how big my balls are."

"Sweet Mary, mother of Jesus, I don't know about the size, but I know gravity has pulled them between your knees. I imagine you scared those youngsters to death in the shower."

They exited the courthouse, crossed the street to the jail. Joe held up his pants as he walked. The magistrate's clerk checked out Joe's items, including the handgun. Because Joe didn't have a concealed permit in the state, he had to hold the handgun. Out on the sidewalk, he got a few wide eyes and a lot of wide berths. Joe wondered what they were thinking. *Mama, is that man robbing the jail?*

Tony and Joe got into the lawyer's car. He drove to the parking lot where he left the loaner the night before. It was near eleven now. Why not an early lunch? Why not a cold one to wash the roast beef down with? It's five o'clock somewhere. How about one more to hear about the big evening? Joe left the handgun on the floor of the loaner. Not concealed, not really visible. He felt OK with it. He put it there under the advisement of legal counsel—at least, that was his story.

WOOF-WOOF-WOOF. THE SURPRISE alarm echoed in his mind; it was unarmed before. Questions cascaded through his brain. Where was the real dog? Why did Coleman come home late and then leave before daybreak with his dog? Where had he gone? How long would it take to find him?

At his direction, Alberto confirmed that the charter's manifest was filed, Coleman listed as pilot.

Anxiety tugged on Francisco. There was much to do—much to rebuild, much to destroy. He thought about the fragile and violent Mexican cartels. He needed to pick an ally he could invest firepower in and yet still control. He had inserted this to-be-determined group onto his notepad in the shape of a grenade. Once it was armed, he needed to send his as-yet-unchosen ally into a civil war with the other cartels. He would have the same issue as always: How do you keep an ally once they are powerful and wealthy? Hostages. Perhaps like he did with key employees, he'd require the ally's family to live in Colombia. They would live like royalty—beautiful houses, majestic scenery, the wonderful temperature. They'd have mile-long private beaches to ride horses on, trained help, and protection. Royalty, yes. They would never want to leave. They would never be allowed to leave.

He needed to move his attention to these opportunities. Success did not realize itself; it needed to be driven. Of course, success with the Mexican cartels would mean they had destroyed each other, leaving the *norteamericanos'* powdered nostrils ever more desperate to receive his supply.

Choosing to enlarge his myth by personally carrying out this vendetta was proving more of a nuisance than he imagined it could be. Practical concerns filtered through his thoughts. He tried to stoke his anger with memories of his brother and Pablo. He zeroed in on the gunshots to Pablo's back, the bullets entering his flesh, the gut-wrenching fear with El Capo suddenly lying dead within his sight, then the ensuing power vacuum he barely survived to fill. But those memories were old. He had mined that emotional well for too long, and the bottom was now dry. He focused instead on his living family and the need to fuel the force field that protected them.

Francisco sat for lunch at the bar of a busy restaurant a block off the beach, a margarita on the rocks lined with salt and a wedge of lime untouched on the counter. Alberto and the Cuban sat at a table across the room. Alberto sipped a beer and ate chips while the Cuban drank water and watched the room. They knew this mood of Francisco's and kept their distance. Alberto had seen it in Francisco as he had seen it in Pablo. It meant violence, with no concern for collateral damage. This was when buildings were firebombed, when twenty were killed to make certain one was dead.

The restaurant's TVs showed surf video loops. The unnecessary insanity of the activity grabbed Francisco's attention. Waves the size of buildings that went on for half a mile. Guys with long hair or shaved heads almost encircled by a tunnel of water and then riding out. How did the cameraman stay in that spot with the wave breaking and a surfboard coming at him at thirty miles an hour? The requisite shots of beauties in string bikinis preening and laughing made sense to him. Some girls in rash-guard shirts and bikini bottoms rode waves too. A blonde girl with one arm whipped turns at the crest of garage-size waves.

It surprised Francisco how quickly people reappeared after the storm. Young men leaned boards against the side of the restaurant. They entered with wet hair under ski hats. Attractive waitresses hustled and smiled, some young, some career servers. So many tattoos. The place served Baja-style tacos—fresh fish, fresh toppings, hot sauces. Even children were in the restaurant. Surely, the *norteamericanos* would have taken the children away from the storm. This place was too egalitarian for Francisco but was a place of fun for the *norteamericanos*.

Two young women approached in sheer cover-ups over bikini tops. They wore short shorts, presumably over bikini bottoms. They didn't wear the same outfit, but they were a matched pair. They smiled.

"Are these stools taken?"

"No. Please join me."

"Thank you. Are you in town to surf the storm surge?"

Francisco found the question odd, given the difference between his clothing and age and those of the waterlogged people entering the bar. He responded, "No. Just here on business."

"Do I hear a slight accent? Where are you from?"

Francisco hesitated. He wanted everyone to know who he was, where he was from, and what he was doing. Yet he appreciated the value of prudence. This time, prudence won.

"Panama."

He was pretty sure the *norteamericanos* couldn't speak Spanish, but there might have been Mexicans working the kitchen. If he spoke Spanish, they would know he was not Mexican, so he went with something a little less mainstream. He'd been to Panama enough times and worked closely enough with Panamanians to pass a quick inquiry.

"Well, your English is excellent. I could hardly tell. Is it hard to learn another language?"

"Not really. It is, how would you say, situational. Panama is a small country with many outside influences. Because of the canal, of course."

He looked at the girls, not sure they knew what he meant about the canal. He continued anyway.

"America is a big country, and everyone speaks English, every sign is in English. Let me say this another way. What do you call someone who speaks three languages?"

"Umm, trilingual."

"What do you call someone who speaks two languages?"

"Bilingual."

"What do you call someone who speaks one language?"

"I don't know."

"An American."

The girls smiled, somewhat amused, but uncertain whether the handsome Panamanian had insulted them or given them words of wisdom. Then an image of a tall, middle-aged man with sun-bleached hair being towed into a wave caught their attention. Francisco used the lull to return to his thoughts.

He compared the two trips to Coleman's house. He envisioned the driveway. Neither time was a car parked there. He wouldn't have left the dog in the house overnight without letting him out. He assumed the man had left his car at a bar, too much to drink. Perhaps a neighbor let the dog out. The lights had changed—some that were not on the first time were on the second and vice versa—either they were on a timer or someone had been home. Both times, the doors were unlocked, but the second time, the alarm was armed. Someone had been there or the alarm was armed remotely.

Was anything else different? Any reason to think they wouldn't be successful if they went back to the house after lunch? He mentally went through the front yard. No. Side yard. No. Back yard. No.

He motioned to his men. Alberto got up to come over, but Francisco waved him off and motioned for the Cuban. Francisco angled his body to shield the conversation from the women sitting to his side and asked, "Did you notice anything that might help us understand what happened between our two trips?"

The Cuban nodded. With his eyes, Francisco told him to proceed.

"The first time, the boat was on the lift. The second time, the boat was in the water."

Francisco himself had missed that. He was again impressed. The boat was different. The first time, it had been on a lift. The second time, it sat in the water. What did that mean? Was Coleman watching? Why? Was he preparing to go out? Could something have tipped him off—the death of the arsonist? Was he helping friends with their hurricane damage? If he knew he was hunted, it might make the errand more difficult to complete. In the dark with rain hoods on, Coleman certainly would not have seen them well enough to recognize them. That was another reason for Francisco to either succeed quickly or buy his satisfaction.

»» 27

THE GIRLS REPEATED the trail jog, now breathing too fast to carry on a conversation. Their ponytails bounced behind them. They jumped puddles in low spots. Small birds washing their heads took flight at their approach. Berries and blossoms carpeted the ground, and small sticks and trash were bunched against walls where the wind and water gathered them. The girls' shoes were heavy from puddles too large for successful jumping. Their tank tops showed outlines from the sweat soaking through their sports bras.

The clouds showed cracks, brighter light penetrated, the breeze was down—gusty like fall, and the humidity now came from the ground up. Ashley believed that if she stood on the flybridge, she'd be above the humidity. She knew the air would feel awesome there after a swim and a shower.

A steady stream of cars with boards on their roofs passed. Four cars headed onto the island for every car heading off. Ashley wondered where they would all park.

"A quarter mile to go. Let's race from the next light pole back to the boat ramp," panted one of her friends.

"Game on."

Before the light pole, all three girls accelerated.

If the distance had been fifty yards, it would have been close. At a hundred yards, Ashley's long legs and fluid stride helped her pull away by ten feet. At the finish line, she was in front by thirty. She decelerated, put her hands on her knees, and raised her head, drinking in air. Her friends did the same.

They spent a few minutes stretching, kicking one heel at a time over the back of a park bench and leaning forward, pulling a foot up to their gluts while standing on one leg. They only did standing stretches. The ground was still too muddy to sit on.

"Want to take a dip before going to the boat?" Ashley asked.

"Sure, if we don't have to race."

The girls took off their soaked sneakers and socks and waded into the water on the pebbly beach beside the boat ramp. Ashley pondered whether the pebbles came from nature or from crushed gravel running off the parking lot. The girls floated, and the current dragged them down the shoreline. They walked back in waist-deep water against the current, picked up their shoes, and stepped delicately back onto *Framed*.

Ashley sat Indian-style on the dive platform, awaiting her turn for the shower. With Gino and his friends gone, she thought Joe might invite them to spread out to other bedrooms and showers. She checked her messages. There was a message from Tony's number. It was Joe.

"Ashley, why don't youse girls join Tony and me in my freedom celebration party? We are at the same establishment that I started in yesterday afternoon. Didn't bring the heat in here today, not much of a crowd. Things should be OK. Find the captain. He'll procure you a land vessel for the journey. If youse can't make it, we'll be back aboard midafternoon. Ciao."

She enjoyed Joe's voice. She enjoyed hearing *ciao* used and not sounding hipster-like.

She heard the latch open—her turn in the shower.

It was surprising how comfortable a two-foot circular shower could be. The water pressure when the boat was attached to shore water was definitely greater than when they were anchored out. When she finished, she towel-dried her hair, put her black sundress on, and went topside.

She decided to give Cale a call. Her whole life, she'd promised to stay away from violent men, and now she'd been awake four hours without calling him, and it felt like an accomplishment. For the first time, something inside her felt empathy for her mother.

She hoped Cale didn't think the call was too desperate. She told him she'd let him know when Joe was out so he could come down for a meal or a drink. She was just keeping her word, really. *That was good, right?* Cale said today was his last day off before he left town for work; it was now or never.

He picked up on the third ring. All she heard was wind.

"Cale, you there? Can you hear me?"

She heard "Hold on," then more wind. Finally, the wind sound subsided to a manageable level. "This is Cale."

"Hey, Cale, it's Ash. What is all the background noise?"

"Sorry, I'm on the Whaler. Took me a minute to slow down. Sound better now?"

"Yes. Hey, Tony got Joe out of jail like they planned. Wow, that is a sentence you don't say everyday. Anyway, they are at the place we found the pickup last night, having lunch and drinks. They should be back here midafternoon if you want to stop by and say hi."

Did that sound as transparent as it felt? At least she hadn't stayed up all night with her girlfriends talking about how dreamy he was, only to be decimated in the morning when he proved to show no interest. She'd never had the chance to do the teenage forlorn love thing, to talk boys with the girls.

Could you think of a man with two grown daughters, a house, a boat, and a plane as a boy? She was also curious about what the fairly recent photo she'd seen at his house of him holding two babies was about.

On the other end of the line, there was a longer pause than Ashley liked.

"I'm not too far from you now. Want me to swing by, and we'll hop down an island and grab lunch first? Maybe the old-timers will be onboard when we get back."

Well, that improved her spirits. "Yeah, that would be great. You know where we are in the marina?"

"Sure. If you want, bring a bathing suit. The waves are still pretty good, and I have two boards stowed. Maybe we can paddle out somewhere."

Ashley decided this moved into date territory. She would tell her friends what she was doing rather than ask if they wanted to come. He hadn't invited them anyway, not even in an offhand manner.

She told the girls, and they teased her a bit. "So it's the flyboys that can get your attention! All those doctors we've watched trying to break through the ice with you, and to think, all they needed was a career that was a little more daring."

Her friends went to the marina bar for Bloody Marys and chicken Caesar salads. Ashley readied herself for her date by putting a bikini on under her sundress and added her sunglasses. She found and packed a tote bag with a towel, sunscreen, and bottled water.

What exactly was she hoping for? She cut that reasoning off and decided to just enjoy the day. She'd take whatever it offered. If it was just a boat ride and on to normal life, so be it. As much as she'd enjoyed the prior two evenings with Cale, she didn't have a whole bunch of expectations wrapped up in today. At least, that is what she was telling herself while her foot tapped excitedly as she waited.

››› 28

CALE HUNG UP the phone. That was a good call, if not the expected call. Why not ask a beautiful girl out on a date? Until that call, his plan for the day had been to walk the heavy tourist areas looking for three Spanish-speaking gents he could introduce himself to on his own terms (Gunfight at the O.K. Corral style). But sometimes opportunity only knocked once, and you needed to answer the door. Sure, this was a life-or-death situation, but wasn't it always if you were paying attention? This situation was just exceptionally transparent. Was it the re-illumination about life being finite that spurred him to ask her out? Amazing, given the events in his life that Cale needed the finiteness pointed out again.

Maggie, you OK with this? What's that? Funny. Leave a wrinkly, sagging forty-five-year-old you for a taut, shiny, new twenty-five-year-old. No chance. Maybe at fifty-five, but not forty-five. Just kidding. Remember, you left. Cale thought he would have done just about anything to have seen her as a wrinkled fifty-five-year-old.

Cale felt dual rushes of attraction and danger as he idled the Whaler in the channel. He was slow to regroup after the call and the daydream conversation. Jimmy got up and leaned against his leg, uncertain why they were stopped. Cale's mind followed several thought trails. Not much traffic on the water. He was in nobody's way, and took his time putting thoughts, emotions, and worries into their appropriate spots and timeframes to deal with. Again, the phone started dancing in front of him. "This is Cale."

"Cale, it's Sheila. I am going to put you on speaker phone, OK?"

"Sure."

"I have a few colleagues in my office." Several male voices rang out different variations of "Good morning."

Sheila continued, "Can you go over the story you outlined on my voice mail for everyone? Sorry for not returning your call from the other day before now. This second message really alarmed me, so I wanted to get the appropriate parties together."

Not introducing her colleagues meant they were either political attachés or other law enforcement agencies. Possibly a senator's chief of staff. Senator for the committee on what—South American relations? Free-trade agreements? Was there still a cabinet-level drug czar position? If Radcliffe's death was ruled a homicide, it might be FBI. CIA possibly, but they couldn't do anything domestically—at least according to their congressional charter.

Cale parsed Sheila's voice and words to search for warning. For some reason, she was pretending she'd never called him back. He read loud and clear that he was not to mention that conversation. Was this unvoiced reason why she called from the 703 number last time? Had she used a prepaid disposable cell phone, paid for with cash? Those were a pain for investigators to track. She probably wore a hat, glasses, and collar turned up when she bought it. There was warning in that; he'd proceed with caution.

"OK. I noticed when I came home yesterday that I'd had visitors on my back porch, and there is no logical reason for me to have back-porch visitors during a hurricane. For some reason, maybe because of Radcliffe, who I read about on the Internet, it made me unusually nervous. We rarely worked together, only shared one real mission, but for those with the clearance, you'll know it was a substantial one. I decided to be safe and slept in my boathouse."

Shed, boathouse, tomayto, tomahto. Sleeping in your shed based on a gut feeling seemed a little much, might trip alarms of being fore-warned, and Sheila was obviously hiding her complicity.

"I set my house's alarm. When it went off, I looked through the window and saw three men at my house, handguns drawn. One had gray hair pulled back. One seemed younger and faster. He covered a lot of territory. The leader appeared middle-aged, slender, full head of black hair. They raised their voices over the alarm. They were speaking Spanish. A very proper, well-enunciated Spanish, the type I associate with Colombia."

Like the 911 call, this was a slight departure from reality to make reality easier to follow. He'd never heard them speak. Could he explain this caveat on "honesty is always the best policy" to his kids if they were listening? They were parents now; they understood gray. Of course, you could rationalize six outcomes to a coin toss if it suited you. Soon enough, his grandkids would pose the questions. More to their parents than Cale; he'd teach them how to crab.

The Spanish comment was made to ratchet up the likelihood of the visitors' being the Escobars in the eyes of the powers that be. The likelihood was ratcheted tightly enough in Cale's mind that he was a bit afraid the bolt heads were stripping.

Hearing silence from the other side, Cale proceeded.

"With Radcliffe dying in very unusual circumstances and now this at my house within less than a week, I have some questions. How secure are our classified files? If I Google my name, will some report show up talking about my history with the agency? Is there any rea-son to think some very undesirable Colombians are now traveling in the US?"

Presumably, the speakerphone was muted. Cale didn't expect an answer. Well, not a truthful answer. There were too many inter-agency coworkers watching each other for anyone to take a chance with the information they released. There was probably very little trust among the group sitting around Sheila's desk, so ten cents to a quarter their response would be cloaked in national security nondisclosure bologna.

The silence dangled as they discussed the company stance. Cale passed the time by picking out his obit picture. Young man or present day? Formal or outdoors? The funeral was, for obvious reasons, more for the living than the dead, so his daughters could go with what they liked best. He didn't think it would be the one he'd have picked, in which he holds, with arms outstretched to the camera, two seven-pound flounders. The photo he'd picked for Maggie was crystal clear in his mind. Casual. Outside. She was young. But, of course, she was young.

A long minute later, a voice returned.

"Mr. Coleman, we don't have any reason to believe the Escobars or their proxies are operating illegally within the borders of the United States. In fact, outside of the Spanish-speaking countries in South America, their operation is largely shut down."

Hmm, no introductions provided. The speaker wasn't taking any chances that Cale might be recording the call. That's one player with his cards on the table, the rest of the players with their cards in their hands. The voice was hiding behind ubiquitous plural pronouns— *they, we, us*; never *me, I*—*the buck stops here* (at least since Truman made that statement famous). This was the problem with government bureaucracy: *You must understand, it's for the public good, just not yours, but, by happenstance, it is for mine.*

Cale dissected the answer. He was pretty sure only one country in South America didn't speak Spanish. That left—guessing now—a couple of hundred million potential customers. Cale let the silly statement pass—not out of deference, but because he wasn't confident in his South American census knowledge.

"OK. How about my records' status?"

"Your mission work files are classified. We have no reason to suspect this status has been breached. In fact, it took no small amount of effort to get them in preparation for this call. Upon reading them, I thank you for your patriotism."

Patriotism? So it was a political attaché speaking. Someone from law enforcement would have laced the compliment with *doing your duty*. Politicians used *patriotism*. Nothing good would come from this call, but Cale asked anyway.

"So what have the investigators found in Radcliffe's death?"

"Nothing to report, Mr. Coleman. We have yet to receive the report."

No pause before answering that one. Cale wanted to quote Shakespeare, *The lady doth protest too much, methinks*, but let it slide.

"OK. Another question comes to mind." Sure, sure, don't poke the bear. But maybe a firm nudge to the belly wouldn't hurt. "If there is nothing to report, and you think I have nothing to worry about, why are all of you on this call?"

More behind-the-muted-phone-line conversation. Sheila answered this time.

"Cale, I wanted to make sure you knew I took your concern seriously. I brought in all the interested parties to see if anyone knew something I didn't."

After a brief pause, another anonymous man came on the line. "Mr. Coleman, it is not uncommon for agents who have been involved in on-the-job fatalities to later need psychological counseling. In the military and now in the media, they refer to it as posttraumatic stress disorder, or PTSD. Sometimes, people who have been through incredible strain begin to weave stress-filled fantasies into everyday realities. Particularly if there is a trigger, like the death of a coworker or a natural disaster, like a hurricane. May I recommend you consult a psychologist that a grateful country will pay for?"

Grateful country, was it, you son of a string of bad words that Cale kept himself from using to keep from getting himself further riled up? This felt like they were building a case. If something happened, like he stopped breathing, suicide would be a likely cause of death. Given that the way Colombians handled personal retribution was traditionally up close and messy, it might pan out for them: If he ended up with his throat slit, they would already have noted in the files that there had been signs of PTSD. And what was with the need to define PTSD? Did they think he was Rip Van Winkle? You couldn't unplug enough from society not to know what PTSD was after fourteen years of the country being at war.

Sheila's voice again. "Cale, I will keep you updated when we hear about Radcliffe's investigation. In the meantime, take care."

They said thank you and good-bye, and everybody clicked off.

››› 29

CALE PUT THE Whaler in forward and headed toward the marina. The clouds had almost fully dispersed. A good rain on land made the earth glisten. A tropical storm in the Intracoastal Waterway made the water an obstacle course of floating debris. Cale trimmed the engines higher than normal to avoid hidden flotsam and ran two-thirds of normal cruising speed.

Saturday's Caribbean-clear water was now Mississippi murky. You know who likes murky water? Bull sharks. This is when they swim into rivers. Their kidneys function highly enough to switch from processing salt water to processing fresh water. The bulls were mostly blind. The murky water reduced their preys' eyesight advantage.

Alligators liked murky water, too, and it made them blend in easier with all the debris. They were just one more log. After a storm, alligators got flushed toward a river's mouth, the water there not quite salty enough to impair their vision. Cale imagined that the Cape Fear River's mouth today was a Nile Delta of carnivores. He and Ashley would definitely not be swimming on the inside of the barrier islands. If the ocean was stirred up, too, maybe they'd just cruise around for the day.

Framed floated in an outside slip and was docked stern-to. The captain was hosing her down. Ashley sat on a small cooler, with a knapsack resting on her lap. She held her flip-flops in one hand and a magazine flipped open and folded back in the other. The hose's pressurized water, searching for exit, crossed her feet. A prism of light reflected in the water. Cale decided the captain was using soap.

The Whaler pulled along the dock's butt end, and Cale looped a bowline around a cleat, backed up, and put a half-hitch knot on a stern cleat. He killed the engines but left them in the water, hopped on the dock, and approached *Framed*'s gangway steps. Ashley reached the steps from above as Cale reached them from below. She handed over the cooler and descended, holding her flip-flops and magazine in one hand and the flimsy cord rail down the steps in the other.

At the greeting hug, Cale enjoyed the smell of her suntan lotion. She introduced him to the captain, and they exchanged pleasantries before saying good-bye. Cale held Ashley's hand as she climbed aboard the Whaler. Jimmy came up for a rub, then laid back in the shade. The engines turned over, and they cast off, pointed roughly south. They passed the state park where their paths first crossed, which had a significantly smaller flotilla today.

Cale still ran at two-thirds speed. The pair stood in the center console. Their shoulders bumped occasionally, slightly more than the chop necessitated, which Cale noted favorably. Ashley held the tubular aluminum rod holder overhead to steady herself. They passed the outlet of the Cape Fear River. The water was browner and full of more debris, but there were no visible monsters in the water. Visible or not, Cale wasn't stopping for a dip.

They darted out into the open ocean and continued south. At a big, round, bald beach peninsula, they looped back into a protected marina.

A decorative replica lighthouse overlooked the sheltered water. The marina had fuel pumps beside the harbormaster's hut. Nobody was inside, but there was a leathery-skinned man in Vans resetting boat fenders whom Cale assumed was the harbormaster. The Whaler bypassed the fuel pumps and passed the big slips with shore power and water plug-ins. At the farthest dock, where there were no slips, a menagerie of small boats were tied to pylons and cleats. Most of them had six inches of water in them. Cale found a clear path and backed the Whaler to the dock and cleated it. He floated it forward and looped a bowline over a pylon. He and Ashley then climbed onto the dock.

No bridge connected the island to the mainland. Cale knew this place and liked to come here for dinner, especially in late October, just before it closed for the season. The island's homeowners' association documents allowed only service vehicles and golf carts, which was pretty cool. Vacationers didn't have to worry about their kids getting hit by a car when they were out biking. The deer loved the island without their main predator roaring down the asphalt. Of course, coming with a minivan full of kids and missing the ferry wasn't super awesome. Nothing started a vacation better than ending an eight-hour drive from Pennsylvania by watching a ferry depart without you.

They walked over a series of decks. The storm damage looked minimal. There were no missing boards and only a few shingles off the roof of the harbormaster's shack. Several boat fenders either hung on by one end or floated untethered around the marina. The harbormaster would rectify these items today.

A two-story building sat several feet behind the seawall, with a neon light in the window that said *OPEN*. The first floor was a polished restaurant. Cale loved its air conditioning. There were white tablecloths, grass cloth walls, and soft carpet. Cale knew they would do a Sinatra sound track until seven thirty, a Coltrane from then to close. The lighting from the floor-to-ceiling tempered-glass windows with slightly tinted frames was dim but clean. The windows faced southeast, with a view of the marina below to the left, the mainland to the right, and the short channel to the ocean straight ahead. It was a perfect restaurant for a romantic date.

But today, Cale bypassed the restaurant's door, went around back, and took Ashley up an exterior stairwell to the second floor. Upstairs was a fish fry, where the days' catch was deboned, seasoned, and flash-fried in cast-iron pans. No breading. It was always fresh—whatever they bought that morning at the docks from the guides, charters, or enthusiasts who showed up. Was it a little risky not to use commercial crews? It was probably riskier to run multiple deep fryers on the second floor of a wooden building. It was a day after a hurricane, and they were stocked with fresh fish. The food was served in paper trays with sides of okra, corn on the cob, green beans, and slaw. No choices; you received them all. This was probably why the waitresses never delivered a wrong order. Cale always drank sweet tea there.

Inside, the upstairs area was shallower than downstairs, with a long bar where you ordered, paid, and took your number. Cale looked past the cashier and saw the morning's catch being filleted. Red drum it was. You could either sit at the bar or on the deck outside.

They ordered and headed out to the deck. It was lined with rows of oversized picnic tables equipped with built-in benches and covered with waxy red-and-white checked tablecloths. Cale produced two cushions from the Whaler, which would provide a dry place to sit. Who said chivalry was dead? Ashley and Cale sat on the same side of the table facing the water.

Ashley asked, "Is this big white pole behind the building an antenna?"

"No, it's the first part of a range."

Should he ask her whether she knew what he meant, or was that condescending? Did he continue on, assuming she didn't know, or was that too pompous? So many decisions. And he was supposed to worry about narcotraffickers?! He didn't truly sweat this decision, but his mind naturally channeled through the options and possible outcomes, which made him hesitate. Now that he was being tracked by narcotraffickers, he needed to stop hesitating.

Ashley asked, "What's a range?"

See, things usually worked out.

"It's a way to find the deepest part of a channel. Look farther into the island, where there is an even taller pole."

They pivoted in their seats. Cale pointed toward the second pole in the range. She leaned into him. Her eyes followed where he pointed. She nodded. He again enjoyed the scent of her lotion, perfume, shampoo—whatever it was that made her smell so good. Reluctantly, when looking at the taller pole was no longer justifiable, they unwound and turned back to the sea.

"When you want to come into the marina, you get your boat into position to where those two poles look like one long pole and head straight in." He unrolled his napkin and demonstrated with the knife and fork. "Whenever the two poles are in line with each other, you should be in the deepest part of the channel."

"But there is no way *we* did that, coming around the bend so tightly."

"The Whaler doesn't draw enough to worry about it here."

"Does 'draw' mean how deep it is?"

"Basically. Joe's boat draws enough to need to use the range."

Mentioning Joe made her smile. Even Cale got a kick out of him—sort of. That lovable old lug who came calling with a firm handshake and a pistol in his pocket, just checking to see whether his nephew was hit in the back of the head with a tire iron. He was probably all right when he wasn't out of sorts. Tony was definitely all right. Despite Cale's concerns that they were involved in organized crime, he figured the odds were they were the hardscrabble city boys who made good like they said. But he reserved the right to change his opinion and brain Joe if his hand found its way into his rain slicker again.

When the food arrived, Ashley was impressed. Cale was impressed that she drank the island water without complaining. The volume of sugar in his sweet tea overcame the beach-water gravy for him. His paper cup was refilled several times without his asking.

They lingered. The air felt good. Conversation came easy. It stayed in the present tense—not *Some weather we are having*, but not personal history lessons or religious debates either. It floated. Cale found himself enjoying this afternoon even more than the last two evenings with her. He only had to stop once from saying, *My daughters think the same thing.* Weddings always used that verse about love being blind; you never knew what could happen. He'd accept dim lighting; at this point, blind seemed too much to ask.

His phone rudely began vibrating against his leg, and Cale pulled it out, looked at the screen. It was a 703 area code. He said, "Excuse me for a minute, Ashley," and walked to the railing before she could grant or refuse permission.

"This is Cale." His practiced phone greeting was a bit singsong for such a big man. It was optimistic, suggesting he was looking forward to learning who was on the other end of the line and that he was ready to help. Cale could look gruff enough in person, and it was often a client calling.

"Hey, Cale, it's Sheila. Sorry about . . . the way the call went earlier this morning. I had higher hopes for that group. I should know better by now."

"Yeah, OK. Should I ask why you keep calling me on a disposable phone?"

"Don't be an ass, Cale. You know why. I'm trying to get you help."

"Mental help or guys with guns help?" He thought she was on his side, but best to clarify.

Sheila, demonstrating part of the skill set that helped her achieve her rank, didn't dignify the jab. "Radcliffe was dead before the fire."

Not earth-shattering news. The three guys who came to party at Cale's house confirmed it without Radcliffe's autopsy, but it was a step in the right direction and should speed up getting the various anonymous players bought in.

"So now everybody will take appropriate precautions," Cale said leadingly. "Locate the Escobars here in the States. Make sure they know they are under surveillance. Tell them they are suspects. That kind of standard operating procedure stuff, right?"

"I'm working on it. But you should know: When we spoke this morning, everybody in the room except me already knew this information."

That was a mule kick to the gut. Cale's response was an audible "Ugh." Sheila stayed quiet while he searched for an unemotional response.

"Sheila . . . come clean. Is there any set of circumstances where they will allow this to be pinned back to the Escobars, or are these treaties too big and too recent a triumph to have these details muddy it up?"

"I don't know. I'm working on it. The president really put his weight behind getting the deal with the rebels signed, and the other side has wanted the free-trade agreement signed for over ten years. I'm not sure where the sponsors are for bringing up any issues, but I'm looking. This was the grand bargain for both parties to get this done. They are trumpeting it as a blueprint for how they will tackle the bigger domestic issues next."

This was a detailed way of saying, "You are on your own." But there was no reason to shoot the messenger (although she might be off the Christmas card list). Once the message was delivered and received, the perfunctory motions getting to good-bye happened quickly.

The dice now bounced down the craps table. After twenty years of dormancy, the Escobars needed to complete their Old Testament eye for an eye version of justice. Cale needed to find them to get on with his life. He couldn't let them leave; he'd have to look over his shoulder for the rest of his life. And his daughters would have to look over theirs for the rest of their lives. But he was not a SEAL or even a bounty hunter. He wished the Escobars understood MLK Jr.'s words, about only light being able to chase dark and only love being able to chase hate and end this cycle of violence. But he knew that was not their code. The facts were simply that hate was chasing him, and his loving sidearm must be ready for that hate.

But right now, the Escobars weren't on the island, so nobody was murdering anybody this afternoon. Cale's mind strategized most creatively when he was engaged in things he liked doing. It was a beautiful gift to compartmentalize future stress away and enjoy the present. So he'd enjoy his date, assuming it continued to be awesome, and hope some ideas floated up from the recesses of his brain. There was also a small part of him that was looking forward to the challenge the Escobars would present and the opportunity to complete some unfinished business.

He looked toward Ashley, who politely looked out to sea rather than watching him. He wondered whether she thought he was talking to a girlfriend he conveniently hadn't mentioned. The absurdity of trying to explain this development to her cheered him up. Gallows humor. He didn't think he'd explain it. He wasn't putting her in any danger here—at least, no Colombian danger, and he'd already fully disclosed the bull sharks. He knew his mind would keep processing how to handle his predicament, but he would hold off officially worrying about it until after he dropped her off. No matter how well the day progressed, he would drop her off this afternoon; it wouldn't be kosher to invite her back to his place when he expected company.

"Sorry I took that call. It was from my old boss when I worked for the DEA. A coworker died a few days ago, and she was giving me an update on the details."

She offered condolences but didn't request specifics. Whether her actions stemmed from good breeding, disinterest, or trust was hard for Cale to tell. A hint of jealousy might have been nice.

They finished lunch, and Cale stuffed cash in an amount equal to the meager price of lunch in the tip jar on the way out. Back at the marina, they rented a modified golf cart from the harbormaster. Ashley refilled Jimmy's water bowl and set it in the boat. His sleeping spot followed the shade. If he got too hot, he was smart enough to hop in the water and then climb back onboard. Cale pulled the two surfboards out and set them crossways in the back of the cart—probably OK at fifteen miles per hour.

A hundred yards down the path from the marina, the scenery became scrubby, wind-beaten trees five feet on either side of the path. They passed houses built on stilts. Mosquito central, Cale thought, but to each their own. It wasn't beyond the realm of possibility that mosquito leeching was a little-known method for reducing blood volume and pressure passed down from unlicensed barbers throughout the centuries.

The gas-powered cart downshifted to first gear to climb the island's mountain. They reached the plateau, roughly seventy-five feet above sea level. The dune, cleared of trees, was domesticated with zoysia and provided a bit of a view. Cale pointed out the areas of interest: the marina; the ferry dock; the island grocery store; the mainland; the golf course, where a gator, with doves perched on its back, impersonated a statue in the fairway.

The large beach Cale targeted for them was down to the right. The waves looked OK. The water didn't look turbid enough to hide a bull shark, but he couldn't tell for sure. A bull shark is just not a pretty animal and doesn't even look hydrodynamic: big belly, small eyes, mottled coloring. Would Ashley buy it if he just said the waves were no good? But things looked OK from here.

They descended the mountain. The cart's governor kicked in, and Cale got no juice from pushing the pedal to the mat, but he kept it pinned anyways. At sea level, he pulled the cart onto the road's shoulder. They were the only people at the beach.

With the longboard under his arm, Cale walked to the beach. He used the bagged essentials in his other hand as a counterbalance. Ashley carried the smaller board on her head. Cale was giddy to get in the water. His speech and walking pace accelerated. Just short of the water, they set everything down. He traded out his shirt for a rash guard. She pulled off her dress, and Cale became even giddier. He handed her a rash guard to put over her bikini. A strange surge of gravity made his eyes watch her raised-arm wiggle that got the rash guard over her head much too quickly. Even with the guard on, Ashley's gravitational force was still very strong. Fortunately, the extra polyester weakened it enough that he could mind his manners.

A circular bar of green wax was fished out of the bag. It smelled slightly of coconut. He waxed the shortboard and started on the long-board. It was pretty bare; there was plenty of sand in old bumps. He expected Ashley to use the longboard. It had a safer feel. It was easier to catch waves on it, too. The only time the longboard was a bummer was when the water was choppy, when fighting its size could be exhausting.

Cale's world narrowed to one job: waxing. Small circles into big circles. Nose to tail. Rail to rail. He was fully in the present, just like when he was flying. This was a characteristic of a good pilot—immersed in the present, fixated on the little jobs that needed to be done. He hummed tunelessly. When he finished, he looked up.

Ashley was already in the white water. He hadn't noticed her departure. She held the board leeward of her body to keep the wind from slapping it into her face. She walked to waist deep, waited out a breaking wave, took two quick steps, dove forward with the board, and paddled furiously. She made the crest of the next wave at its peak, the last unbroken spot in the wave. Pretty cool. Cale wouldn't mention that since he got to use the longboard, he wasn't as nervous about the bull sharks.

He dropped the wax in the sand, ran the longboard into the water, and used the bigger board's superior paddling speed to catch Ashley as she turned perpendicular to shore to await her set. She flicked her hair back as she sat up, straddling the board. She wiped the water out of her face with both hands. Cale paddled slightly past her. As he sat up, straddling the board, he slowly slid down toward the board's tail.

The lower center of weight helped him quickly spin around and, by kicking his feet in opposite directions, he sped up the turn, spinning in a circle.

The first wave passed. They both caught the second. He went left; she went right. It was a nice first ride for both of them. Cale made it back to the surf zone first. She paddled back calmly, with a steady rhythm, not at the furious pace she broke through the breakers with. She must have been giddy to get out there too.

Cale said, "Well, you could have told me."

She showed a mouthful of the type of straight white teeth you find only in America. God bless the US orthodontics industry.

Cale continued, "I had worked up this whole 'feel the spirit of the ocean' guru routine."

She replied, "I told you, I'm from San Diego. I thought you knew that was on the ocean. Pretty big surf town."

Unfazed by the flirty taunt, he replied, "I know where San Diego is. It's the first place I killed a man."

Ashley gasped audibly. "You are such an animal. I feel so safe yet so vulnerable with you here alone in the ocean."

Of course that exchange never happened, but Cale liked the thought of it. But when calculating the odds in his head, the estimated chances for a net positive response from mentioning that he'd killed someone were precisely none too good. His response instead was a smile coupled with a wizened look down the shoreline (this would have been part of the ocean guru routine anyway). He assessed the break of the waves and made certain they were in an optimal location. That was the biggest key to enjoyable surfing: being in the right location. Too far out, you didn't catch many waves; too far in, you had waves breaking on your head.

As a surfer, she proved distinctly not bad. Good etiquette. Good wave count, particularly considering she was using the shortboard. Nothing radical. They stayed on the water longer than he'd meant to.

Cale came in tired, but Ashley seemed energized. There were no side-to-side-moving fin sightings. Several fins swam by bobbing up and down, which seemed a positive harbinger.

They dried off, and Ashley undid her bikini and got into her dress from behind a beach towel—a both incredibly sexy and incredibly cruel San Diego Beach Betty trick.

The wind picked up. This time, she drove the golf cart while Cale kept an arm across the boards. Back aboard the Whaler, Ashley cast off the bowline and pushed the boat's bow away from the dock. Cale let the stern line tighten, the bow swung around, he unhooked the stern line, then engaged the engines to forward, and they headed to the channel.

Outside the barrier island, the Whaler bounced across intermittent whitecaps. At the next channel, Cale ducked the Whaler inside to the waterway. They again found themselves crossing over the debris coming out of the Cape Fear River. The sun was warm now, and it felt like August again. When the journey was over, Cale tied back onto the butt end of the pier where *Framed* was docked and killed the engines.

When they arrived, Ashley's roommates were sunning their hides on the bow deck, out of the wind. Their hands pecked at smartphones. The captain was working in the storage locker under the rear salon benches. Joe and Tony walked to the flybridge rail as the welcoming committee. They each wore clean Tommy Bahama shirts and held a highball in one hand. Tony fanned playing cards in his other hand. They had magnanimous greeting smiles on their faces.

Tony said, "It's about time youse two made it back. We was getting ready to deputize a posse. We'da had seafarers from Norfolk to Daytona Beach on the lookout."

Ashley responded, "Thanks for the concern," and asked, "Joe, how did you sleep last night?"

That was a very polite way to ask the burning question.

Joe answered, "Not too bad, really. Think I'll sleep better tonight. Bring Mr. Coleman onboard with you if he has a moment. He and I only met briefly . . . and not over the sunniest of circumstances."

Ashley went to see her friends. Cale climbed the flybridge ladder. At the summit, Tony handed him a Scotch on the rocks. Not his normal order, but when in Rome (or, in this case, transplanted Brooklyn) . . . Cale scanned Joe's boating attire over and concluded it was an impossible outfit in which to hide a weapon except in the small of his back.

Joe started the conversation. "Youse know I don't blame you for Gino."

"Thanks." It was amazing how little he'd thought about this recent conflict today. You want to forget your little problems? Get big problems.

"My sister—his mother—called me today. She is likely to find an old Sicilian to curse you, though."

"Don't worry about those curses," Tony added. "They only work if they have a little of your blood to start with."

"Well, curse or not, I hope the guy recovers quickly."

The three men moved into more cocktail party-caliber get-to-know-you conversations, reviewed the day, the water, Cale's current business. He felt a bit like a teenager being vetted in the front parlor before the homecoming dance. *You kids have fun tonight, but not too much fun.* His twenty years in the DEA came up.

"Yeah, it was terrible to see in the eighties what happened to some neighborhoods. Crime—so much property crime. And the things people would do. Moms turning tricks behind dumpsters for a fix. Glad they cleaned up the crack problem. Dinkins just fed the beast; Giuliani showed the difference you can make when you don't accept problems as unsolvable.

"It sounds so silly, but one of the main things he stopped that turned the city around was the guys washing windows at intersections. When that kind of harassment stopped, it just turned things around."

"How much did you tip those goombahs for washing your windows, Joe?" Tony goaded. His eyes twinkled at the jab.

"Only tip they got from me was . . . " Joe let it pass. Maybe he couldn't come up with the right comeback. Maybe he didn't want to let a carnal insult or racial diatribe flow out in front of a stranger or, more likely, where it could be overheard by the girls.

Joe turned back to Cale. "So where were you in the DEA?"

"All over. Here, DC, Southern California, Northern California, Texas, Florida, Mexico, even South America."

"You ever get in any tight spots?"

"Yes."

"Undercover?"

"No."

"Busting into a crack house with a SWAT team?"

"No."

But this got Cale thinking. There were so many more frontline jobs than pilot. How did he get in this position? His risk was supposed to be from turbulence. Updrafts. Downdrafts. Instrument failure. Worst case, a surface-to-air missile that the agency rehearsed dodging but to Cale's knowledge nobody actually ever faced. Certainly not long-suppressed revenge.

The captain brought snacks up, which provided a momentary diversion in the conversation. But before Cale could get traction heading in a different direction, Tony was back on him.

"So youse going to tell us what kind of tight spots?"

The difference between Brooklyn gentlemen and Southern gentlemen: The Brooklyn gentlemen would make you say no. But for some reason unknown to himself, Cale chose not to say no. He'd been queried for years on the topic and always clammed up before. Today, he answered, "I can tell you about one incident. It got a decent amount of press at the time. The other stuff is still classified."

At least officially. It didn't feel quite as classified as he'd like it to be. Maybe that was why he told them about San Diego.

The captain, who was sitting in on the conversation, pulled up an old newspaper article on the tablet about the incident. He read the relevant sections aloud. Cale really didn't like how easy that was to find. Joe and Tony's expressions changed slightly. They were perhaps surprised by the brutality. Their visitor stabbed a person to death. Did they question how a blade felt cutting through a man? Cale would have answered, "Same as deer." That wouldn't help. They had never field dressed a deer.

"So why'd you retire?"

"I needed a change. After Maggie—my wife—passed, I took more and more back-office assignments. I couldn't let something happen to me while my girls were growing up. The back office is not where I was meant to be. I'm no good at it. So when I got my years to qualify for retirement, I mustered out to the real world. My girls were away in school by then. I borrowed heavily, bought a twin-engine turbo prop, and started my charter business."

"Sorry to hear about your wife. I was wondering about you spending this whole day with Ashley, thinking maybe you and your friend who's about to tie the knot again were two peas in a pod."

Cale laughed, "Thanks for that comparison."

"Now I feel like a real prince with that comment I made asking about what you told your wife. My wife passed, too. Last year. You know, Tony isn't going to believe this, but I think I was jealous of you and Ashley. Sadly, I was more fired up about that than my dear sweet muscle-headed nephew. For what it's worth, I've switched my feelings on Ashley to paternal, so watch yourself, I've been known to pack heat."

"I'm sorry to hear about your wife too. Hard to believe the things you take for granted about loved ones until they're gone."

For the first time, the two men felt the similarities in their lives' flight paths, including their attraction to Ashley. The mood turned respectful, and there was palpable longing for the dead, but it wasn't somber. Tony decisively broke the mood.

"My wife is still alive. Look, I've got the voice mails to prove it." He held up his phone and showed seven unchecked voice mails with the name Sofia beside each.

Joe laughed, "Tony, when did you tell her you were coming home? Between the storm and you not returning her calls, she's worried you're coming home before she can get her cabana boy out of the house!"

"Cabana boy. Yeah, now that I'm retired, I should be a cabana boy out in the Hamptons. That's a good gig. 'Miss, may I apply your sunscreen? No, ma'am, rubbing it in won't be any trouble at all.'"

The banter picked up speed. Cale's wit wasn't quick enough to catch the ride, but he enjoyed watching the carousel. Eventually, the girls came up. Joe wanted to treat for a large steak dinner. Cale took off, with promises to return in time for a seven-thirty topside cocktail and an eight o'clock reservation at the steak house.

»»» 30

CALE MOTORED HOME at full cruising speed. There was no less debris in the water, but he had acclimatized. That didn't make going full speed smart; it was the intellectual equivalent of, after several hours' driving in the rain, finding yourself traveling at eighty miles an hour despite the decreased visibility, increased stopping time, and unpredictable hazards.

He realized his calendar was suddenly full. He'd planned on Googling for pictures of Escobar today, but the date with Ashley had somehow superseded that in importance. Now he had a dinner party tonight, a charter tomorrow through Friday, and finding and killing narcotraffickers this weekend. The last part needed to be done without ending with a seat in Old Sparky. Busy times. But first he needed to dock, get in the house, pack for the charter, and get back on the Whaler without anything bad happening.

Tonight, Cale would pay to leave the Whaler at the marina with *Framed* until Friday. He'd then get a hotel room after dinner for shuteye. A good night's sleep would keep up his energy reserves, and the FBO was a quick cab ride away. He needed to get there earlier than normal, closer to three hours before flight time than the normal one hour before. He hadn't checked his plane since the storm. The guys from the hangar said everything was fine, but they didn't have as strong an interest in its maintenance as he did. What's that saying about a pig and chicken at breakfast? They both are invested but the pig is committed. Old pilots didn't get old by saving money on their airplane maintenance.

Without slowing, Cale passed his house. Nothing caught his eye. He did a one-eighty, pulled back the throttle, and passed again, now heading south. He came back, stopped at a crab pot buoy with a good view of the house. He raised the pot, hoped the pot's owner wasn't in eyesight, pretended to unload and rebait the trap while studying the house. It seemed OK. He dropped the pot, reengaged the engines, and pulled into the boat lift slings. Cale chose not to raise the slings and wrapped only one line around a cleat.

Jimmy hopped out and trotted up the yard, changing the pH mix in several locations as he made his way toward the house. He wasn't on edge, but he wasn't a trained guard dog either. Cale pulled the Beretta from the console box, pointed it down with his right hand, and stepped onto the dock. He jogged off the edge of the dock, turned left, and walked into the pines. After pausing and resurveying his surroundings, he walked out of the pines into the outdoor kitchen, ducking behind the counter. After another pause, he picked his head up and looked around. Jimmy stood at the back porch screen door waiting. Cale went back into the trees. The back of his flip-flops slung dirty puddle mud up his backside as he ran. He now circled to the front to study the driveway. It still seemed OK. He had a feeling that right after the bullet pierced his ribs, the thought *Well, it seemed OK* was going to run through his mind.

Jimmy didn't ask questions and walked around to the front door without complaint. Cale decided Jimmy was right and he would enter the front door. The door was too thick to shoot through, and he'd know if anybody was inside as soon as the door opened. If the alarm started beeping, all was kosher. No beeping, and it had been cut from the inside; there was a battery backup if the power had been cut from the outside. Straight to *woof-woof-woof* meant somebody had tripped it already.

Cale sprinted from his hiding spot to the front door and pushed completely against it. His hand on the knob, he turned and pushed. *Beep-beep-beep.* He hustled in, locking the door behind him. He turned off the alarm, went through the house, locked the back door, then returned to the front door to let Jimmy in. Cale then relocked the front door, armed the alarm to STAY, and exhaled.

He gathered his stuff for the work trip. Packing was a core competency for a charter pilot, and it took two minutes to complete. Cale then selected an evening outfit before wavering—to shower or not to shower? He decided to get clean and keep the shower door open. Jimmy rested on the bath mat, not minding the occasional splashing water. The Beretta waited on the counter, two short steps away if he didn't trip over the dog.

Cale dressed in nicer-than-normal summer wear: A white button-down, beige cords. It was a nice restaurant with a nice girl. He donned lace-up running shoes, letting practicality trump style. If he needed to run, he would need to run fast. He calf-holstered the Beretta. It had been so long since he'd worn the ankle holster that he was surprised it wasn't dry rotted. He hefted his bag, changed the alarm to AWAY, and left the house.

Outside, he set the bag down and walked Jimmy up the driveway and down the street to his sitters. He chatted with the parents while their elementary school kids rolled Jimmy on his back. Four small hands scratched the big belly. Cale walked home slightly faster than his natural pace. In his front yard, he grabbed the bag without breaking stride and followed the stepping stones to the Whaler, careful not to splash mud on his pant legs.

Job one was surviving the trip home and with that accomplished, he motored toward the marina. He'd had no mental progress on finding and eliminating his pursuers. Might inspiration strike over a glass of red and a porterhouse?

Mid-trip, he radioed the marina and was directed to an interior slip where the entrance geometry proved advanced but ultimately solvable. Cale removed cushions to access a bench seat locker and dropped the bag inside, affixed a padlock, then replaced the cushions to recreate a comfortable seat. He set fenders but wouldn't need them. It took several minutes to secure the lines properly because the slip was oversized for the vessel. The harbormaster took Cale's credit card info efficiently, and when Cale departed the harbormaster's office, the digital clock read 7:25 p.m.

As he approached *Framed*, laughter spilled over her flybridge. The calm sound of drips on the dock rippled outward, starting Cale's transformation from predatory animal into social being. He noticed that the captain had joined Joe and Tony in sporting a Tommy Bahama shirt over khakis and boat shoes. The captain's shirt sported vertical rows of a Polynesian hula girl bobblehead doll. The nurses wore summer dresses and various forms of angled heels. Ashley's heels appeared to be four-inch-high bamboo wedges that put her height close enough to Cale's that he semiconsciously improved his posture.

He boarded unnoticed and without invitation, climbed the ladder, and received a warm greeting at the top. The captain poured a drink from a pitcher. Sangria, slightly chilled and full of fruit. Appropriate. Delicious. Cale picked the fruit out with his fingers and ate it. Somehow, Ashley's friends had already severed Cale from the group and had him cornered. Joe and Tony had Ashley to themselves as the captain tidied his bar and appetizers.

"Did you and Ash have fun today?"

"It was great. Ended up a beautiful day, didn't you think?"

"Sure was. She says y'all went to an island that only had golf carts. That sounds fun."

"It was super fun. There are lots of fun islands between South Carolina and the Chesapeake Bay. Just north of here, you have islands with wild horses. To the south, you have the Gullahs. In the Chesapeake, you have two islands where the red-haired, blue-eyed islanders have a British accent. Blackbeard was caught hiding behind islands not too far away. When I was a kid, I knew a German who'd been on a U-boat hiding around these islands. When he told me that, it made the big World War II cannon compounds on Cape Lookout make more sense."

"Umm, OK. Will your friends come back this weekend?"

So historian slash tour guide was not what she was looking for? Misreading a youthful social situation like that had the potential to make you feel out-of-date if you let it. Cale didn't let it. He thought about amusing himself by continuing his island history lessons. He put an over/under on one minute for the shine to dry up in their eyeballs, and he could talk about Fort Sumter alone for five minutes. But, instead, he chose mercy and answered her. "One of them is. He's returning my car."

The one friendly with Blake wanted to ask questions. He recognized the antsy look in her face. Was he the one coming back? Was he really getting married? Cale felt a bit sorry for her. Not as sorry as he felt for Blake's fiancée, ex-wife, or others who'd found themselves in his crosshairs. Somehow, he'd assumed that, with age, Blake would get less rather than more misogynistic or selfish or whatever it was. Blake had a bad combination of charisma and a cloudy moral compass, with his intent and messaging frequently misaligned. Cale found it interesting that he labeled Blake as having a cloudy moral compass when he, himself, would be disappointed if he didn't kill three guys this weekend.

The conversation with the two girls ran the length of Cale's drink. They were young, attractive, and smart. They were unseasoned with judgment, not jaded by life's cycles. Their cynicism levels healthily hovered between no longer excited for the high school pep rally and betting at wedding ceremonies on the marriage's length.

Normally, he'd enjoy the conversation. He appreciated a look into his daughters' peer group, but, in the end, he was also still an animal in its prime. Maybe the backside of prime, but still somewhere within the bounds of prime. Right? He was the alpha lion with two shredded ears sitting on the termite mound in the sunshine, surrounded by lounging lionesses and his progeny tormenting meerkats in the dirt, awaiting the night's hunt. Life was good. But even sleeping, the big cat scanned the horizon and watched for the next young nomad whose papa sent him on his way and told him to find his own pride. Each time an interloper showed up, it was a little harder for the big lion to get off the mound. The desire to service the lionesses had grown less pressing as time marched on. Now it was the desire to keep the progeny going that brought the roar, the teeth, and the claws out.

That was a wonderful analogy, but Cale needed to leave the savannah grasses behind. He was slightly impatient, ready to pick back up with Ashley. He decided to be assertive in dinner's seating arrangements.

He heard Ashley laugh, and it drew his eye. Her neck tilted back, mouth open, she brought a hand to her mouth and covered the informality of her laughter. She was in the present, a beautiful moment. Cale could bear it no longer, excused himself from her friends, and intruded on the other conversation. Quickly, Tony and Joe had him laughing too.

The group walked the half mile to dinner, which, without a shepherd, took the herd of cats nearly thirty minutes. The restaurant was in a small outdoor mall that housed high-end clothing stores, three fine-dining establishments, and one small nightclub. The restaurants and the nightclub had large outdoor patios that overlooked the same central courtyard and oversized koi pond. After a rain like yesterday's, it would not be surprising if a small gator had a new home in the shallows and there were fewer giant koi. The patios bustled with the noise of people and the competing music coming from the various establishments.

Their party sat inside, at a semiprivate table behind a Chinese paper screen. The otherwise modern restaurant used an old-style salad bar beneath an angled glass sneeze guard. Spinach. Lettuce. Cherry tomatoes. Unpeeled cucumber slices. Baby carrots. Diced peppers.

Bacon bits. Croutons. Sunflower seeds. French, thousand island, and creamy Italian in inset buckets. Oil and vinegar in decanters on the bar counter. It was nothing fancy, no modern food trends, but everything was in good form. The word *fusion* was absent from the menu.

Seating worked out, with Ashley sitting beside Cale. It was a good time. Everyone enjoyed side conversations between laughs at Brooklyn stories. Tony and Joe could take their show on the road.

Dinner ended at nine forty-five, when Tony suggested a nightcap at the nightclub next door. Cale's only drink of the night took place on *Framed*. He only counted the sangria, because he really hadn't enjoyed the Scotch from this afternoon. He never drank more than one the night before a charter. The sangria supplanted the previously envisioned cabernet, but the others shared three bottles, all red. Yes, Cale's water with lemon was quite delicious and left him an untarnished palette to enjoy the meat.

At the nightclub, a one-man band played a guitar through a loop pedal. He banged on the side of the guitar to record a drumbeat. He played and recorded rhythm guitar. He was now playing lead guitar. Then he looped in the drum and the rhythm behind it while he took the song where he wanted it to go. His sound was very full. Not for the first time, Cale was amazed at the amount of talent in this country. (This is what people can do when they don't have to spend half their day walking to the well and back.) Every church had a singer who could make you cry. Every town had a running back who could play in the NFL if things went his way. Painting. Pottery. Photography. Writing. Dancing. So much ability it was hard to see why the famous rose to the top. Again he wondered why they were so well compensated when they were so replaceable. Maybe it was like diamonds, and the issue wasn't rarity but who controlled the supply. Surely the Internet would bust the bottleneck at some point.

The three girls took to the small dance area. The guitarist looked pleased, but Cale wondered whether the girls' flame was too bright for a Monday night. Would they prove too intimidating for suitors? Too formidable for competitors? Cale took the guys' orders and bought the first round plus his own standard mocktail of tonic and lime in a highball glass. On the dance floor, Ashley moved half as much and looked twice as good as the other two. She isolated different body parts—hips first, shoulders now, then arms up, hands intertwined. She spun somehow without Cale seeing her move her feet. He kept watching, waiting for her to go back to hips.

Team Tommy Bahama found the Yankees game behind the bar. A public flogging was preferable to watching baseball for Cale. Backing the boast, he headed for the dance floor. The first guy on the floor received a special amount of attention. To the brave was given the world. And to the well-coiffed, intelligent, and successful man leaning on the wall, it should be said that a coward died a thousand deaths.

Cale didn't embarrass himself, thankful once more for his three most valuable college credits. After a few songs, the dynamic moved to where Ashley and Cale were dancing. The guitar man slowed it down with Van Morrison's beach town standard, "Into the Mystic," and Ashley's friends receded.

Cale and Ashley slow danced a modified shag, since neither knew the exact steps. Cale was pretty sure they looked good, for what it mattered, simply because she looked so good (*kind of like how he and his daughters looked at their weddings*, he thought before he could stop himself). The dance provided plenty of opportunity for violating the principal's six inches of separation rule, yet the pair maintained fluidity and a PG rating. There were short windows of close talking, mouth to ear. Cale barely defeated his adolescent desire to have every inch of their fabric and skin pushed together.

The dance changed the evening's tone. As they left the dance floor holding hands, something unspoken transpired. Between Cale and Ashley. Among the entire group. Tony delivered the clean break.

"Hey, Joe. Let's me, youse, and Cap go to the ship and play hearts. Dollar a point."

"Nothing better than found money. Tony, I thought youse knew better than to play when youse was in the cups."

The captain nodded in agreement.

"Good evening, ladies," Joe said. "We cast off at nine. If you miss us, rent a car and find us in Virginia Beach tomorrow night. Cale, I have your card. I'll give you a call for visiting or transporting some grandkids this fall. Good night."

Cale thanked Joe again for dinner. There was a round of handshakes and hugs as the men exited. Ashley and Cale sat outside, and her friends returned to the dance floor. Then her friends were saying good-night. Time slipped by. The entertainer packed up. It was an exciting ride. Infatuation? Check. Lust? Definitely. Love? No. But possible.

Cale couldn't remember thinking that was a possibility in this decade. This was sort of his and Ashley's third date, and he couldn't remember a third date since Maggie where he didn't already know it was a temporary assignment. Temporary assignments were fine as long as both parties were on the same page, which was rare in his experience, regardless of how much it was discussed.

Cale noticed he was spinning his wedding ring. Perhaps he hadn't given the others a true chance. He conversed silently, *Mags, are you OK with this if it goes somewhere? It has been a long trek in the emotional wilderness.*

It was near midnight, and Cale needed to be at the FBO by seven to perform the extra poststorm checks. He didn't want the night to end, but for him to do his job, it had to. His brain couldn't navigate the logistical obstacles needed to take this further tonight anyway. *Why the hotel room? You already had a packed bag? Did you think I was in the bag?* He could navigate those shoals without mentioning the throat slitters who were, he assumed, watching *Simpsons* reruns at his house. *Why is that pistol strapped to your leg?* That was a trickier reef. One truism in boating: Sandy shoals forgive more than coral reefs.

Of course, even if he read the chart correctly and ran the gauntlet, he needed to be fair to his passengers and get five hours of sleep. Nobody chartered a plane to have a grumpy, sleepy pilot. The sales brochure promised a confident, tanned man with a smile and a kind, calming demeanor.

The next thought escaped Cale's mouth before he was aware of it. This is what people meant when they said "thinking out loud" but meant "talking out loud."

"Would you like to come on my charter with me? I can sign you on as a pilot in training."

"What about my stuff?"

Positive momentum. "Bring it. I'm staying in a hotel nearby tonight. It's tough to get cabs at my house."

See, he knew he'd think of something for that one. Maybe he could have overcome the pistol thing too. But not the sleep. Remember the sleep.

"I'll have the cab pick you up off *Framed* around six forty-five."

He could see she was somewhat surprised he'd given up on tonight. *Trust me, love, it was not age or desire. Or ability. Don't give that seed of doubt a chance to germinate.*

"Don't you pilots call that 'oh six hundred something something?'"

"Not when talking to civilians." A small jest.

"Will I get back to Charleston for work in time?"

"If you want." A borderline cocky jest. "My charter ends Friday, then I'll fly you home."

They figured out the logistics during the walk back to *Framed*. Cale received a good-night kiss. Very sweet. It put more sorrow in the parting but more excitement in thinking about what was coming.

With Ashley back aboard *Framed*, Cale quickly retrieved his bag from the Whaler, found a cab, and checked into the hotel. As he lay down, the bedside clock read one thirty in the morning.

››› 31

DESPITE THE COOL shower, Francisco's forehead beaded with sweat as he dressed. The hard morning workout had cleared his mind.

Francisco decided to vacate the hotel this morning. If they failed today—he would not fail today—he would pay for Mr. Coleman's removal. Torturing him would yield twenty-year-old information. Given the opportunity, he would enjoy the process of extracting that information. But there were enough ghosts to chase. And now, today, he didn't think he'd have the opportunity. His best outcome was reduced to a kill that wouldn't alert the authorities. Being there personally enhanced his mythology but was not essential. He did yearn for the rush of excitement of vengeance extracted, the intoxication of vindicating a brother's death, a proxy kill to represent all the *norteamericano* soldiers who coordinated the hunt and murder of El Capo. This kill would be personally satisfying, given the past, but was mostly a bedside note left for his future pursuers that their success might mean their demise.

Last night had ended in frustration for Francisco. They returned to Coleman's house and cut the power before entering, but the alarm had a backup. *Woof-woof-woof.* They rapidly searched the small house. With spotlight-mounted guns and night-vision goggles, they moved quickly through the rooms. He was not home, and his boat was gone too. When they left the house, they waited out the responding officers' sirens deep in the driveway of the lot where no house was ever built.

Returning to the hotel, he'd had a drink with his men at the bar. They switched to speaking Spanish to convey sharper nuances to their thoughts and ideas. Sleep was fitful as Francisco's subconscious tried to find solutions to his problems in his dreams. He eventually relented and started his workout early.

While dressing, Francisco reviewed his plan for Mr. Coleman's death at the airport. Board the chartered plane first. He was confident Coleman would not recognize him, would be ignorant of the danger. While the four men were alone in the cabin, the Cuban would slip a wire over Coleman's head, strangle him before the plane powered up. Francisco had heard the Cuban was legendary with such work in close quarters, and he looked forward to seeing it. After ending Coleman's life, they would stuff him in his own plane's locker closet, deplane, cross the tarmac, board the Gulfstream, and take off for Savannah. If things went poorly, they'd take off for Bogotá. If they went really badly, Caracas. Even with Chávez dead, America had no influence there. If needed, twenty minutes after takeoff they could be over international waters. This was not the type of crime where the United States would scramble fighter jets to retrieve or destroy the perpetrators.

He met Alberto and the Cuban in the hotel's restaurant. A bowl of fruit and a mug of coffee waited in front of his empty seat. Each man's travel bag was at his feet. They were properly prepared.

Francisco asked, "Anything to discuss before going to the airport?"

Alberto looked at the Cuban, who turned away, distancing himself from what Alberto was about to say. Undaunted, Alberto continued, "Mr. Escobar, look at these photographs I took from the house last night."

Alberto handed over several pictures. A tall man with a wife and two young daughters at a sporting event. The tall man in a semicircle with friends, all holding large fish. The tall man and the grown daughters at a wedding. The tall man on the beach, shirtless, holding a baby under each arm, his grown daughters beside him and their husbands beside them.

"Yes, Alberto, this is Mr. Coleman. We had a picture of his face before we came. What do you want me to know?"

"Mr. Escobar, this *hombre es muy grande*. I think we should use guns."

Francisco felt a flush of anger color his cheeks. He glanced about to make certain no one overheard and felt safely out of earshot. Alberto looked at him pensively and expectantly. The Cuban had coldly angled his body away from the conversation to keep the stain of cowardice off of himself.

Francisco let the idea rattle. Alberto had served him well, if for far too long. He was mad at himself for not preparing his younger men for this opportunity. Alberto should be enjoying guarding an empty villa at this point in his life.

Francisco disdained the idea of putting a bullet into Coleman's head from a distance. It was frustrating enough that they would not have time to drag out his death with nicks and slices, and small threats about his children's futures. Mind games mixed with physical pain— that was what vengeance looked like. Whether the plea was spoken or unspoken, he especially relished the look of recognition in the eyes when death was certain, and a speedy death was all that could be prayed for. Radcliffe had given him this, and he had forgotten how intoxicating it was.

Maybe a gut shot if they had to. Yes, maybe the gut.

"Let us each put on our silencers. We will attempt, as discussed, with the wire first. But, Alberto, you will have your firearm drawn to help quickly if necessary."

The men nodded agreement. They finished breakfast and left for the ten-minute drive to the municipal airport at eight-fifty—an hour before flight time, in case their plans needed to be adjusted.

»» 32

DUNT-DA-DA-DUNT, DA-DUNT-DA-DA-DUNT, DA-DUNT *da-da-dunt dun dun da*. Cale turned his phone's alarm off mid reveille. If he dreamed last night, he didn't recall.

He slipped out of bed, showered, brushed his teeth, and got dressed. He wore a tucked-in golf shirt and a baseball cap, both with his company's logo, with sunglasses hanging from Croakies around his neck and his bag hanging off one shoulder. He took the stairs down, because the elevator was too slow for just two flights. Then he stopped at the continental breakfast, ate yogurt, drank orange juice, and decided to grab coffee at the FBO.

Stepping outside and into the cab, he felt anxious giving instructions for two stops—the marina first, then the municipal airport. Would she have changed her mind? The cabbie questioned his airport choice. Yes, he did mean the municipal airport. He should have thanked the cabbie for his diligence instead of being annoyed at the question. Cale took off his wedding ring, unzipped his bag, found an unused pocket in his Dopp kit, secured the ring inside with a Velcro strip, rezipped the bag, stared at the pale strip on his finger, and involuntarily took a deep breath.

Ashley stood in the parking lot with Joe. Joe had a newspaper tucked under the arm in which he held his coffee cup and was waving his free arm as he spoke. She wore the dress from Saturday night, and Cale still very much approved. At the cab's approach, Joe and Ashley gave each other a long hug good-bye. They held a close conversation. Cale envisioned Joe's parting words being something along the lines of Bogart telling Bacall "Give 'em hell, kid." As they separated, Joe waved at Cale and turned the motion into a thumbs-up. Cale almost shook back a two-handed hang loose before he went conventional and returned the thumbs-up.

One anxiety left Cale as Ashley slid in the back of the cab.

"Good morning." A quick greeting kiss before he could stop smiling.

Very nice. A flush of warm emotions. Cale worried he might be too distracted to fly safely.

Fifteen minutes later, the cab arrived at the chain-link fence separating the runway from the parking lot. The cabbie stopped, and Cale paid. They got out, walked to the fence, pressed the buzzer, and were buzzed in.

Cale indulged his hobby and scoped out the nearby aircraft. A Gulfstream V with its distinctive windows reflected the rising sun—a beautiful plane. It looked new. Most of the other planes were single-engine props, or what in professional pilot parlance were called *doctor killers*. A few twin-engine turbo props like Cale's King Air were visible. Two jets besides the Gulfstream were parked on the tarmac. One was a small Brazilian Embraer: four-seater, fully pressurized, a great jet for short runways with steep climbs. Think Eagle-Vail. St. Barts was too short for takeoff, although the landing would be fine. The other jet was a faster, more fuel-efficient four-seat HondaJet. Its unique engine configuration—with the engine over instead of under the wing—might change the industry. The HondaJets were made in North Carolina, which seemed fair if John Deeres were made in Japan.

The small general aviation terminal was empty except for the shift manager who buzzed them in. They walked through the terminal and headed across the tarmac toward Cale's craft to drop their bags. When Ashley remarked on it, Cale explained that general aviation terminals outside of major cities (and Lincoln, Nebraska, on fall Saturdays) rarely had more than a handful of people in them at any one time.

Ashley looked puzzled. "Hey, Cale. Where are the security checks?"

"There aren't any. Saving hassle is what you're paying for."

They locked eyes. She was processing but didn't quite get it yet.

"Ashley, you're going to love this so much it's going to ruin your life!"

"But people could bring guns or drugs or llamas—whatever they want—on their trip."

"Yes."

Sometimes the simplest answers said it best. Cale loved witnessing the understanding that came into her mind that there were still some freedoms left.

He was spoiled. He only found himself in commercial aircraft terminals when doing Caribbean island hops, where most airports were too small to separate general and commercial aviation entrances. Of course, even while working and going through metal detectors, it was hard to complain in the Caribbean. Inside the United States, the quality-of-life differences in air travel between general, meaning private, and commercial aviation were gargantuan. The price difference was pretty gargantuan too, but you picked your luxuries: Do you want a five-thousand-square-foot house, a new Mercedes, and to fly commercial? Or a twenty-five-hundred-square-foot house, a thirty-year-old Toyota, and to fly private? He knew what he'd choose—or, in this case, chose.

They dropped their bags behind the back-row seat in the plane's elevated storage compartment, leaving the large lower part of the closet with the hanging rack empty for the clients. There were three men booked on this charter, and they indicated this was a business trip, so Cale wasn't worried about fitting in golf bags. The plane sat six in the cabin, plus two in the cockpit. There was plenty of room for three passengers, the newest crew member, Cale, and everybody's luggage (and there was no fee for a bag over fifty pounds).

They went back into the general aviation terminal to pick up drinks and snacks for the flight. The charter clients requested only sodas, waters, peanuts, pretzels, and M&Ms. The plane's wet bar was always stocked. The hospitality group would have the provisions box assembled, along with bags of ice ready to load in the built-in cooler.

As they reentered the terminal and headed to the hospitality pick-up in back, the crew from the Gulfstream stood at the coffee bar. The stewardess was assembled in a beauty factory. Now, it was sexist to assume she was the stewardess, but Cale let this small personal imperfection—his, not hers—pass without feeling guilty. The crew spoke Spanish and was joking about the quality of the complimentary coffee.

Cale's phone vibrated in his jeans pocket. He glanced at his watch. A quarter after seven was a little early for a social call and a little late to cancel a charter. He pulled the phone out. It was a 703 area code but not the number he'd seen before. He guessed who it was and gave Ashley the universal "one minute" sign with his finger and walked ninety degrees away from her to answer.

"This is Cale." Four hours and forty-five minutes of sleep and as chipper as ever. He was a professional.

"Cale, it's Sheila."

"Are you FedExing my old Kevlar vest?"

"Hey, jackass, I'm working on this for you!"

It was meant as a joke but getting yelled at raised his temperature.

"Based on the new disposable number, I'm thinking none too successfully!"

The outburst done, he cooled. Sheila had the ability and desire to help. She might be risking her career with this call.

"Sorry, Sheila. I had my mind on a job. Your call brought me back to reality."

Actually, his mind was on Ashley, which was a very pleasant mental vacation from what might be a very unpleasant and imminent future. He was *about* to get his mind on his job. But he figured the apology itself was the important part, not the facts of the backstory. Was this ethically equivocating or just conversationally efficient?

She sighed. "Understood. You must be afraid and under a lot of stress."

She felt bad that her former subordinate was dangling on a line without a hook. She should feel bad, but only in a misplaced maternal way, because it wasn't her fault. It was the machine's. As high as she was, she wasn't high enough to call a press conference to discuss the Escobars that wouldn't get her labeled as crazy within a half hour if the rest of the machine didn't want the Escobars discussed.

But she was wrong about how he felt. The mandatory post-work-related-death psychiatrists and psychologists never got it either: It was indecision that troubled him. Once he knew Big Brother wasn't stepping in and he understood the dynamics of the situation, the decisions were made, and that's when fear left. The stress of the situation was stowed in a footlocker he'd unlock and deal with on Saturday, just like dragging the lawnmower out of the shed on a normal August weekend.

Without Big Brother, he'd created his own marching orders. Priority one: Eliminate the three Colombians. Priority two: Do it in a manner that would keep him from going to jail. Priority three: Do it without anybody knowing he did it. Best to not have four avenging the three who were here avenging the two. He needed to make sure whatever transpired didn't go in a report preformatted for HTML.

But he needed to fill in the *how*. *How* started with Cale finding the Escobars on his terms.

At this point, as usually occurred, he received help. Sheila informed him, "We know where your friends are staying."

Again the *we* instead of an *I* in government conversations—more

Trotsky *we* than royal *we*. And this was a good employee, not a go back and fill this form out in triplicate employee.

"How did you put that together?"

"We started by finding the rental car from your description of the make, model, and color."

Impressed, he asked, "You have that kind of information electronically?"

"Yes and no. If everybody was onboard, yes. But in this case, no. I sent human assets with badges to the local rental places. We came up with a dozen options. We then searched local hotels. Found about half our options, staked those out, and one of those turned out to be your three friends."

Good old boring gumshoe work, sitting in a car waiting with a newspaper on your lap. You couldn't pay Cale enough to do it, but he was glad others were willing. That Sheila organized this caused a lump of emotion to catch in his throat. She had used her autonomy for cross-purposes from the folks diagonally above her. There was career jeopardy in taking those actions. He felt worse about all his smart comments now and, at the same time, thought the disposable phone might be a bit pointless if fifteen agents had done legwork, but you never knew what broke the trail or created plausible deniability. It was probably not enough to save her job but maybe enough to keep her from being prosecuted.

She named the hotel where the Escobar men were staying. He was familiar with it. In fact, he'd left it just an hour before.

He asked, "Have you been able to figure out their schedule?"

"No. They were scheduled to check out Monday but rescheduled to check out today."

That made sense. He had foiled their diabolical plan Sunday night, so they extended a day. Squeezing a bit of flesh between his thumb and index finger, he confirmed they didn't achieve success Monday night either. He hoped they were patient and extended their rooms through the weekend. Guys, if you waited twenty years in the jungle, what was an extra few days at the beach?

"Sheila. Thanks for the info. I know what you're jeopardizing." Then he hated to ask, so he told her, "I hate to ask, but I'm leaving on a charter in a couple hours. Return Friday. Can you let me know their location Friday?"

"No promises. But yeah, I'll try. Have a safe trip. I'm still pushing on the other fronts."

"I know. Thanks again for what you're doing."

Ashley procured the hospitality box while he was on the phone. When he rejoined her, she didn't pry about the call. They retrieved the ice together and carried everything to the plane.

The King Air's cabin was pretty self-explanatory, and she took the lead stocking provisions. Cale began his visual examination of the plane's exterior. The metal rivets looked good, tires good, flaps good, and props good. He grabbed an A-frame ladder and set it up in several spots around the plane, looked for anything amiss topside, but found it all shipshape.

He ascended the steps into the cabin. The low ceiling height made him bend forward at the waist, which was less painful than bending at the knees. He squeezed past Ashley, who was doing her work on young knees, and he found the plane egregiously too wide for maximum incidental physical contact. He stepped into the cockpit and tested the instrumentation. Radio good. Flaps good. Rudder good. He continued his extended preflight check routine and found nothing the worse for wear from the wind and rain.

"Ashley, you want to check out your seat?"

"Sure." She came forward with one of his logoed ball caps on her head. Part of the crew. She was in character. Discovering another fun side to her personality so early in their courtship was a bit titillating. Down boy.

She slid past him, choosing to have her perfectly shaped bottom face him before stepping into her seat well. She settled in and figured out how to buckle up. He then gave her the instrumentations' CliffsNotes.

Mid-tutorial, she asked, "Why do so many small planes crash in the water like JFK Jr.'s?"

It was a non sequitur unless you remembered this was probably her first flight on a small plane. Cale answered, "I don't know what happened to him, but the main reason is because when you're flying, the ocean and sky look a lot alike. If someone is flying by sight rather than by instruments and is not checking their altitude, they sometimes just cruise down into the ocean, for no reason other than they think they're going level. They won't even try to jerk up the controls. Amazingly, if someone was fifty feet off the water and just hit their autopilot, it would raise them up. Truthfully, if they were upside down, the autopilot would right them."

"So do you have autopilot?"

"Yes, on this plane. Not on the helicopters I flew." He pointed to the button. "If I have a heart attack, press this button."

She nodded.

"We have about an hour before departure. I'm done with all my checks. What do you want to do?"

"Can we check out the other planes?"

Good girl. How did she know he wanted to check out the three jets?

They walked to each jet in turn. They circled, then lingered outside the big boy with the oval windows. They started to giggle as they'd made their circling conversation unnecessarily loud, hoping the Gulfstream's crew would notice their interest and invite them inside for a tour. But the crew proved unwilling to notice them—which was really hard to believe, because everybody noticed Ashley. Perhaps that beautiful stewardess demanded absolute fealty from her coworkers. Also, every time-killing pilot wanted a tour, so they'd probably learned not to notice.

Ashley asked questions about the jets and prop planes. She talked about her grandfather, who served on a carrier and always labeled the jets buzzing San Diego for her. At nine thirty, Cale told her they should use the facilities. Never looked good to a new charter customer if the pilot got up and took a whiz midflight. And the pee tube wasn't a favorite of most lady passengers (or crew).

Ashley said, "If *our* clients show up before you're done, I'll show them to the plane."

He grunted his appreciation, thinking it sounded like she thought he was going to be in there longer than to just take a whiz.

BEFORE REACHING THE bathroom, Cale's phone vibrated. Same 703 number as earlier this morning.

"Calling with good news?"

"I'll deliver it. You judge whether it's good or not. Your friends checked out this morning."

"Are they being tailed?"

"Sorry, we didn't have the resources."

"Did you attach a birddog tracker to monitor via the computer?"

Sheila paused, and Cale remembered she did that when delivering news she didn't want to deliver, supported by a reason she didn't agree with. "No. That would be against the law. That would be criminal harassment of a minority group that has, to our official knowledge, not committed a crime."

How could she deliver that line with a straight face? Of course, he couldn't see her face, so maybe she was wincing with a crooked smile and one closed eye when she said it. Next time, they'd talk on a video feed.

Also, that logic hadn't exactly stopped the DEA on any assignment before. You might notice ninety percent of individuals arrested for drugs were black or Hispanic. And to be factual, if Escobar wasn't speaking, you'd have thought he was another white guy with a nice tan. But this wasn't really a DEA assignment, and everyone knew Escobar spoke Spanish. But Sheila could face country club prison if she was discovered and prosecuted, so he understood her reluctance.

"I don't suppose you figure they just wanted to make me think a bit about my past sins and have now gone home?"

"Your guess is as good as mine, but I don't think that is what either of us guesses."

"True. Anything else?"

"They haven't returned their rental yet. We put an asset there once we knew they checked out."

"OK. Thanks again, Sheila."

"No problem. If we can get them on any infraction to keep them from leaving the area, we'll do it. I'll call you Friday afternoon with an update."

"Thanks." To lighten the mood, he added, "Maybe trick me with a phone with a different area code next time."

They finished the conversation. Cale walked into the bathroom more pleased with his behavior and less pleased with his predicament.

›››

BEFORE ENTERING THE small airport, Francisco spoke to his jet's crew. He told them to stay on the plane and prepare for departure; he had a quick meeting to inspect a King Air he was considering purchasing. He expected the jet to depart within two minutes of his boarding. The ability and desire to follow precise instructions without question was something Francisco had prized above all else when he'd interviewed for these crew positions.

The three men walked into the FBO. Alberto wore a sport coat over slacks, the Cuban wore a tight polo shirt tucked into tight pants, covered with a tight-fitting sports coat, and Francisco wore a long-sleeved linen shirt over linen pants that were tailored to his frame.

Francisco had been unable to find a new guayabera in his American shopping excursions but was enjoying the new linen shirt except for the wrinkles. A tall, tanned American Athena wearing a dress and a baseball cap stood in the lobby with a smile, waiting for someone. Her long legs caught Francisco's attention before he turned his back to her and talked with the Cuban in hushed tones. Alberto motioned that he was going to the restroom.

〉〉〉

CALE DID HIS business. Both legs fell asleep, and he realized he must still be a bit dehydrated from the bachelor party. He read the sports section left in the tray on the back of the stall door. Freaking baseball. He had to keep up hope. Football started soon. He washed his hands and used the folded paper towels out of the tray on the counter to dry them.

FBO bathrooms were full-service and usually spotless. This one was no exception. It was high quality and low traffic. There were shower stalls with big wooden, louvered doors; oversized fluffy towels; and often a steam room. They catered to a high-end clientele. Actually, they catered to the highest-end clientele.

Cale gurgled and spit mouthwash, dispensed sunscreen from the pump jug on the counter, and lubed up his face and ears. He usually forgot the ears. He examined himself in the mirror to make certain no white globs remained. Satisfied, he washed his hands to get the oily lotion off and dried them again. If he'd thought to put the lotion on before using the bathroom, he could have saved a hand washing and the world a paper towel. This probably wouldn't be his biggest mistake of the day.

〉〉〉

AS THE THIRD man disappeared around the corner, Ashley approached the two men standing in the middle of the room. They had their backs to her, facing north out the floor-to-ceiling windows at the tarmac's loading area. The young man pointed at something outside. It raised the back hem of his jacket, and she glimpsed the black metal in the small of his back. Her brain registered this as a pistol. She stopped her approach.

Why did he have a gun? Was he the other man's bodyguard? The customers who can afford private air travel might need—or at least be able to afford—bodyguards. She would tell Cale about it before they took off, in case he had an issue with it.

She gathered herself and finished her approach. "Mr. Garcia?" she said to their backs.

>>>

FRANCISCO AND THE Cuban turned, responding to the proximity of the comment, not the use of the pseudonym, which didn't register when coming from an unexpected source. Francisco's eyes scanned up to the ball cap on her head. He recognized the logo.

"Oh, yes. Are you our pilot for today? I thought I saw a man's name as our pilot on the paperwork. A Mr. Coleman, I believe."

"My name is Ashley Walker, and I am only your copilot today," the woman responded, with a small stage curtsy. "Truthfully, I'm in the early stages of training, so I will be mostly observing. You are correct: Mr. Coleman will be our pilot today. He is very experienced. He has been a professional pilot for twenty-five years, so we are all in good hands."

"Wonderful. Is our plane ready?"

"Yes. If you're ready, I will take you out and return for your friend. Do you have any luggage other than these small bags?"

"No, this is all we will bring, and yes, we are ready to board the plane."

>>>

CALE STARTED TO leave, and as he reached for the door, it opened inward. He stepped back slightly, startled because the older man entering was slightly startled too. Cale said, "Excuse me."

The older man responded with an accented "Pardon."

They looked in each other's faces. The older man recognized Cale. Cale recognized him without knowing his name. He was the largest of the three men who'd visited his house. The older man recognized Cale's recognition of him. Cale had never been good at cards.

The older man reached behind his back. Cale lunged for the man's throat and both hands grabbed it. His thumbs dug into the Adam's apple. The older man tried to peel the hands off his throat. A SEAL would have possessed the mental toughness to ignore the choking, grab the gun, and shoot Cale. But this was a goon past his expiration date, and Cale wondered how he got so lucky. The older man pulled at Cale's hands. He swung his knee toward Cale's balls. Cale angled his hips in the way. The kneeing didn't feel good, but it didn't crumple him.

He pushed the older man against the closed door. He was worried the man would start banging the door and wall to get attention, but he was too focused on the oxygen restriction. Cale never appreciated all that survival training. It always seemed so intuitive. Watching these mistakes, he appreciated it now. It was kind of how Fort Benning had to teach soldiers to return fire. You wouldn't think that people would need to be taught to shoot back at people who were shooting at them, but apparently they did.

Cale's thumbnails punctured the skin of the man's neck; a trickle of blood dripped down under the man's collar. Cale didn't want to create a hole to his trachea that might keep him functioning longer but still kept squeezing as hard as he could. The wingspan difference between the men was enough that the older man's hands couldn't reach Cale's face, so the frantic clawing was contained to the back of Cale's hands and triceps, where blood was beginning to drip. The protests were frenzied as the man fought for oxygen. Then he weakened, but before he passed out, Cale released his throat. The man slouched forward drunkenly into Cale's arm and gasped for air. Cale wrapped his arms in counter directions around the man's head. There was no resistance. A quick twist, with a pivot of the hips, and the neck snapped.

The body went limp, Cale wrapped his arm around the waist, leaned slightly backward, and took on the body's weight while keeping the dead man's lower body still pushed against the door. Cale searched with his free hand, found the thumb latch, and locked the door. He reached into the man's back pocket and removed his wallet. Nice to meet you, Alberto. He laid the body down and took a good look at him. Mid-sixties, he guessed. Strong frame gone soft. Slight nicotine discoloration of the mustache, the same discoloration on the left hand's middle and index fingers.

When he frisked the corpse, he found—as he'd suspected—a gun in the small of the back. Wouldn't that have been a pisser if he was reaching for a handkerchief? He left the gun alone. Alberto's passport was in his front shirt pocket, a cell phone in his front pants pocket. Cale took all identification from the wallet, the man's passport, and his cell phone and put them in his own pockets, then slipped the wallet back into Alberto's.

Bending at the knees, he picked Alberto up and carried him to a stall. Dead people were amazingly heavy, especially their floppy heads. Cale propped him inside on the commode, locked the stall door, and scaled over it. He scrolled through the cell phone. There were group text messages in Spanish to two numbers. Those were the only numbers used in the phone. They were both 919 area codes, for phones obviously bought recently. Cale's conversational Spanish was sufficient if someone was speaking to him, but if he was watching two Spanish speakers talk to each other, he was lost. He could comprehend written Spanish even better, because he had more time to figure it out before the next set of words needed comprehending. His written Spanish, however, *no es muy bueno*. But he wanted an advantage. So he gave it a shot. Texting language wasn't particularly proper anyway, between the phone's autocorrect function, typing shortcuts, and fat fingering.

He group texted the two numbers. "*En el baño—diez y seis minutos.*" He wanted to say fifteen minutes, but couldn't remember if the word for fifteen started with a "c" or a "q."

〉〉〉

AS THE TWO men followed Ashley out of the lobby, a text pinged in both men's pockets. The men stopped and looked at the news. They discussed it in frustrated tones.

She wondered how she'd lived near Mexico her entire life and only had an elementary understanding of Spanish. She did understand when the young man said, laughing, "*¡Dios mío, el viejo necesita diez y seis minutos!*"

She waited while Mr. Garcia typed in his reply.

〉〉〉

ONE OF THE numbers texted back. "*Hay un copiloto. Estamos en el avión.*"

Cale texted back, "*Claro.*"

For the first time, he regretted the decision to bring Ashley. Was it hubris to think he wouldn't put her in harm's way? Maybe this would be a story to share and laugh about years later, in the old folks' home. *Remember the first time you went flying with me, got taken hostage, and I killed those three guys? What a hoot!*

It probably wouldn't go that way. She wouldn't be ready for the old folks' home until Cale was long dead. He hoped she wasn't a hostage, but just part of the scenery. This reminded him again that hope was not a strategy. He'd find an excuse to get her out of the plane before the violence started.

He popped Alberto's phone open, took out the memory card, washed the phone in the sink, dropped it into the trash, and covered it with paper towels. The memory card, he flushed down the toilet. Cale removed the Beretta from his ankle and slipped it in his back pocket to make it easier to reach. He untucked his shirt and covered the handle sticking out of the pocket. Not a very professional look, but he was no longer interested in having this client as a repeat customer, and he doubted they'd post a review to his website. *A trip booked for three guys? He should have figured this out sooner. Nice work, detective.*

Was it time to get the authorities? And charge what? No, there was no charge sufficient to hold them—maybe enough to hold Cale, though. He had significantly upped the stakes. The Escobars' pride gave them no choice but to finish Cale off, while they'd given Cale no good choice but to finish them. If they left, they'd come back at a time and in a manner of their choosing. But if he went the authorities route, it was safer for Ashley.

He decided he'd see whether he could get her out of the plane first, before there was any confrontation. If he could get her out, he'd finish this. If he couldn't, he'd bring in the police—at least, that is what he told himself.

Taking paper towels, Cale dabbed the blood off. Thankfully, his navy blue shirt and blue jeans hid stains well. His sunglasses hanging on their Croakies and ball cap somehow never got displaced in the tussle. Cale unlocked the bathroom and started the walk toward the plane. He scanned the FBO terminal for people; there was still only the shift manager behind the desk, staring at a computer screen.

>>>

THE THREE WALKED outside in the sunshine. Enjoying her role as concierge, Ashley made small talk.

"Did you have any trouble with the hurricane?"

"No. Only we did not get to work on our suntans as much as we had hoped."

As they walked, she pointed out the different types of prop planes and mentioned interesting trivia about them. She waved at the jets and regurgitated the information she'd digested this morning from her tour with Cale. Standing in front of the twin-engine turbo prop, she explained the King Air's features, it's flying altitude parameters, the speed range, the odds of turbulence in the wake of the hurricane, the deviations from the direct route that air traffic control would assign them.

〉〉〉

CALE SAW ASHLEY standing on the tarmac speaking with their passengers. He gathered she was in copilot character, pointing out physical characteristics of the plane and contrasting those with neighboring planes. These were things she'd heard just once from him. She was a quick study.

As he neared shouting distance, she motioned everyone inside. Cale waved but she didn't see him. He cupped his hands into a megaphone and called to her, but a rumbling engine drowned his voice out, and she followed her clients into the aircraft. As he drew near the plane, Cale repeatedly and fruitlessly tried to beckon her out.

〉〉〉

FRANCISCO WAS ONLY half listening to the information the pretty copilot was providing. He smiled, thinking how jealous Estella would be if he brought this one aboard his plane. But it was not to be, and it was a shame that one so beautiful would have to die, but he saw no choice.

Francisco scanned the tarmac before boarding the plane, looking for Mr. Coleman. He saw the man starting the two hundred yard walk across the tarmac to the plane. It would not be long now. He wondered where Alberto was. He nudged the Cuban, who turned and saw Coleman in the distance.

>>>

INSIDE THE CABIN, Ashley asked, "Can I fix you a drink? Leaded or unleaded?"

She winked with her sales pitch. It was a habit that her patients seemed to love. She originally picked it up waitressing, where it kept her average tips over 25 percent.

Both men declined the drink, so she showed where the refreshments were stored, pointed out the pee tube in back with a modest giggle. With the men settled in their seats, she stepped past them into the cockpit and slid over and down into shotgun position.

A minute later, she watched Cale moving across the tarmac and involuntarily wondered, if he really needed that much time in the bathroom, what day-to-day life with him would be like on this trip. Despite his exterior form, had his interior become *viejo*? She giggled like a girl with a crush, which felt good, and realized he was covering the distance very quickly, without looking like it took him any effort. His face appeared stern, and she wondered why he had let his shirt come untucked right before meeting his clients. Then she lost sight of him as he got too close to the plane to see out the cockpit window.

»»» 34

THE KING AIR'S steps were located on the copilot side of the plane. (Cale was always tempted to say *starboard*, but that was just for boats.) The pilot—and in this case, the copilot—entered the cabin and then turned right, passed the front-row seats that faced the back of the plane, and stepped through into the cockpit. It was not an easy step to navigate and a hard location from which to get quickly in or out. If there was a run on parachutes (if the plane actually contained parachutes), the passengers would have a distinct advantage. Given the narrowness between the pilot and the copilot seats, the console between the seats, the fact that you didn't want to kick any expensive instruments on the dash, and the low ceiling height, it took effort getting in and out.

Cale tried to look into the cockpit to see if he could make eye contact with Ashley, but the reflection of the sun off the glass kept him from seeing inside. He walked faster until he drew abreast of the plane, paused to look around, and stepped in. The two passengers sat talking softly with each other in Spanish. Ashley wasn't visible.

"Ashley?"

"Yes, sir?" She responded. From the sound, he figured she must have been seated in the cockpit.

The "sir" was a nice touch. Excellent role-playing—he hoped they could revisit that later. Although, given the age difference, maybe "sir" wasn't exactly the role he wanted to play.

At the top of the three steps, Cale poked his upper half inside the plane and asked, "Can you come out and help me with something?"

"Sure, just give me a minute to unstrap."

Escobar and the young hit man turned toward Cale in greeting. Cale went into captain mode and provided a confident smile. The two men sat in the front seats, Escobar on the far side of the cabin with his hands resting innocently on his knees. The smaller, more dangerous man on the door side had his hands pushed together in his lap, knuckles up, possibly hiding something in his palms. They were between Ashley and Cale. Escobar half stood, reached in front of the other man, and extended a hand. Always the boss.

He said in accented English, "Forgive our third traveler, Captain, as he is delayed. I believe the saying is, 'He is answering the nature's call.'"

Under other circumstances, the near miss on the colloquialism would be endearing, Cale thought as he hunched over and took the proffered hand. Escobar placed his left hand warmly on top of Cale's right in the manner politicians used to express connection and to secure votes from barbecue-eating constituents. Cale's ears registered the sound of Ashley's buckle clicking open. As they clasped hands, Escobar made strong eye contact, which Cale did his best to return without menace. Before they had released hands, Cale started backing out of the plane to create space for Ashley to walk through.

Escobar pulled his hands back and felt and then saw the blood on them. He looked at Cale's arms and saw the clawing on the triceps, which had begun to ooze anew.

Escobar shouted, "*Mátenlo ya.*"

Cale recognized the command before its intended recipient did. His left foot was wedged against the side of the plane in the doorway, his right foot on the top step. He transferred his weight instantly to his left foot and pushed off, lunging toward the hit man. The Cuban, delayed by his reaction time to the command, likewise moved forward, spreading something between his hands, with his face up and soulless eyes.

Cale closed the space quicker than the Cuban expected and led with the top of his head, which was also unexpected. It caught the Cuban in the nose, and his head snapped back. Cale drove through him, wrapping his arms around the man's back. The Cuban's head rocked backward between his shoulder blades as he hit the wall forehead first, then nose, then chin, then chest as Cale tried to drive the body through the bulkhead. When the Cuban's neck bent backward at an angle that didn't support life, Cale knew he would cause no more trouble and released him.

He pushed off the Cuban and scrambled back into a crouch. His mind registered that Ashley had stood up and was leaning forward between the pilot and copilot seats. Without pause, he lunged for Escobar but lacked the force or leverage he'd had with the Cuban. Escobar moved away from his seat, toward the seat that faced forward. Cale got a hand on his shirt. As he jerked it down, the buttons popped off, and Cale's knees landed on the cabin carpet. His right elbow dented Escobar's former seat, and his left arm held the tail of the buttonless shirt. This was too vulnerable a position, but, at least for the moment, he was between Escobar and Ashley.

Cale released the shirt and pulled his arm back. Escobar's right hand swept toward Cale's back as Cale rotated away. Cale hadn't realized that Escobar held a knife until it nicked his shoulder. Escobar overextended on the swing, but Cale's weight was all wrong, and he couldn't counter the attack. It was all he could do to get on his feet. But he did know now that Escobar was not good with a knife. Then again, how good did you have to be?

Both men reset their ready positions and stood crouched forward on the balls of their feet with their heels off the ground. Escobar swayed, the knife in front of his body, the blade pointed up. The distance separating the men was too small for either to reach for their guns, and there was no space for them to circle each other in the narrow cabin aisle. They each made small feints and shifts of weight. Cale did quick stutter steps and half-arm pumps, trying to get Escobar to make a mistake.

The speed of Cale's feints put Escobar slightly off balance, despite his advantage of holding the knife. Cale adjusted positions to get his left leg in front of his right, his natural attack position. The knife was in Escobar's right hand. Cale could likely swat it with his left hand without stepping but chose to wait for Escobar to swing the knife wide of his body.

Reacting to a feint, Escobar attacked, his hand drifting wide, and Cale shot in on him, visualizing his high school wrestling coach's proud eyes. He drove off his right foot. His right knee dropped to the ground first, his left leg bent in front. His right arm swung up into Escobar's groin. The bend in his elbow exploded upward against Escobar's testicles. Cale's left arm blocked Escobar's knife hand wide of his body, and he noted another nick from the blade, this time on the forearm. Cale's feet lifted off the ground, and he dumped Escobar over. Escobar landed on his right side knocking himself in the ribs with his own elbow.

Escobar held onto the knife, but his knife hand was on the carpet. Cale could see that the knife arm bore all Escobar's weight. Before Escobar could shift that weight, Cale pinned Escobar's right forearm to the carpet and began smashing Escobar's chin with his right fist. Again. Again. Again. Escobar's body slackened, and the knife left his fingers as his consciousness drained. Cale pushed Escobar's mouth closed, pinched his nose shut. He leaned all of his weight onto him. Escobar half consciously tried to fight. He lost. Cale won.

›› EPILOGUE

CALE NEEDED TO remove himself as far from the killings as possible. The US justice system was not the primary concern, although that would entail a long, burdensome process. Ashley had heard the order to kill. All three men carried handguns and knives. The youngest man's hands also contained a very nasty wire. Cale's concern was about the next set of family members taking their attempt at vengeance.

With that in mind, his decision was clear. Concern number one: Ashley. She just witnessed two murders within ten feet of herself. *Self-defense killings* was perhaps a more appropriate description, but the result was the same: There were two fewer souls breathing. Working in a hospital, she had the psychological advantage of having watched multiple people breathe their last breaths. And although he was concerned for her mental health, the truth was less noble and more pragmatic: He needed her cooperation to restore his unfettered freedom—not freedom from prison but freedom from an overhanging vendetta.

When Cale rolled off Escobar, Ashley was watching him, still standing frozen in the same spot. He raised his index finger, indicating he needed a moment. Adrenaline pulsed through him in such doses that physically he didn't need a moment. Physically he could have jumped through the plane's metal roof. He needed a moment to get his words together. Fortunately, the adrenaline helped his brain, and his ideas came together quickly.

When he was gathered, Cale, with a slow, steady speech rhythm, described his "clients" to her. Who they were. Why they wanted him dead. He mentioned the third dead guy in the bathroom.

Not shockingly, these words alone didn't put her at ease. If he wasn't physically between her and the door, he thought she would have left the plane at a full sprint. He then made the hard pitch of explaining why he didn't want to alert the authorities.

"Ashley, for me, my children, and my grandkids to not live in fear every day, no one can know what happened here this morning." He hated to play the grandkid card but was willing to use all the tools at his disposal. Particularly since it was the truth.

Slowly, she answered, "You killed this man when he was already unconscious."

"Ashley, what choice did I truly have." He wanted to say he'd done the world a favor but refrained. "I haven't faced an Escobar in over twenty years, and they came to kill me. The leader of the entire cartel came to kill me. This was personal and not business for them."

She grew silent, then asked, "Would those men have killed me after they killed you?"

Her focus shifted from his behavior to her self-preservation. Gordon Gecko was wrong when he said greed is good as it relates to interpreting the works of Adam Smith, but Adam Smith was right: Self-interest was a force for good. In this case, as Ashley's brain was beginning to register, hers and Cale's self-interests were in alignment.

Cale nodded yes in response to her question.

"If they know what happened, and they know I was here, will they try to find me?"

"Ashley, I don't know. They will certainly try to kill me again if this comes to light. If this gets reported to the authorities, your name will be known around the world by tonight, and if they want to find you, they'll be able to. They waited twenty years to find me."

Silence again overtook them. They sat, breathing in the plane's cabin, in the presence of two impossible-to-ignore warm dead bodies when Wikipedia came to Cale's rescue. He flipped Escobar around until he found his passport and handed it to Ashley. On her phone, she Googled his name and explored the various links describing his life. While she was occupied, he retrieved Escobar's cell phone. There was a third number in his text history, this one with a 702 area code. All the texts concerned travel schedules, and Cale felt confident this was the number for his plane's pilot. The last message indicated the plane was here and ready for travel when Escobar was ready. The texts were a mix of English and Spanish. Cale chose English for Francisco's response.

"Making alternative travel plans. Go to Miami this morning. We will meet you Thur." Before delivering, he changed "alternative" to "other" then hit send. Within a minute, there was a return text acknowledging the new itinerary.

Cale again sat quietly watching Ashley read and learn. She started nodding her head, and Cale took this as a good sign. After ten minutes of reading, he slipped his phone into her hands. He had pulled up Radcliffe's Facebook page. There were hundreds of sympathy posts from DEA colleagues. He then took her to his own page. There were dozens of new posts from DEA colleagues saying simple messages like, "CC be careful," "Cale take a vacation," "Don't be a hero (moron); please get some protection," and "Coleman, want me to come house sit with you this week?"

When she looked up and said, "OK, what do we need to do?" he realized he'd been holding his breath. As he started to thank her, the big Gulfstream's engines overpowered his vocal cords, but she knew what he was saying.

With some ingenuity, two oversized black garbage bags, and a roll of duct tape, Cale retrieved Alberto from the men's room. Ashley kept the FBO's shift manager occupied as Cale carried the last piece of luggage over his shoulder, fireman-style, to the King Air.

He then registered a change of flight plan for the Abacos, and reduced the passenger list to one. Before reaching Abacos air traffic control, he made a stop at an old runway known from his DEA days. The strip was on an uninhabited piece of sand and crushed coral. Circling low, they could see submerged planes in the clear water on either end of the runway. The planes had slid off the runway, been blown off in a hurricane, or were pushed off by a rival. This was one of hundreds of no-name strips in the Bahamas. This one, like most, appropriately enough, had been constructed by the Colombians or their accessories in Panama during the 1980s. It was a fitting final resting place for these three.

So Cale landed with more bumps than he would have liked, but he'd had worse runways (just not with his own plane). Cale unloaded the three men while Ashley gazed into the water. He stripped the bodies, dumped them near a reef, and pocketed their money. It was more than the fuel would cost but not enough to retire on. He kept Escobar's cell phone and piled the rest of the stuff in an oyster-shell fire pit. With the help of a little jet fuel, the belongings ignited nicely. Ashley walked back and sat in silence with Cale while everything turned to ash. With the ashes still smoldering, they boarded and took off for the Abacos.

The rest of Tuesday was a day of rest and stony quiet. He and Ashley shared a room, but it contained an unspoken divider down the middle of the king bed. Cale soaked his flesh wounds in the patio hot tub.

Wednesday, they ventured out. Conversation returned, and they rented a rigid inflatable dinghy and explored the giant and shallow Abaco Bay. Cale dove for conch and wet a line, Ashley read a book, and they both reinforced their tans. At sunset, they put their teetotaling days behind them with gin and coconut-water cocktails and watched the sun sink into the water. Just as the sun dipped below the horizon, Ashley stood and jumped.

"What are you doing?" he asked.

"Seeing the sunset for a second time," she smiled.

With that, he knew she had made her way back, was enjoying a silly little West Coast tradition on the west coast of the Abacos. This realization forced him into reflection.

Six months after Maggie died, he started attending chicken dinners. And it was nice and necessary, but too soon. A year after Maggie died, he starting going on dates. After two years, he stuck his toe into nightlife, going out with single, mostly divorced friends to the places single people met each other, where alcoholic and musical lubricants featured prominently. Unfortunately, he found himself experiencing it as a sociologist did a previously unknown society—that is, with interest and awe but without engagement.

Pretty women just out of college and starting new careers frequently approached Cale and, at first, he had difficulty understanding their interest. They had so many experiences waiting for them that would never be mind blowing for him again. He worried that by being with someone his age, they would be giving up too much for whatever they might gain in return. Eventually, he stopped viewing the real-life fantasy he'd lived with Maggie as attainable for most people. He accepted that, even with these women's limited experiences, he had a lot to offer. He also knew some would call this rationalizing the trip to young skin.

He left prudishness behind, but his growing number of experiences became, in a word, boring. So he became a snob. He no longer wondered why young women had an interest in him, but wondered instead why he had an interest in them. Beyond his appreciation of aesthetics and the sense of touch, how was the next dalliance going to nurture his brain and spirit?

He came up with a challenge for himself. When he found himself falling into the date rhythm with a new woman nearer his daughters' age than his own, he developed a trick of finding ways to carry on a conversation with his eyes closed and without physical contact. If, without aesthetics and touch, he enjoyed himself, then he would carry on with the relationship. He had yet to find one relationship that passed the test.

So as Cale faced the darkening ocean, he held his cocktail in the hand nearest Ashley to stop himself from reaching over and touching her. He closed his eyes as they talked. And talked.

Thursday morning, he texted the Gulfstream's pilot, "Meet me in Vancouver Sunday."

Cale called Sheila on her office line. The call went to voice mail. The message he left said, "Sheila, hey, it's Cale. I think your coworkers were right. Just too much stress. Getting some therapy. Not sure if it was post- or pretraumatic stress disorder they said I had. I don't think I'll be imagining those three guys breaking into my house ever again. Just wanted to let you know. No need to call back. Take care."

He hoped the message would bring a smile to her face.

That afternoon, he and Ashley enjoyed a couples massage. The massage therapists draped different parts of Cale's and Ashley's bodies with sheets as they worked their fingers into the muscles. The oils' scents were mint and jasmine. After the rubdown, they were dotted with hot stones, and Cale fell asleep. When the stones were put away, Cale and Ashley languorously drifted back to their room. For the first time, they experimented with their newly limbered bodies. The experimenting was loud and lasted longer than Cale could remember. In the late afternoon, the general manager knocked on the door and asked if they'd like to move to a private cabana, where there were—ahem—no guests below or to the sides. He mentioned this all with a smile buried below his professional demeanor.

Thursday evening, they became acquainted with the new accommodations. The view was better, and the four-poster bed larger, although the decorative mosquito netting at times proved an encumbrance. The cabana was significantly more expensive than the room, but Cale was using Francisco's cash and didn't think he would mind the up-charge. Extravagance, he assumed, was Francisco's style.

The couple broke briefly for a late dinner of mahimahi sandwiches and bottled Caribs before returning to their cabana for another go. Finally, sleep overtook them.

Friday morning came, and responsibility hung heavy in the air. Reality had set its hooks and was reeling them in. So, begrudgingly, they did their duty.

Ashley called in and asked for the week off.

ABOUT THE AUTHOR

 **SETH COKER SPENDS** his days developing and building apartments in North and South Carolina. He splits his time between Greensboro and Wilmington, North Carolina, and passes far too much time on the water. He freely acknowledges that his wife, Melissa, and their four children, Tyler, Sienna, Lexi, and Cale, are more patient with his pursuits than he deserves. *Salty Sky* is Seth's first book.